Widely regarded as Bengal's earliest and boldest feminist writer, ROKEYA SAKHAWAT HOSSAIN (1880–1932) was a woman of many talents. She was a pioneering and creative educationist. The school she founded in Kolkata, the Sakhawat Memorial School for Girls, still thrives. She was also a social activist who organized middle-class women in undertaking slum development and training poor women in income-generating activities. Her best-known publications are "Sultana's Dream" (1905), *Padmarag* (1924), and *Abarodhbasini* (1931). She is an iconic figure in South Asia, especially among Bengalis in Bangladesh and India.

BARNITA BAGCHI is a feminist translator, literary and cultural critic, and cultural historian. She is associate professor in Comparative Literature at Utrecht University, the Netherlands. She has published widely on utopia, histories of transnational and women's education, and women's writing in western Europe and South Asia.

TANYA AGATHOCLEOUS is professor of English at Hunter College and the Graduate Center, CUNY. She is the author of *Urban Realism and the Cosmopolitan Imagination in the Nineteenth Century* (Cambridge University Press, 2011); *Disaffected: Emotion, Sedition, and Colonial Law in the Anglosphere* (Cornell University Press, 2021); a Broadview edition of Joseph Conrad's *The Secret Agent*; a Penguin Classics edition of *Great Expectations*; a YA biography of George Orwell; and several academic articles on nineteenth- and twentieth-century literatures in global, transnational, and imperial contexts. She has also written for *Public Books* and *LARB*.

ROKEYA SAKHAWAT HOSSAIN

Sultana's Dream
and
Padmarag

TWO FEMINIST UTOPIAS

Translated by
BARNITA BAGCHI

Introduction by
TANYA AGATHOCLEOUS

PENGUIN BOOKS

PENGUIN BOOKS

An imprint of Penguin Random House LLC
penguinrandomhouse.com

First published in India by Penguin Books India 2005
This updated edition published with an introduction by Tanya Agathocleous and
two additional essays translated by Mohammad Quayum in Penguin Books 2022

"Sultana's Dream" was originally published in *The Indian Ladies' Magazine*, Madras, India,
1905, in English. First published in book form in 1908 by S. K. Lahiri, 44 College Street, Calcutta.
Padmarag was first published in Bengali, in book form, in 1924 by the author,
86A Lower Circular Road, Calcutta.
"God Gives, Man Robs" was first published in *The Mussalman*, edited by Mujibur Rahman, in 1927.
"Educational Ideals for the Modern Indian Girls" was first published in *The Mussalman*, edited by
Mujibur Rahman, in 1931.
"God Gives, Man Robs" and "Educational Ideals for the Modern Indian Girls" were translated into
English by Mohammad Quayum in *The Essential Rokeya* by Brill, in 2013.

LIBRARY OF CONGRESS CATALOGING-IN-PUBLICATION DATA
Names: Rokeẏā, Begama, 1880-1932, author. | Bagchi, Barnita, translator. |
Agathocleous, Tanya, 1970- writer of introduction.
Title: Sultana's Dream and Padmarag : two feminist utopias / Rokeya Hossain;
translated by Barnita Bagchi ; introduction by Tanya Agathocleous.
Description: New York City : Penguin Books, 2022. | Includes bibliographical references.
Identifiers: LCCN 2022001375 (print) | LCCN 2022001376 (ebook) |
ISBN 9780143137054 (trade paperback) | ISBN 9780525508557 (ebook)
Subjects: LCSH: Rokeẏā, Begama, 1880-1932—Translations into English. |
LCGFT: Science fiction. | Utopian fiction. | Short stories. | Novels. | Essays.
Classification: LCC PK1718.R55 S85 2022 (print) | LCC PK1718.R55 (ebook) |
DDC 891.4/487109—dc23/eng/20220426
LC record available at https://lccn.loc.gov/2022001375
LC ebook record available at https://lccn.loc.gov/2022001376

Printed in the United States of America
1st Printing

Set in Sabon LT Std

Contents

Introduction

Solar power. The end of war. Gender role reversal. Dirigibles. First published in 1905, Rokeya Hossain's short story "Sultana's Dream" is steampunk *avant la lettre*, strikingly advanced in its critique of patriarchy, conflict, conventional kinship structures, industrialization, and the exploitation of the natural world. Notably speaking to the concerns of our contemporary world as much as its own, it is also striking for being a parodic critique of purdah by a Muslim woman. At a time when British colonialism was using the treatment of women in India as justification for colonial intervention there (a rhetorical strategy still in use by the West today), Hossain's story imagines a world in which men rather than women are kept inside, thus framing her protest against Islamic patriarchy within a larger feminist vision that takes on Western as well as Islamic forms of gender hierarchy.

"Sultana's Dream" is not just one of the first science-fiction or utopian stories written in India by a woman; it is an integral part of the emergence of sci-fi as a form of speculative fiction at the turn of the nineteenth century, more often associated with male Western writers such as H. G. Wells, Jules Verne, and Arthur Conan Doyle. At the same time, it is one of the first feminist utopias in modern literature, published a decade before Charlotte Perkins Gilman's *Herland* (1915), and part of a wave of fin de siècle utopias that includes Edward Bellamy's *Looking Backward* (1888) and William Morris's *News from Nowhere* (1890). It is also one of the first literary works in English by a Muslim writer in South Asia. In all these ways,

Hossain's story is an important part of Anglophone literary history that has yet to be fully recognized as such.

It is all the more remarkable, then, that "Sultana's Dream" was written in her fifth language by a woman who was denied a formal education (she also knew Urdu, Persian, Arabic, and Bangla). The Muslim community in India at the time largely did not approve of education for women, and the colonial government, though it had a college for Hindu women, did not open one for Muslim women until 1939, close to the end of the British imperial rule in India. Promoting education for girls and women was thus Hossain's passion, as evidenced by the stories and essays collected in this volume; it also shaped her career and political work and is one of her enduring legacies.

ROKEYA HOSSAIN IN HISTORICAL CONTEXT

Rokeya Hossain (1880–1932), known by the honorific Begum Rokeya, is widely recognized in South Asia today as a pioneering educator, feminist, writer, and activist. Because she lived and worked in a region of colonial India that is now part of independent Bangladesh, she is a particularly revered public figure there and is celebrated every year on December 9, otherwise known as Rokeya Day.

India was ruled by Britain from 1857 to 1948. The idea that the English language and English literature was superior to Indian languages and literatures, and should therefore be taught as widely as possible, was a racist justification for Britain's prolonged rule and a tactic of governance: many desirable government jobs required an English education, so it came to be seen as crucial to social, economic, and political advancement. This is part of the reason Hossain educated her children in Britain, wrote "Sultana's Dream" in English, and argued that Muslims should pursue English educations so they would benefit from the vocational advantages that accrued to those who could speak and write in English. But she was also deeply critical of British rule and its imposition of cultural norms on India; in

Padmarag, Tarini Bhavan, a women's school, workshop, homeless shelter, and hospital, offers a broad and Indian-centered education so that its students would not be "forced to memorize misleading versions of history and end up despising themselves and their fellow Indians."

Hossain grew up in a traditional Muslim family. Her father had four wives, favored education for his sons but not his daughters, and imposed purdah: a Muslim practice, also employed in some Hindu communities, where women live in separate quarters to conceal themselves from men, and sometimes unknown women as well, and use veiling to cover their bodies when in public. As a result, Hossain had to largely educate herself by reading on her own, though she was helped by her brother, who taught her English (and to whom she gratefully dedicated *Padmarag*), and her sister, who taught her Bangla, the language in which she published most of her writing. Like many women at the time, she was married young, at the age of sixteen. It was an arranged marriage, but her sympathetic brother deliberately helped match her with a man, Sakhawat Hossain, who he knew to have more progressive views about women's education than their father. Her husband ended up not only being supportive of her writing—he encouraged her to publish "Sultana's Dream," for example—but also left her money when he died to set up a school for girls, thereby paving the way for her autonomy and ability to pursue her ideals.

"Sultana's Dream" was first published in 1905 in *The Indian Ladies' Magazine*. Edited by Kamala Satthianadhan, it was the first English-language periodical in India run by, and targeted at, Indian women; Satthianadhan's daughter, Padmini Sengupta, wrote for the magazine and later served as its assistant editor. Both a Christian and an Indian, Satthianadhan saw herself as a syncretic blend of East and West and imagined her magazine this way as well, blending sympathy for Indian nationalism with expressions of friendship with Britain. Thus while hers was one of the first magazines to publish the poems of Sarojini Naidu, who would later become a prominent figure in the nationalist movement, it tended to shy away from publishing the kind of overtly anti-imperialist articles that came to dominate the Indian press by the early twentieth century. But like Hossain's story, *The Indian Ladies' Magazine* was more explicitly part of the burgeoning conversation about women's rights and published the work of several influential feminists and activists. As well as Hossain and Naidu, it showcased writing by lawyer and reformer Cornelia Sorabji, socialist and politician Annie Besant, and educator-reformer Pandita Ramabai.

Satthianadhan's gender politics, like her nationalism, were cautious; on the one hand, she promoted the idea that women should stick to the domestic sphere, on the other, she was interested in women's rights and strongly believed in their education and right to participate in public discourse, as evidenced by her own path and that of her daughter. She was also, like Hossain, against the strictures of gender segregation and purdah, which no doubt motivated her inclusion of "Sultana's Dream" in *The Indian Ladies' Magazine*. But in a move consistent with the political balancing act typical of her journal, she went on to publish a satire of the story, "An Answer to Sultana's Dream," in the next issue of the magazine, which ends by restoring the gendered division of labor that Hossain's story so gleefully subverts. The fact that this counterargument may have been authored by her daughter (the author's name is listed simply as "Padmini") suggests how radical Hossain's story was and how careful Satthianadhan felt she had to be in disseminating it.

Although it was one of Hossain's first published pieces, "Sultana's Dream" would end up being her most famous. But she wrote for a number of contemporary periodicals and in a range of genres, including essays, stories, poems, and reportage, most often in Bangla. Her choice of language was an intervention in itself. Bangla was a regional language, whereas Urdu was considered the proper language of educated Muslims; as a girl, she had had to learn Bangla on the sly to skirt her father's disapproval. Yet she developed a passion for the Bengali language, and since her goal was to shift public opinion in Bengal about women's rights, she used Bangla as a way to address her community directly; she also made a point to teach it to her students. Her influential works written in Bangla include *Motichur* (translated as "A String of Sweet Pearls"), a collection of feminist essays in two volumes, and *Padmarag* (translated alternately as "The Ruby" or "Essence of the Lotus"), reprinted here. Though published in 1924, more than twenty years after "Sultana's Dream," it reprises many of that story's themes, focusing on the injustices of gender disparities, on utopian female community, and on women's education.

Another influential work by Hossain, *The Secluded Ones*, was published in 1931. Initially serialized in the periodical *Mohammadi*, it was later released as a single volume. Audacious both in form and in content, it documented the adverse effects of purdah on women's lives by gathering together forty-seven anecdotes of absurd and/or tragic situations resulting from inflexible approaches to gender segregation. Hossain drew from her own experience as well as that of other women; for example, one of the anecdotes describes how as a small child she once had to hide under a bed in a dusty attic for four days so that visiting maids, who wandered freely around the house, wouldn't come across her. *The Secluded Ones* was not only a significant feminist intervention but also important for having been written by someone who had both experienced purdah herself and who celebrated her Indian and Muslim identities, since many of the accounts of purdah that circulated before this were exoticized traveler's tales by Western writers who often held derogatory views of Islamic culture and relied on second- or thirdhand accounts of gender seclusion.

The bulk of Hossain's writing, as we have seen, promoted the cause of women's education, either directly or indirectly. In an essay included in this volume, "God Gives, Man Robs" (1927), for example, she invokes the Prophet Mohammed to support her arguments. Since he commands that all men and women should acquire knowledge, she contends that it is wrong for men to stand in the way of the education of their wives, daughters, and sisters: not only is this a disservice to women and to Islam, she notes, but it also puts Muslims at a further disadvantage relative to the Hindu community (the dominant religious community in India), which was at the time engaged in a number of reforms related to women's rights, including increased access to education.

"Educational Ideals for the Modern Indian Girls" (1931), meanwhile, spoke of uniting the religious and moral emphasis of traditional Indian education ideals with the secular knowledge important to twentieth-century life: "We must assimilate the old while holding to the now." She advocated for a diverse and well-rounded curriculum that included art, physical education, science, horticulture, and health care—a pedagogical vision that is reflected in the utopian communities depicted in both "Sultana's Dream" and *Padmarag*. Education for women, considered a break from tradition, is associated with modernity and thus with "the adoption of western methods and ideals." But as in *Padmarag*, Hossain argues in this essay against the "slavish imitation" of the West and contends that domestic duties and older forms of knowledge should be integrated into female education, along with the kind of vocational training passed on from parent to child. While her appeal to the importance of feminine duty may have been in earnest or may have been an attempt to harness more widespread support for women's education, this essay also contained an unambiguous and bold statement: "The future of India lies in its girls."

Alongside this writing, Hossain devoted much of her relatively short life to hands-on educational work. In 1911, not long after her husband's death, she founded the Sakhawat Memorial School for Girls in Calcutta (now Kolkata). A letter she wrote to the editor of the periodical *The Mussalman* appealing to the Muslim community for support shows how challenging and potentially controversial this undertaking was, despite the money left to her for this purpose by her husband:

To
The Editor
The Mussalman

Sir, Permit me the liberty of asking the courtesy of your paper to inform the Mohamedan public that I intend to start a Girls' school in Calcutta in strict observance of Purdah at an earliest opportunity possible, which is not only the crying need of the time but the want of which, I believe, is keenly felt by all right thinking men and women.

My beloved husband, the Late Moulvie Sakhawat Hossain, B.A. of the Provincial Executive Service, has bequeathed Rs. 10,000 for female education, the income (Rs. 6,000 annually) of which is at my disposal. I am therefore not only ready to spend that amount but I shall rather be glad to personally conduct the school and am prepared to devote my time, energy, and whatever knowledge I possess, towards its furtherance.

But as the fund in hand is not sufficient to meet the requirements, I appeal to the generous Moslem public to extend their helping hand and thus contribute to the success of the project which deserves the hearty sympathy and practical patronage of well-wishers of the community.

Mohamedan gentlemen desirous of helping me in my scheme are requested to kindly communicate with me direct, while my Moslem sisters who wish to associate themselves by their cooperation to the movement are invited in my house to discuss the subject, or I shall be glad to call on them should they inform me of their addresses.

Though Hossain ended up starting the school with only eight students, she persisted against bias in the Muslim community and had over eighty students in her school by 1915. Even while teaching and running the school, she was engaged in other forms of activism to promote women's rights. In 1916, she founded the Bengali Muslim Women's Association to cater to less privileged women (since women at her school tended to be from the middle and upper classes); much like Tarini Bhavan in *Padmarag*, it provided a variety of forms of aid, including shelter, community, financial help, and education. She was also involved in the organization of an All India Muslim Ladies' Conference in Calcutta in 1919, where women's education and polygamy were debated in the context of modern Muslim community. In a letter to *The Mussalman* in which she publicized the conference, she demonstrated her commitment to female solidarity by proposing to meet women traveling to the conference from remote areas at the train station and offering them free room and board at her school.

While Hossain is celebrated in the present day for her contributions to feminism and education, she endured bitter criticism in her own lifetime. Many members of the Muslim community, especially religious leaders, deplored her feminism and declared her irreligious and overly Westernized, even though she remained a practicing Muslim and dedicated her life to helping Indian women. But she also inspired a younger generation of activists, who used works like *The Secluded Ones* to campaign for women's rights, and her activism and writing helped to change public attitudes toward women's education. Shortly after her death at the age of fifty-two, her school for girls started receiving government funding. It still exists in Kolkata today, evidence of Hossain's work and lasting effect on Indian education. And her influence continues to spread—though Hossain's crucial contributions to feminism are still not that well known outside of South Asia, "Sultana's Dream" is increasingly included in Anglophone literary anthologies. In 2018, it was also the subject of an art exhibit by South Asian American feminist artist Chitra Ganesh, "Her Garden, a Mirror," that illuminated how eloquently and urgently Hossain's utopian visions continue to speak to the crises and injustices of the present.

ROKEYA HOSSAIN
AND SPECULATIVE FICTION

Because it could be labeled both utopian literature and sci-fi, "Sultana's Dream" is perhaps best described as speculative fiction, an umbrella category that includes these genres as well as horror and fantasy. Speculative fiction encompasses any form of imaginative literature with nonrealistic elements: objects, situations, places, or beings that have never existed in the past, and don't exist in the present, but—in the case of much sci-fi and utopian and dystopian fiction—could potentially exist in the future. Margaret Atwood, for example, uses the term to describe her dystopian novels, such as *A Handmaid's Tale*, because they present worlds that might emerge out of present-day political conditions. The term has also been used more broadly to describe fiction, like that of H. P. Lovecraft, that is nonmimetic but also nonpredictive. While some critics argue that this definition is too broad to be helpful as a description of a literary genre, speculative fiction as a label for a wide variety of works has emerged more prominently in recent years, partly because nonmimetic genres have proliferated and partly because it captures the way that the genres encompassed by it tend to intersect and overlap, particularly in the work of contemporary writers of color like Octavia Butler (see Suggestions for Further Reading).

In "Sultana's Dream," the protagonist, a Muslim woman living in contemporary India, falls asleep and wakes up in a transformed future world: a utopia in which women are free to explore the world at will and pursue an education. Their society is peaceful and just, run by a queen who uses scientific principles to put an end to war, conquer disease, harvest clean energy from the sun, and live in harmony with nature. The sci-fi elements of "Sultana's Dream"—electric flying cars, the use of science to harness the power of rain and of the sun—are particularly notable for their prescience and innovation. Hossain draws on other genres as well, namely satire and parody, to accentuate her critique of purdah. If satire works through poking fun at its object in order to lambast it, parody imitates the form of its object of critique but incorporates a key difference that indicates why the object is worthy of ridicule. The parody of "Sultana's Dream" operates by replicating the conditions of purdah in Sultana's utopia but reversing the gender roles, so that men, rather than women, must stay indoors and take care of the home and the children, while women run society and roam the streets happily, free from harassment and exploitation. The unlikeliness of male seclusion is part of the story's humor, but this detail also draws its strength from the logic of purdah; if women need to be covered and cloistered because of their own weakness and because of male desire, as supporters of purdah believe, then this desire and male strength (or physical aggression) is the problem that needs to be contained. To the degree that the story seems to hold a low opinion of men—who are held responsible for the prior woes of the world and, more comically, are depicted as lazy and hapless—it does so by leveraging and rearranging real-world assumptions about gender.

More pronounced than its sci-fi or satiric elements, though, is the story's utopianism, and the way it uses those elements as building blocks. The utopian tradition spans most of literary history; it has been traced back to Plato's *Republic* (375 BC) and Thomas More's *Utopia* (1516), among other influential texts, and has long been an occasion for feminist imaginings. Christine de Pizan's *The Book of the City of Ladies* (1405) builds an imaginary city of famous women (both real and fictional) in order to advocate, as Hossain does, for female education. *Millenium Hall* (1778) by Sarah Scott is also similar to both "Sultana's Dream" and *Padmarag* in its vision of female community as crucial to the advancement of both the self and society.

Influential theorists of utopia, such as Ernst Bloch (see Suggestions for Further Reading), argue that utopian thought is a key component of human aspiration. Since the word "utopia" means "no place," utopias are not necessarily meant to be direct road maps to social transformation. Instead, they are designed to show us what's wrong with the current world and ask us to imagine it differently; they strive to startle their readers into the perception of new possibilities. "Sultana's Dream" does just this in its reversal of gender roles and in its transformation of the world into Ladyland: a safe and joyous space in which women are able to live productive lives and nature and culture are harmonized. If the fact that this vision entails keeping men separate and inside the home is the story's most unrealistic element, it is also its most poignant in its indictment of both purdah and gender-based violence.

When is the time of utopia? Generally, both utopias and dystopias are associated with the future; "Sultana's Dream" seems like futuristic sci-fi because of its visionary space-age details. But according to the Queen of Ladyland, her country exists *alongside* India, which she refers to as "your country" when addressing Sultana. Sultana's dream world, then, is a parallel world that might be accessed, the story suggests, via female education, since this is the key reform the Queen instituted that allowed for the radical transformation of society. Hossain's novella *Padmarag* is similarly utopian in its depiction of female community; the institution at the center of the story, Tarini Bhavan, functions as a home for widows, a school for girls, and also as a "Home for the Ailing and Needy." It welcomes women of all ages, ethnicities, and religions and supports them equally, giving them the opportunity to become self-sufficient by supplying work training or allowing them to work on the premises. By forming a collective, the women free themselves from the need for support from husbands or family: entities that the story often depicts as selfish, abusive, or uncaring. The intentional community of Tarini Bhavan, on the other hand, is one of mutual care and sustenance, both material and emotional.

The utopian component of the story, then, inheres in the overcoming of differences between women and the success of their enterprise, but there are also many realistic elements to the story. Rather than occurring in "no place," *Padmarag* seems to be set in contemporary India, and the depiction of the school and ancillary institutions that make up Tarini Bhavan clearly draw on Hossain's experiences running her own school and the Bengali Muslim Women's Association (such as the letters of complaint from parents that Tarini reads out loud to her friends in chapter 19). If in "Sultana's Dream" the utopian Ladyland contrasts with the imperfect state of contemporary India for women, in *Padmarag*, Tarini Bhavan is a small island of utopian community within a real world of grossly unfair gender disparities. As we learn the stories of the different women who live there, we also learn of the different forms of exploitation and bondage to which women can be subject.

Yet Hossain is careful to wrest the critique of gender roles in India away from Western commentators by showing how British colonialism itself perpetuates oppression. Helen, the British member of the Tarini Bhavan community, demonstrates that women in Britain are subject to similar forms of discrimination, while one of the central villains of the story is a British indigo planter whose greedy machinations lead the heroine Siddika (aka Padmarag) to Tarini Bhavan to join the other women who are seeking refuge from patriarchy there. At the end of the story, Siddika foils both the romance plot that would have her reconcile with her true love, Latif, and a utopian ending, by leaving Latif *and* Tarini Bhavan behind to return to seclusion in her hometown. Her motivations, beyond a sense of duty and a desire to determine her own destiny, are not adequately explained, but the story as a whole seems determined to flout expectations of genre and gender in order to show us both a deeply flawed world and people struggling to carve out a better one. As one of its inhabitants puts it, Tarini Bhavan exists to redress the injustices of the society it inhabits: "Come, all you abandoned, destitute, neglected, helpless, oppressed women—come together. Then we will declare war on society! And Tarini Bhavan will serve as our fortress." Seemingly disarming in their innovation and humor, both the utopian stories collected in this edition are formidable as well, presenting themselves to the reader as mental fortresses against pernicious gender ideologies and other conventional ideas.

TANYA AGATHOCLEOUS

A Note on the Text

The appendix contains Rokeya Hossain's essays "God Gives, Man Robs" and "Educational Ideals for the Modern India Girls." "God Gives, Man Robs" was first published in *The Mussalman* (ed. Mujibur Rahman), on December 6, 1927. "Educational Ideals for the Modern India Girls" was first published in *The Mussalman* (ed. by Mujibur Rahman), on March 5, 1931.

To ease readability, a small number of typographical and grammatical inconsistencies in the original manuscript have been silently emended for this edition.

"SULTANA'S DREAM"

One evening I was lounging in an easy chair in my bedroom and thinking lazily of the condition of Indian womanhood. I am not sure whether I dozed off or not. But, as far as I remember, I was wide awake. I saw the moonlit sky sparkling with thousands of diamond-like stars, very distinctly.

All of a sudden a lady stood before me; how she came in, I do not know. I took her for my friend, Sister Sara.

"Good morning," said Sister Sara. I smiled inwardly as I knew it was not morning, but starry night. However, I replied to her, saying, "How do you do?"

"I am all right, thank you. Will you please come out and have a look at our garden?"

I looked again at the moon through the open window and thought there was no harm in going out at that time. The menservants outside were fast asleep just then, and I could have a pleasant walk with Sister Sara.

I used to have my walks with Sister Sara, when we were at Darjeeling. Many a time did we walk hand in hand and talk lightheartedly in the botanical gardens there. I fancied Sister Sara had probably come to take me to some such garden and I readily accepted her offer and went out with her.

When walking I found to my surprise that it was a fine morning. The town was fully awake and the streets alive with bustling crowds. I was feeling very shy, thinking I was walking in the street in broad daylight, but there was not a single man visible.

Some of the passersby made jokes at me. Though I could not understand their language, yet I felt sure they were joking. I asked my friend, "What do they say?"

"The women say that you look very mannish."

"Mannish?" said I. "What do they mean by that?"

"They mean that you are shy and timid like men."

"Shy and timid like men?" It was really a joke. I became very nervous when I found that my companion was not Sister Sara, but a stranger. Oh, what a fool had I been to mistake this lady for my dear old friend, Sister Sara.

She felt my fingers tremble in her hand, as we were walking hand in hand.

"What is the matter, dear?" she said affectionately. "I feel somewhat awkward," I said in a rather apologizing tone, "as being a purdahnishin woman I am not accustomed to walking about unveiled."

"You need not be afraid of coming across a man here. This is Ladyland, free from sin and harm. Virtue herself reigns here."

By and by I was enjoying the scenery. Really it was very grand. I mistook a patch of green grass for a velvet cushion. Feeling as if I were walking on a soft carpet, I looked down and found the path covered with moss and flowers.

"How nice it is," said I.

"Do you like it?" asked Sister Sara. (I continued calling her "Sister Sara," and she kept calling me by my name.)

"Yes, very much; but I do not like to tread on the tender and sweet flowers."

"Never mind, dear Sultana; your treading will not harm them; they are street flowers."

"The whole place looks like a garden," said I admiringly. "You have arranged every plant so skillfully."

"Your Calcutta could become a nicer garden than this if only your countrymen wanted to make it so."

"They would think it useless to give so much attention to horticulture, while they have so many other things to do."

"They could not find a better excuse," said she with a smile.

I became very curious to know where the men were. I met more than a hundred women while walking there, but not a single man.

"Where are the men?" I asked her.

"In their proper places, where they ought to be."

"Pray let me know what you mean by 'their proper places.'"

"Oh, I see my mistake, you cannot know our customs, as you were never here before. We shut our men indoors."

"Just as we are kept in the zenana?"

"Exactly so."

"How funny." I burst into a laugh. Sister Sara laughed too.

"But dear Sultana, how unfair it is to shut in the harmless women and let loose the men."

"Why? It is not safe for us to come out of the zenana, as we are naturally weak."

"Yes, it is not safe so long as there are men about the streets, nor is it so when a wild animal enters a marketplace."

"Of course not."

"Suppose some lunatics escape from the asylum and begin to do all sorts of mischief to men, horses, and other creatures; in that case what will your countrymen do?"

"They will try to capture them and put them back into their asylum."

"Thank you! And you do not think it wise to keep sane people inside an asylum and let loose the insane?"

"Of course not!" said I, laughing lightly.

"As a matter of fact, in your country this very thing is done! Men, who do or at least are capable of doing no end of mischief, are let loose, and the innocent women shut up in the zenana! How can you trust those untrained men out of doors?"

"We have no hand or voice in the management of our social affairs. In India man is lord and master. He has taken to himself all powers and privileges and shut up the women in the zenana."

"Why do you allow yourselves to be shut up?"

"Because it cannot be helped, as they are stronger than women."

"A lion is stronger than a man, but it does not enable him to dominate the human race. You have neglected the duty you owe to yourselves, and you have lost your natural rights by shutting your eyes to your own interests."

"But my dear Sister Sara, if we do everything by ourselves, what will the men do then?"

"They should not do anything, excuse me; they are fit for nothing. Only catch them and put them into the zenana."

"But would it be very easy to catch and put them inside the four walls?" said I. "And even if this were done, would all their business—political and commercial—also go with them into the zenana?"

Sister Sara made no reply. She only smiled sweetly. Perhaps she thought it useless to argue with one who was no better than a frog in a well.

By this time we reached Sister Sara's house. It was situated in a beautiful heart-shaped garden. It was a bungalow with a corrugated iron roof. It was cooler and nicer than any of our rich buildings. I cannot describe how neat and how nicely furnished and how tastefully decorated it was.

We sat side by side. She brought out of the parlor a piece of embroidery work and began putting on a fresh design.

"Do you know knitting and needlework?"

"Yes; we have nothing else to do in our zenana."

"But we do not trust our zenana members with embroidery!" she said laughing, "as a man has not patience enough to pass thread through a needle hole even!"

"Have you done all this work yourself?" I asked her, pointing to the various pieces of embroidered teapoy cloths.

"Yes."

"How can you find time to do all these? You have to do the office work as well? Have you not?"

"Yes. I do not stick to the laboratory all day long. I finish my work in two hours."

"In two hours! How do you manage? In our land the officers—magistrates, for instance—work seven hours daily."

"I have seen some of them doing their work. Do you think they work all the seven hours?"

"Certainly they do!"

"No, dear Sultana, they do not. They dawdle away their time in smoking. Some smoke two or three cheroots during the office time. They talk much about their work, but do little.

Suppose one cheroot takes half an hour to burn off, and a man smokes twelve cheroots daily; then you see, he wastes six hours every day in sheer smoking."

We talked on various subjects, and I learned that they were not subject to any kind of epidemic disease, nor did they suffer from mosquito bites as we do. I was very much astonished to hear that in Ladyland no one died in youth except by rare accident.

"Will you care to see our kitchen?" she asked me.

"With pleasure," said I, and we went to see it. Of course the men had been asked to clear off when I was going there. The kitchen was situated in a beautiful vegetable garden. Every creeper, every tomato plant was itself an ornament. I found no smoke, nor any chimney either in the kitchen—it was clean and bright; the windows were decorated with flower gardens. There was no sign of coal or fire.

"How do you cook?" I asked.

"With solar heat," she said, at the same time showing me the pipe through which passed the concentrated sunlight and heat. And she cooked something then and there to show me the process.

"How did you manage to gather and store up the sun-heat?" I asked her in amazement.

"Let me tell you a little of our past history then. Thirty years ago, when our present Queen was thirteen years old, she inherited the throne. She was Queen in name only, the Prime Minister really ruling the country.

"Our good Queen liked science very much. She circulated an order that all the women in her country should be educated. Accordingly a number of girls' schools were founded and supported by the government. Education was spread far and wide among women. And early marriage also was stopped. No woman was to be allowed to marry before she was twenty-one. I must tell you that, before this change we had been kept in strict purdah."

"How the tables are turned," I interposed with a laugh.

"But the seclusion is the same," she said. "In a few years we had separate universities, where no men were admitted.

"In the capital, where our Queen lives, there are two universities. One of these invented a wonderful balloon, to which they attached a number of pipes. By means of this captive balloon, which they managed to keep afloat above the cloud-land, they could draw as much water from the atmosphere as they pleased. As the water was incessantly being drawn by the university people no cloud gathered and the ingenious Lady Principal stopped rain and storms thereby."

"Really! Now I understand why there is no mud here!" said I. But I could not understand how it was possible to accumulate water in the pipes. She explained to me how it was done, but I was unable to understand her, as my scientific knowledge was very limited. However, she went on, "When the other university came to know of this, they became exceedingly jealous and tried to do something more extraordinary still. They invented an instrument by which they could collect as much sun-heat as they wanted. And they kept the heat stored up to be distributed among others as required.

"While the women were engaged in scientific researches, the men of this country were busy increasing their military power. When they came to know that the female universities were able to draw water from the atmosphere and collect heat from the sun, they only laughed at the members of the universities and called the whole thing 'a sentimental nightmare'!"

"Your achievements are very wonderful indeed! But tell me, how you managed to put the men of your country into the zenana. Did you entrap them first?"

"No."

"It is not likely that they would surrender their free and open-air life of their own accord and confine themselves within the four walls of the zenana! They must have been overpowered."

"Yes, they have been!"

"By whom? By some lady-warriors, I suppose?"

"No, not by arms."

"Yes, it cannot be so. Men's arms are stronger than women's. Then?"

"By brain."

"Even their brains are bigger and heavier than women's. Are they not?"

"Yes, but what of that? An elephant also has got a bigger and heavier brain than a man has. Yet man can enchain elephants and employ them, according to their own wishes."

"Well said, but tell me please, how it all actually happened. I am dying to know it!"

"Women's brains are somewhat quicker than men's. Ten years ago, when the military officers called our scientific discoveries 'a sentimental nightmare,' some of the young ladies wanted to say something in reply to those remarks. But both the Lady Principals restrained them and said they should reply, not by word, but by deed, if ever they got the opportunity. And they had not long to wait for that opportunity."

"How marvelous!" I heartily clapped my hands. "And now the proud gentlemen are dreaming sentimental dreams themselves."

"Soon afterward certain persons came from a neighboring country and took shelter in ours. They were in trouble, having committed some political offense. Their king, who cared more for power than for good government, asked our kindhearted Queen to hand them over to his officers. She refused, as it was against her principles to turn out refugees. For this refusal the king declared war against our country.

"Our military officers sprang to their feet at once and marched out to meet the enemy. The enemy, however, was too strong for them. Our soldiers fought bravely, no doubt. But in spite of all their bravery the foreign army advanced step-by-step to invade our country.

"Nearly all the men had gone out to fight; even a boy of sixteen was not left home. Most of our warriors were killed, the rest driven back, and the enemy came within twenty-five miles of the capital.

"A meeting of a number of wise ladies was held at the Queen's palace to advise as to what should be done to save the land. Some proposed to fight like soldiers; others objected and said that women were not trained to fight with swords and guns, nor were they accustomed to fighting with any weapons.

A third party regretfully remarked that they were hopelessly weak of body.

"'If you cannot save your country for lack of physical strength,' said the Queen, 'try to do so by brain power.'

"There was a dead silence for a few minutes. Her Royal Highness said again, 'I must commit suicide if the land and my honor are lost.'

"Then the Lady Principal of the second university (who had collected sun-heat), who had been silently thinking during the consultation, remarked that they were all but lost, and there was little hope left for them. There was, however, one plan which she would like to try, and this would be her first and last efforts; if she failed in this, there would be nothing left but to commit suicide. All present solemnly vowed that they would never allow themselves to be enslaved, no matter what happened.

"The Queen thanked them heartily and asked the Lady Principal to try her plan. The Lady Principal rose again and said, 'Before we go out the men must enter the zenanas. I make this prayer for the sake of purdah.' 'Yes, of course,' replied Her Royal Highness.

"On the following day the Queen called upon all men to retire into zenanas for the sake of honor and liberty. Wounded and tired as they were, they took that order rather for a boon! They bowed low and entered the zenanas without uttering a single word of protest. They were sure that there was no hope for this country at all.

"Then the Lady Principal with her two thousand students marched to the battlefield, and arriving there, directed all the rays of the concentrated sunlight and heat toward the enemy.

"The heat and light were too much for them to bear. They all ran away panic-stricken, not knowing in their bewilderment how to counteract that scorching heat. When they fled away, leaving their guns and other ammunitions of war, they were burned down by means of the same sun-heat. Since then no one has tried to invade our country anymore."

"And since then your countrymen never tried to come out of the zenana?"

"Yes, they wanted to be free. Some of the police commissioners and district magistrates sent word to the Queen to the effect that the military officers certainly deserved to be imprisoned for their failure; but they never neglected their duty and therefore they should not be punished, and they prayed to be restored to their respective offices.

"Her Royal Highness sent them a circular letter intimating to them that if their services should ever be needed they would be sent for, and that in the meanwhile they should remain where they were. Now that they are accustomed to the purdah system and have ceased to grumble at their seclusion, we call the system 'Mardana' instead of 'zenana.'"

"But how do you manage," I asked Sister Sara, "to do without the police or magistrates in case of theft or murder?"

"Since the Mardana system has been established, there has been no more crime or sin; therefore we do not require a policeman to find out a culprit, nor do we want a magistrate to try a criminal case."

"That is very good, indeed. I suppose if there was any dishonest person, you could very easily chastise her. As you gained a decisive victory without shedding a single drop of blood, you could drive off crime and criminals too without much difficulty!"

"Now, dear Sultana, will you sit here or come to my parlor?" she asked me.

"Your kitchen is not inferior to a queen's boudoir!" I replied with a pleasant smile. "But we must leave it now; for the gentlemen may be cursing me for keeping them away from their duties in the kitchen so long." We both laughed heartily.

"How my friends at home will be amused and amazed, when I go back and tell them that in the far-off Ladyland, ladies rule over the country and control all social matters, while gentlemen are kept in the Mardanas to mind babies, to cook, and to do all sorts of domestic work; and that cooking is so easy a thing that it is simply a pleasure to cook!"

"Yes, tell them about all that you see here."

"Please let me know how you carry on land cultivation and how you plow the land and do other hard manual work."

"Our fields are tilled by means of electricity, which supplies motive power for other hard work as well, and we employ it for our aerial conveyances too. We have no railroad nor any paved streets here."

"Therefore neither street nor railway accidents occur here," said I. "Do not you ever suffer from want of rainwater?" I asked.

"Never since the 'water balloon' has been set up. You see the big balloon and pipes attached thereto. By their aid we can draw as much rainwater as we require. Nor do we ever suffer from flood or thunderstorms. We are all very busy making nature yield as much as she can. We do not find time to quarrel with one another as we never sit idle. Our noble Queen is exceedingly fond of botany; it is her ambition to convert the whole country into one grand garden."

"The idea is excellent. What is your chief food?"

"Fruits."

"How do you keep your country cool in hot weather? We regard the rainfall in summer as a blessing from heaven."

"When the heat becomes unbearable, we sprinkle the ground with plentiful showers drawn from the artificial fountains. And in cold weather we keep our room warm with sun-heat."

She showed me her bathroom, the roof of which was removable. She could enjoy a shower bath whenever she liked, by simply removing the roof (which was like the lid of a box) and turning on the tap of the shower pipe.

"You are a lucky people!" ejaculated I. "You know no want. What is your religion, may I ask?"

"Our religion is based on Love and Truth. It is our religious duty to love one another and to be absolutely truthful. If any person lies, she or he is . . ."

"Punished with death?"

"No, not with death. We do not take pleasure in killing a creature of God, especially a human being. The liar is asked to leave this land for good and never to come to it again."

"Is an offender never forgiven?"

"Yes, if that person repents sincerely."

"Are you not allowed to see any man, except your own relations?"

"No one except sacred relations."

"Our circle of sacred relations is very limited; even first cousins are not sacred."

"But ours is very large; a distant cousin is as sacred as a brother."

"That is very good. I see purity itself reigns over your land. I should like to see the good Queen, who is so sagacious and farsighted and who has made all these rules."

"All right," said Sister Sara.

Then she screwed a couple of seats onto a square piece of plank. To this plank she attached two smooth and well-polished balls. When I asked her what the balls were for, she said they were hydrogen balls, and they were used to overcome the force of gravity. The balls were of different capacities to be used according to the different weights desired to be overcome. She then fastened to the air-car two winglike blades, which, she said, were worked by electricity. After we were comfortably seated she touched a knob and the blades began to whirl, moving faster and faster every moment. At first we were raised to the height of about six or seven feet and then off we flew. And before I could realize that we had commenced moving, we reached the garden of the Queen.

My friend lowered the air-car by reversing the action of the machine, and when the car touched the ground the machine was stopped, and we got out.

I had seen from the air-car the Queen walking on a garden path with her little daughter (who was four years old) and her maids of honor.

"Halloo! You here!" cried the Queen, addressing Sister Sara. I was introduced to Her Royal Highness and was received by her cordially without any ceremony.

I was very much delighted to make her acquaintance. In the course of the conversation I had with her, the Queen told me that she had no objection to permitting her subjects to trade with other countries. "But," she continued. "No trade was

possible with countries where the women were kept in the zenanas and so unable to come and trade with us. Men, we find,
are rather of lower morals and so we do not like dealing with
them. We do not covet other people's land, we do not fight for
a piece of diamond though it may be a thousandfold brighter
than the Koh-i-noor, nor do we grudge a ruler his Peacock
Throne. We dive deep into the ocean of knowledge and try to
find out the precious gems, which nature has kept in store for
us. We enjoy nature's gifts as much as we can."

After taking leave of the Queen, I visited the famous universities, and was shown some of their manufactories, laborato-
ries, and observatories.

After visiting the above places of interest we got again into
the air-car, but as soon as it began moving, I somehow slipped
down and the fall startled me out of my dream. And on opening my eyes, I found myself in my own bedroom still lounging
in the easy chair!

PADMARAG

(THE RUBY)

Letter of Dedication

This book
is placed in the hands
of my most beloved elder brother,
Abul Asad Ibrahim Saber

ELDER BROTHER,

I have basked in the warmth of your love from my very
infancy. It is you who have raised and shaped me. I have no
idea what a father, a mother, a guru, or a teacher is like—I
only know you.

My mother disciplined me from time to time. You never
did. So, it was in you that I sought and found the tenderness
of maternal love,

"Rewards, reproaches, prayers for one's welfare."

You are also the teacher who offered me the same
blessings. Dear brother, only rewards have you reserved for
me, never reproaches. Even honey has a mildly bitter
aftertaste, but your affection was sweetness itself—honey
without its bitterness—like the nectar of the gods. Brother: I
dedicate to you the portrait I have painted during my leisure
hours. It is my first composition, born out of my very first
efforts. My composition has not adhered to social norms. I
have merely painted the portrait of one whose love embraced
the whole wide world.

YOUR BELOVED LITTLE SISTER,
RAKU

Preface

This novel was written nearly twenty-two years ago. The manuscript was shown to the famous writer, the late Jnanendralal Ray. He expressed satisfaction on reading it and in many places, wrote down his comments, such as "Beautiful" and "Most Beautiful." His advice was that the manuscript should be neatly rewritten. But for a variety of reasons, I was unable to get down to revising it all these years. In the process of rewriting it now, modifications, interpolations, and deletions have been carried out in many parts of the original text. Only the Letter of Dedication remains intact.

I remember today, a story about religion and society that my revered elder brother had narrated to me. I cannot recall the complete story, only the following parts:

A man thirsting for religion went to a certain dervish to learn yoga. At that, the dervish said, "Let us go to my guru." That guru was a Hindu. Said the Hindu ascetic, "What can I teach you? Let us go to my guru." His guru was a Muslim dervish. When the student asked the dervish the reason for this intermingling of Hindus and Muslims, he replied:

"Religion is like a three-storied mansion. On the ground floor are many rooms—for Hindus and their many castes, like Brahmins and Shudras; for Muslims and their various sects like Shias, Sunnis, Hanafis, Sufis, and others; so also for Christians—Roman Catholics, Protestants, and so on. On the first floor, you will see Muslims—all Muslims—or Hindus—all Hindus and so on. Then go up to the second floor and you will see just one room with no divisions. That is, there are no Muslims or Hindus or anything else of the kind. Just human beings. And the object of their devotion is one God. If one starts a detailed analysis, nothing remains: everything becomes null and void; only God remains."

No part of the novel, *Padmarag*, has appeared before in any magazine. So, this time, readers will not be able to claim that it is "a stale item; I had seen it in such and such a newspaper!"

Mr. Binaybhushan Sarkar, a professor at the David Hare Training College, has been kind enough to read the proofs of *Padmarag* from beginning to end and has written its preface. I am especially grateful to him.

Any other errors that may have been overlooked in *Padmarag* are due to the author's lack of erudition. I hope that readers will forgive them.

ONE

JOURNEY INTO
THE UNKNOWN

When the train stopped at Naihati station at eleven p.m., a passenger dressed in English attire got off. Avoiding the crowd, he went toward the waiting room. Standing there, he gazed at the sights and beauty of the station. It seemed that he had not seen such a place or a station or a crowd ever before. That is why he was looking around him with eyes full of wonder.

Trains had to be changed here, if one wanted to go to Calcutta via Hooghly. There was time yet for the arrival of the train that would go to the various river ferries on the Hooghly. In the meantime, the passenger in question went down to the other end of the station. Some stationary trains stood there in a row. He began to pace up and down in the small patch of darkness created by the shadow of the trains. The row of trees nearby, the field of grass, all seemed to be bathed in the early autumn moonlight. But our traveler did not notice any of this. He was around eighteen or nineteen; his face was pale, deeply melancholy, but etched with tenderness. It seemed as if his heart would break. Although he was pacing, his feet barely seemed to move.

He was immersed in a deep sea of thought. Meanwhile, the train arrived and departed. Gradually, the lamps went off in ones and twos. He remained oblivious to it all. After a while, as though awakening from a dream, he went over to a station official and asked, "How long before the train leaves?" He learned that the train had left a long time ago. Moreover, there would be no other train going that night to the river ferries

from which one could take a boat to Calcutta. The news struck
him like a thunderbolt. He felt the world closing in on him and
silently moved away.

He had been planning to go to Calcutta but could not. He
would have to spend the night there. He was thinking: then
what do I do? Where do I go? What should I do in Calcutta?
Whom do I know there, after all? Whom can I go to, and what
should I say?

One might ask: why go from Hooghly to Calcutta? It is possible to go directly from Naihati to Calcutta. Certainly, there
must be a reason. This young man was in some kind of danger; so, he had disguised himself. Since he was escaping from
danger in disguise, why would he go by the direct route? The
enemy was following him. It might even be that the enemy was
going with him to Calcutta. That was why he was waiting
here, hoping to go to Hooghly.

Our traveler looked all around him with aching heart and
wistful gaze. The pleasant early autumn skies, the sparkling
garlands of stars, the soothingly beautiful creepers—none of
these showed him any sympathy. Rather, the moon seemed to
be mocking him because he had missed the train. He looked at
the moon listlessly and seemed to say,

Cruel, heartless moon! Perched in the distant sky,
What are you watching? The sins and jealousies of the world?
You see me and want to laugh at me?
Your heart must be very hard
If seeing my sorrow, tears do not come to your eyes,
And you only laugh.
Why can I not laugh?
He who made me also made you;
While you smile divinely always,
Why do I languish in tears?
The sorrows and fears of the world are not your companions,
Sin and penance do not touch you;
Why then do they make me cry?
You go everywhere; do you face obstacles anywhere?

Does anyone say to you, "This is our room,
Do not come here, stranger!"
In the land of the blue sky, you float at will,
As if the endless sky is your home!
Why then, can I not find a refuge?

TWO

HOMELESS

Walking absentmindedly along in this manner, the young man ended up some distance from the station. Although it was late, he was not overcome by drowsiness. Even the Goddess of Slumber, who relieves one of the burden of care and offers repose, is the companion of the happy man, not the sorrowful one. The traveler was careworn with anxiety, his main concern being to find shelter.

Now, with the night waning, the moon's radiance paled. A light veil of darkness hung over the earth. A constellation of stars gently lit up the expanse of sky. The young man was unaware of where he had ended up. The place was completely unfamiliar to him.

The melodious call to morning prayers from a mosque nearby awakened the silent earth, delighting and molding it into the *rasa* of devotion. Hearing that call, nature roused itself; all the birds awoke. The breeze carried the sound far, still further. That celestial sound was enough to make the traveler oblivious to the fatigue of having stayed up all night. I cannot describe what kind of joy he felt, since it can only be experienced; he who has experienced it, knows it.

Our traveler thought that it might not be a bad idea to go and seek shelter at the mosque. All he had with him was a handbag, so he would have no problem staying at the mosque for a couple of days. However, having arrived at the entrance to the mosque, he could not muster the courage to go in. What was wrong with him? He was weeping! No, he would not enter the mosque. He sat down helplessly by the road.

At that moment, three Brahmo women who were walking

that way for reasons unknown stopped near the young man. With no shelter to retire to, the latter gathered up courage and rose to his feet. Greeting the three women, he asked, "Would you be kind enough to help me?"

The first lady replied: "Help? Tell us what sort of help you need; we shall try."

"Would you accommodate my sister for a couple of weeks? I have work to attend to elsewhere. There is no one at home. Please keep her for two weeks. Then I shall return and do whatever needs to be done."

The first lady: "We have no objections, but where do you live? Who are you? You don't know us at all. Yet, you wish to entrust your sister to us—what could you mean by this? Moreover, we, too, are travelers like you. We are going to Calcutta today itself. Try the house of one of the locals."

The traveler looked at them with sad, tired eyes and pleaded, "Please take pity on me and give me—no, my unmarried sister—shelter."

The three women conferred among themselves and said, "We would have taken your sister home, but we really are going to Calcutta today."

"She will also go to Calcutta with you. Please do allow me to take her to your home there. She will pay her own train fare."

The first lady (to her companions): "What do you think?"

The second lady: "Whatever you deem fit. I have no objections. But it isn't our own house—how can we suddenly take a strange woman there without informing Mrs. Sen about it beforehand? What do you say, Bibha?"

Bibha: "Well, my advice would be to leave for Calcutta today; we shall then explain the situation to Mrs. Sen and keep her mentally prepared." (To the traveler) "Go there tomorrow. Here—take this. Our address is written on this paper. It is not our own home—we are employees at Tarini School. Go there and take your sister along with you."

THREE

DINA-TARINI,
OR THE SAVIOR OF
THE DISTRESSED

The distinguished lawyer, Tarinicharan Sen, had died young. He left behind no offspring; only his second wife, the young widow, Dina-Tarini, remained. For four years, she suffered from various ailments along with the trials of widowhood. Then, the city's reputed doctors attending to her gave up hope. But Dina-Tarini did not die.

Going against the wishes of her brothers-in-law, the older and the younger, and those of other relatives, Dina-Tarini set up a home for widows. She named it Tarini Bhavan. Encouraged by its success, she established a school and formed a society called the Society for the Upliftment of Downtrodden Women. Located at one end of the huge mansion housing Tarini Bhavan was the girls' school; at the other end stood the home for widows. But as time went by, Dina-Tarini also felt impelled to found a Home for the Ailing and the Needy next to it.

Having returned from death's door, Dina-Tarini received a fresh lease on life from the vast field of work stretching before her. Her relatives were not exactly pleased by the work she had dedicated her life to. In fact, they were quite unhappy about it, scorning her various activities and lamenting over the lakhs of rupees she was apparently squandering for this purpose.

Where would a widow find refuge, when she had no one in the world to turn to? In Tarini Bhavan. Where would a young orphan girl with no relatives be educated? At Tarini School. Where would a wife go, when she was forced to leave her marital home because of her husband's intolerable brutality? To the same Tarini Workshop.

Having thus been virtually ostracized by her own relatives, Dina-Tarini lived in seclusion. But to use the term "seclusion" would be misleading, because apart from the regular students (the day scholars), more than a hundred girls lived in the boardinghouse. Apart from them, there were the teachers and, of course, the matron and the maids. The number of people living in Tarini Bhavan was also not negligible. Tarini's relatives would remark, "Where will Tarini find people? Will any wife or daughter from a respectable family go anywhere near her? Every prostitute, every leper, and every worthless orphan is now a member of Tarini's extended family!"

Such comments failed to dishearten Tarini. Rather, they made her laugh. She would retort, "Is everyone given the honor of serving others?"

That evening, Dina-Tarini was very busy. A host of details pertaining to the school needed to be taken care of. She would have to serve as arbiter for the complaint that the collection-and-purchase clerk had, for some reason, beaten up the coachman. That afternoon, the female attendant who accompanied the schoolchildren traveling in Bus No. 5 had exclaimed, "Deary me! Never again will I escort a policeman's daughter home. The inspector said, 'I'll impound your bus, and toss your coachman into jail!'"

Tarini asked, "Why?"

"The horse is lame."

"Then tell him, 'Impound the horse and toss the syce into jail.'"

But that evening, a letter had arrived from the Society for the Prevention of Cruelty to Animals, stating that they would file a lawsuit against the school because the horses drawing Bus Nos. 3 and 5 limped. A charge of theft had been leveled against two syces for siphoning off the feed purchased for the horses. That afternoon, a wheel from Bus No. 7 had broken off after the vehicle collided with a tram. It was with such

problems that Tarini was grappling when Miss Bibha Chakrabarti came in with the news that the unknown woman from
Naihati had arrived.

Tarini said: "Keep her in Tarini Bhavan for tonight; I won't
be able to make inquiries about her today. We can meet early
tomorrow morning and discuss the subject. Please leave me
alone now—I am terribly busy."

FOUR

TARINI BHAVAN

Bibha escorted the stranger, Siddika, to Tarini Bhavan.

Usually, when people referred to Tarini Bhavan, they not only meant the house that was so named, but also the school, the workshop, and the Home for the Ailing and the Needy next to it. The school section, naturally, had Brahmo, Hindu, and Christian teachers. When the number of Muslim students increased, a couple of teachers were appointed to impart religious instruction to them. What commendable egalitarianism! Muslims, Christians, Brahmos, Hindus—all working in harmony, as though born from the same womb.

The school did without financial assistance from the government. It was, therefore, under no obligation to include in its curriculum any textbook featuring in the "government-approved" syllabus. Dina-Tarini selected the textbooks herself after consultations with highly learned women. The students were not branded, anyhow, with the mark of education as many universities were wont to do and turned into mere objects of luxury and pleasure. Science, Literature, Geography, Astronomy, History, Mathematics—all these subjects were taught, but the method of instruction was quite exceptional. The students were not forced to memorize misleading versions of history and end up despising themselves and their fellow Indians. Greater emphasis was laid on ethics, religious studies, and the inculcation of sound moral values. The girls were encouraged to grow up into good daughters, housewives, and mothers, inspired by high ideals, and to love their country and their religion more than life itself. Particular care was taken to ensure that they became self-reliant and not lifeless puppets, burdens on their fathers, brothers, husbands, or sons.

Only a select few in the whole country helped the school financially. Special care was taken to ensure that handouts were not accepted from the ruling aristocracy of native Indian states that had declared their allegiance to the British Empire.

The sick and the destitute were picked up from the streets and given shelter at the Home for the Ailing and the Needy. They left after they had recovered. Only the lepers and the physically disabled stayed on.

Many offered financial aid for the home. Several Muslim women offered donations anonymously. Such philanthropy was practiced in secret for fear that the divine grace earned by the act would be lost if the identity of the donors became common knowledge.

Most of the expenses of Tarini Bhavan were borne by the Society for the Upliftment of Downtrodden Women. Many Muslim women had become clandestine members of this society. Old women, impoverished widows, and ailing wives who were unfit for work lived in Tarini Bhavan.

In the workshop, all categories of women—spinsters, wives, and widows—were to be found. They were occupied in various kinds of work—sewing, spinning, weaving cloth on a loom, binding books, and preparing different types of sweetmeats and selling them. Some were given training that would make them eligible for a teaching job; some learned typing, while others trained to become nurses. To sum it up, the women belonging to this section earned their own living. It was here, too, that training was imparted to those who would become teachers at the Tarini Bhavan School and to nurses who would go on to work at the Home for the Ailing and the Needy. Moreover, women from this section were involved in other welfare work as well. They would, for example, distribute rice, clothes, and medicine and provide nursing care to people suffering the aftermath of famine, floods, and epidemics.

Siddika stood for a while, gazing in wonder at the house in all its beauty. The stone floor was scrupulously clean. The place was spare, devoid of luxury items like tables and chairs. All that was provided for each member was a pallet to sleep on. A big clock on the wall carried on its own functions without a pause.

The women's attire was nearly identical: white garments, easily soiled, were avoided. Everyone wore saris and dresses in blue or saffron. Shoes and socks, the badges of "civilization," were conspicuous by their absence. No one wore any jewelry; at the very most, some wore *shankhas* or bangles. None bore any signs of extravagance. All they seemed to be garbed in was simplicity and generosity. It was as if the daughters of sages and ascetics had renounced their ashrams in the wilderness for the material world. Such beauty lay in their austerity! The "sisterhood" seemed to be compassion personified.

Here, everyone addressed each other by using the familiar *tumi*, irrespective of age. They would refer to each other by the term "*di*" *(didi* or elder sister), or, if the lady was a Muslim, "*bi*" (*bubu* also meant sister). Dina-Tarini was usually known as "Mrs. Sen." Everyone used the formal *apni* to address her with respect. She, too, used the same form of address for nearly everyone.

Bibha introduced Siddika to the following three women:

1. Charubala Datta—thirty-eight years old, a spinster.
2. Saudamini—forty-three years old, married. Fair and beautiful. Her radiance had not diminished with the years.
3. Mrs. Helen Horace—Englishwoman, forty-one years old, known to all as a widow.

Siddika was very touched by their warmth and hospitality. She felt that if she could live here, even heaven would be dispensable. Since she fell fast asleep from sheer exhaustion soon after the evening meal was over, the women were unable to get acquainted with her.

The accommodation of the school's teachers was rather different from that of the women engaged in the workshop. The former were each allotted individual rooms and they weren't

saffron-clad nuns either. The other women did not have rooms
to themselves. On the floor along the vast veranda were
stretched out their individual pallets, along with their separate clothes racks and trunks. Siddika spent the night on
Saudamini's pallet.

FIVE

PADMARAG,
OR THE RUBY

A restful night without cares cheered up Siddika and restored her natural radiance. Breakfast over, Bibha and Usharani led Siddika to Tarini's room.

When she was brought to Dina-Tarini, Siddika stood shyly before her. Tarini asked her, "What is your name?"

"Siddika."

"Siddika, or Padmarag, the ruby with the lotus hue? Your complexion is as pretty as the rosy blush on a lotus. I hope you had a peaceful night's sleep here?"

"Oh yes, I slept well. What could possibly befall me in your care?"

"Oh, please! You really musn't say that! You must look upon this place as your own home. We have three Muslim teachers here. You will be staying with them. If any problems crop up, please don't hesitate to tell me about it. Where did your brother go after leaving you here?"

"To a faraway place."

"What reason could he possibly have for leaving his sister here, just because he has gone to a faraway place?"

"But there is no one else at home to leave me with."

"Bibha! What did her brother tell you when he left?"

Bibha: "I was not able to meet him. He apparently arrived in a horse-drawn carriage, handed her down, then left before I could go downstairs."

"Strange fellow! He leaves his unmarried sister in a strange place yet does not bother to exchange a few words with the people in whose care he leaves her!"

Bibha: "It just proves that the general public has great faith in you!"

Tarini: "But what convinced you that this young girl was the sister of the gentleman from Naihati?"

Bibha gazed at Siddika's face and said, "She looks exactly like him—as if they were twins. And she was carrying the piece of paper on which I had written down our address, as well as the handbag which—"

Tarini burst out laughing, "All right, that'll do! No further evidence is called for. Instead of keeping her in Tarini Bhavan, let her share a room with a teacher. So, will you entrust her to Jafri Khanum or Koresha-bi?"

"Koresha-bi is the more courteous of the two. And she herself has expressed a wish to have Siddika with her."

"Well, here's Koresha-bi now. Well, there you are—do take good care of this young girl."

Koresha: "That goes without saying. That is why I'm here in the first place." (To Siddika) "Come . . . what is your name?"

Bibha: "Mrs. Sen has named her Padmarag."

Koresha: "Padam-raj? What kind of name is that, pray?"

Tarini: "Take no notice of Bibha's pranks; this lady's name is Siddika Khatun."

Bibha: "Koresha-bi! You really degrade our Bengali names. You called Padmarag Padam-raj—that's very unfair of you."

Mrs. Usharani Chatterjee said, "You should hardly lament over this! Don't you remember how initially, you would distort the pronunciation of Muslim names? You'd call Rasekha 'Rasika,' Saukat Ara 'Suktara'?"

Bibha: "I also remember that I nearly came to blows with Jafri Khanum on that subject. Well, our Koresha-bi speaks Bengali quite fluently."

Usha: "She certainly does! She has just invited me for tea with the words, 'The tea will drink you'!"

Koresha (softly to Tarini): "Isn't that correct Bengali?"

Tarini: "That's quite all right; don't let these Bengali women bother you."

After evening prayers were over, a group of teachers, excluding Koresha and the members of the workshop, gathered in Usharani's room. The subject of discussion was Siddika.

In a tone backed by wisdom and vast experience, Jafri Khanum commented, "No woman from a respectable background ever comes to a place like this in quite this manner."

Charubala: "Even if her twin brother leaves her there?"

Jafri: "That is precisely what I am saying—no gentleman behaves this way."

Usharani: "Is there a book of etiquette in which it is clearly stated, 'A gentleman does nothing but this and this' and 'does not do that'?"

Bibha: "You're really annoying me! Gentlemen are allowed to commit all kinds of offenses like cheating, lying, betraying promises, and so on—all they're not permitted to do is leave their sisters in a respectable place, is that it?"

Charu: "Is there any crime that gentlemen don't commit? Robbery, embezzlement, theft, the deadly sins . . . is there a vice for which they don't have a license?"

Usha: "If a man doesn't swindle his widowed aunt of everything she possesses and reduce her to abject penury so that she's no better than a beggar on the street, how can he earn his pedigree as a gentleman? His Haj, his pilgrimages, his piety—all would be pointless! Oh, forget it! What I want to know, Khanum Sahiba, is if you can tell by looking at Sidikka whether she's the offspring of some lowly laborer or tribal."

Jafri: "I haven't mastered the art of reading people's faces. But there's a tenderness in the beauty of her face that is common in women who belong to respectable families."

Nalini: "Well, Khanum Sahiba, what kind of work are your gentlemen from Lucknow engaged in?"

Bibha: "They perfume their mustaches and apply clarified butter on their clothes!"

Jafri: "Oh, how you do go on, Bibha-di! I refuse to listen to another word of yours!"

Saudamini: "Life's cruel vicissitudes must have forced poor Padmarag to fall here like a bud torn from its stem. Even if she doesn't come from a respectable background, we will help her to become respectable."

Nalini: "Tarini Workshop will turn her into gold, as though at the touch of a philosopher's stone."

Usha: "I wouldn't mind either if she turned into a padma-rag, a ruby, instead of gold."

SIX

ALL ALONE

Siddika had been in Tarini Workshop for around ten months, but no one had, as yet, been able to discover her real identity. If the sisters (the women belonging to Tarini Workshop and the school's teachers were usually known as "sisters of the poor"; people, therefore, used an abbreviated form of address, "sisters," to refer to them) made tender queries about this, she would either run away to another room or burst into tears and plead, "Please excuse me. I can't tell you a thing. I am all alone in this world with not a soul to call my own."

If confronted once more with the question, "Where do you live?" the reply would be: "I live everywhere. At Tarini Bhavan, in particular."

In all this while, Siddika had not written a single letter to anyone. Nor had she received a letter from anyone. So, there was no way of knowing who she was. Even her brother who had, ostensibly, left her here for a mere two weeks, had not sent a postcard inquiring about her. And no one from Tarini Bhavan had actually seen this brother. Siddika had alighted from the carriage with her handbag and had paid off the coachman herself. After Bibha had come down, she had followed her upstairs. The fact was, that in no way could they discover her true identity. Siddika was always melancholy. The sisters would resort to many witty remarks to make her smile, but in vain. Like an immovable mountain, she remained still and grave. At times, the aged medical compounder, Ishan Babu, would exclaim, "Goodness! I've seen many folks, but never a girl quite like this one! Truly, the hard-hearted daughter of a hard-hearted mother!"

The teachers and nurses would discuss Siddika among themselves and remark, "Is Padmarag not really human? Does she not understand the language of human beings? Is she actually a divine creature descended from some unknown paradise because a curse has been laid on her? Alas! Who could have put such a curse on her?"

"Perhaps, she is a celestial being who, having lost her way, now finds herself on earth. It is as if she were unfamiliar with the ways of the world."

"Indeed it seems so! She looks like the pale full moon of dawn or like a wilting rosebud. Alas! How tragic for her to have been indelibly marked so early in life by a hostile world!"

"This ashram is an ideal haven from the ravages of this cruel life. Sister, we have come to Tarini Bhavan to heal wounds inflicted by a remorselessly cruel world. But what could this adolescent girl possibly know of life to renounce the material world so soon and come here?"

Saudamini: "Who knows, sister? Who can understand another's pain? But you know, some ripen prematurely. Others wither before their time. There are so many stars, big and small, in the vast firmament of life:

> In silence they rise, in silence they set;
> Who keeps track, who keeps an account?"

Nalini: "Yes, I recall the poet's words:

> Full many a gem of purest ray serene,
> The dark unfathom'd caves of ocean bear:
> Full many a flower is born to blush unseen,
> And waste its sweetness on the desert air."

Saudamini: "How is your patient? You probably haven't been to see him even once today!"

Nalini: "Oh, no, sister, how could I not? I have just been to see him. He is sleeping quite soundly."

Charubala: "Nurse Nalini is not one to overlook her responsibilities. While you discuss precious stones, I ponder over Nalini. She

> Would in the humming of the bumblebee
> Hear so many alluring words of hope;
> Creating a world of flowers in her imagination
> Where she was the queen."

Nalini, a child-widow, was, indeed, as cheerful as a lotus bloom; she was around thirty-eight years old. She said with feigned displeasure, "Shame on you, Charu-di! A little more seriousness is in order!"

Charu: "Very well, in that case,

> The lotus bud in the lake of life
> Looked at the sun of hope;
> To the blossoming fullness of Nalini, the lotus,
> Evening came instead of noon."

A few days later, came Siddika's request: "Please allow me to take up some work as well."

Saudamini: "What kind of skills do you have?"

Siddika: "I don't have any special skills; I shall do whatever I am bidden to do."

Saudamini: "Suppose I asked you to chop wood?"

Siddika: "I wouldn't be able to chop wood. Why not entrust me with some chore that does not involve hard physical labor? How about some sewing?"

Saudamini: "Sewing . . . what kind of sewing can you do? Can you tailor our clothes? Are you an expert at cutting petticoats, blouses, shirts, and so on?"

Although Siddika was adept at various kinds of fine embroidery, she had not learned how to sew clothes for everyday use. Whatever little education she had received was not of the income-generating variety. In other words, Siddika's education was akin to the kind that zamindars' daughters were given. It consisted of language skills and training in various kinds of fine embroidery, knitting, and so on. Siddika realized that no part of her learning would be useful for earning an income. Since she had not been taught mathematics, her education would be in vain. When she resigned herself to sewing, the problem of cutting cropped up. Finally, it was decided that she would sew clothes, curtains, sheets, and pillowcases for needy patients.

From that day onward, Siddika was always busy with needle and thread. She would also participate in other activities as far as she was able. She would prepare mixtures as prescribed for patients and cook the latter's meals. She would undertake the minor chores that the other nurses did not have time for. There was no task to which she did not apply herself with diligence. From want of habit, however, she could not, initially, ably perform any of the tasks she undertook.

One day, when she went to the office room in Tarini Bhavan and found some women typing, she assumed that this work would be quite easy. When she approached Rafiya Begum and expressed her wish to type, the latter asked her, "Do you know how to?"

Siddika: "Well, I've never done it, but I'm sure I will be able to. Watch me . . ."

But watching her type, everyone burst out laughing.

Siddika felt quite embarrassed and began to wonder: "I know English; I can read the letters on the typewriter keys. Then, how is it that my fingers refused to move along the keyboard the way they should have?" Later, when she underwent formal training (following the blind system) to learn typing, she realized that even typing a simple two-letter word like "is" involved the use, first of a finger from the right hand, then of a finger from the left hand.

Although Siddika often met all the male employees of Tarini Bhavan in the course of her daily duties, none of them knew her well. Knowing her to be reticent, they made no attempt to speak to her about inconsequential things.

When the day's work was done, the women would go out in the evening for a stroll to the riverbank or the fields. At first, Siddika would not go out with them. Later, Sakina and Nalini persuaded her to accompany them.

A boy named Sarat had come to the Home for the Ailing and Needy. Siddika devoted herself to his care. This gave her an opportunity to learn nursing. Earlier, the sight of patients would make her fearful; Sarat taught her the virtue of serving others. In the course of nursing Sarat, her intimacy with Saudamini increased, since Saudamini loved Sarat dearly, as much as life itself.

SEVEN

THE PATIENT

When Tarini Bhavan closed for the summer vacation, Tarini went to Kurseong along with a few teachers. Koresha and Siddika, too, had gone along with the rest.

Usharani, Koresha, and Siddika had been out one afternoon, walking through a valley. Night was nearly upon them by the time they returned home along Bordillon Road. Bibha's mother had been ill. Having procured medicine for her, Usha came across a shortcut and suggested, "Let us take this path. It'll be quicker this way."

While walking down this path, they noticed something lying near a bush. It looked like a man. After hesitating awhile, they made their way in and saw what lay there: good Lord! It was, indeed, a man, with blood gushing from his body. It was rather dark here, as the moonlight failed to penetrate the area. A shiver went down their spines. Usha felt the man's pulse and realized that he was still alive; with proper nursing care, he might survive. But he needed it urgently.

The hospital was a good distance from that spot, whereas the house where they had put up was nearby. Bibha suggested, "Let us take him home for the time being. Later, we can do whatever is appropriate. But what if it displeases Mrs. Sen?"

Koresha: "Surely not. If she is displeased about it, I shall explain the situation to her."

Usha: "Mrs. Sen will not object to our helping a man on the verge of death. Now wait here while I fetch a *dandi*."

A dandi is a kind of stretcher, carried on the shoulder by a couple of coolies. At the time of which we are speaking, there

was no transport available in Darjeeling district apart from
rickshaws, horses, and dandis.

Fortunately, a dandi was obtained very quickly and they returned home with the critically injured man.

*

Tarini: "I would not worry if it was a woman. But who will
take care of this man? You all know that I'm not exactly exag-
gerating when I say that I keep no male servants; the odd-jobs
boy is too young to count; the bearer and the water-supplier
are not live-in employees. The only other male is the cook—
and he is holed up forever in the kitchen."

Koresha: "Well, what can we do? Now that we have already
brought him here."

Tarini: "Very well, then, you will take care of him together.
I want no part in this particular responsibility. Bibha will, of
course, work hard. Koresha-bi! It won't do for you to be in
purdah . . . please ensure that you take proper care of this patient. And Padmarag, you too—"

Siddika: "But I know nothing about first aid or nursing!"

Tarini: "Well, if you don't, you have to learn! Bibha—quick!
The doctor is here to see your mother. When he has finished
examining her, please ask him to have a look at this poor
fellow."

Bibha hurried out. The doctor came in at once. Koresha ran
to the kitchen to fetch hot water. Usha came forward to help
the doctor examine the patient's wounds. Siddika held up the
hurricane lamp for the doctor. Two maids handed them medicine, water, and so on. And Tarini? She had declared she
would do nothing, but she was now engaged in preparing bandages from discarded old clothes.

*

The patient was asleep in a room; seated on a chair by the bed,
Siddika stared into a book. She was certainly looking at the
book, but it was difficult to tell whether she was reading it at
all. In order to force herself to stay awake, she would occasionally look at the book or knit absentmindedly. Needless to

say, she was not making much headway with either, because her eyes were weighed down with sleep.

Once, the patient turned on his side and uttered a plaintive cry. Siddika perked up a little, gladdened by his return to consciousness.

The patient called out, "Karim Baksh! Karim Baksh!"

Expressing no surprise whatsoever at his words, Siddika said softly, "Karim Baksh is asleep."

The patient: "Is it night, then? How late is it?"

Siddika: "Nearly three a.m."

The patient: "Then why are you still awake? Who are you?"

Siddika: "I am a poor sister. I just came to find out whether you wanted something to eat."

The patient: "Rafika! When did you arrive?"

Siddika: "It's been three days since I arrived on hearing about your illness."

The patient: "Oh, am I ill? I see! That's why I can't get up. My body aches all over."

"Don't fret over it; if Allah wills it, you will recover soon." Having said this, Siddika brought him a bowl of milk to drink.

The patient sat up, looked around him, and exclaimed in surprise, "Whose house is this? It isn't that sanatorium!" He gazed at Siddika and said, "And you are not Rafika either! Please explain how I ended up here."

Siddika: "I shall, later. Now you are very tired, so do drink up that milk, will you? You have absolutely no cause for worry."

Without another word, the patient drank up the milk. Meanwhile, Nalini had come in. Seeing her, Siddika heaved a sigh of relief.

Nalini was a trained nurse. She put the patient at ease with a few gentle words. Later, with Siddika's help, she dressed his wounds.

Nalini was about to leave after putting the patient to bed, when Siddika caught hold of the free end of her sari and said, "Why don't you sit for a while? The night is nearly over."

Nalini: "That's why I was leaving. I shall try to catch some sleep."

Siddika: "Oh . . . have you been awake all night? But tonight—"

Nalini: "Yes, you're right. I had no duties tonight; but that wretched sleep has been eluding me. That's why I've been wandering around and dropped in to see you."

Siddika: "And everyone's collective sleep seems to have overpowered me. I can hardly keep my eyes open. Why can't I stay up nights like you do?"

Nalini: "Once you're accustomed to it, you will. Now, I have to be off."

By then, night had given way to day. Siddika opened a window and noticed the blush of dawn spreading across the expanse of sky. The patient did open his eyes once on hearing that it was morning. He remained silent, his eyes shut the way they had been before.

Several days went by in this manner. Until now, no one had even asked the patient his name. The hapless man would silently gaze at everything and listen to all that was being said. But not a word would he utter himself. It was as if he remained submerged in deep thought. Every day, he would see a different nurse attending to him. If Nalini stayed up one night to look after him, the following night it would be Siddika's or Usha's turn. Whenever he woke up at night, he would find what seemed like a heavenly creature seated at his bedside. It would make him feel that these were, indeed, "sisters." Could Rafika have tended to him with such devotion?

One afternoon, when Siddika was sitting by him, working on a piece of crochet, the patient asked her, "Please, do tell me the truth: where am I? Whose house is this? How have I ended up here?"

Siddika: "You are in Kurseong. This is the home of a Brahmo lady called Mrs. Sen. We are all members of her household. You were lying injured on a path leading off Bordillon Road; we found you and brought you here."

At this moment, someone called from outside, "Siddika, come here for a minute."

Siddika got up at once and left the room. That marked the

end of her conversation with the patient. The latter thought, so, this girl is a Muslim. A Muslim in a Brahmo household . . . what sort of an enigma was this? Anyway, how did it matter to him?

Tarini came to check on the patient and found him stronger, healthier, and sitting up in bed. She told him how glad she was to notice his progress and asked him how he was feeling.

The patient: "I am deeply indebted to you. I owe my life to your people, who nursed me back to health. I am now able to recall how I injured myself. I had arrived in Kurseong from Darjeeling that day. Intending to spend the night in a hotel, I had gone out for a walk after dusk. On the way, I was accosted by three men who wanted to snatch away my watch, chain, spectacles, and other belongings. The moment I shouted for the police, they attacked me with knives and sticks. I fell unconscious. You know the rest."

Tarini: "You were on the verge of death because you had bled so much. Your condition was so critical after we brought you here, that we dared not risk putting you through the ordeal of sending you to a hospital. Our main concern was to save your life. Anyway, don't worry. We, your poor sisters, will take care of you to the best of our ability. May I ask you your name?"

The patient: "Latif Almas. I do not have words to express my gratitude. I doubt whether even a mother or a sister could have shown as much devotion as you did."

When Mr. Latif Almas's condition improved a little, the sisters rarely came to see him. Only the compounder, Ishan Babu, would dress his wounds twice a day. A rapport of sorts developed, in this manner, between Ishan Babu and Latif. From him, Latif obtained a brief account of who the sisters were, and a fuller account of Dina-Tarini's particulars. Ishan Babu was able to offer little information about Siddika, however.

Latif: "Don't you feel hesitant about giving shelter to a woman with no known antecedents? She could well be a murderer and a fugitive from justice. Or she could have come from some really disreputable place."

Ishan: "Whatever she may or may not have done, our Tarini Bhavan is like the Ganga—a single dip is enough to purify anyone."

Ishan Babu was known to everyone as Ishan-da. That is what Latif began to call him as well.

EIGHT

SARATKUMAR

Saratkumar, a nine-year-old boy, had come to Tarini Bhavan. Dhirendra Babu was a highly religious Brahmin. Once upon a time, he had been a wealthy man. Now, the complex manipulations of fate had robbed him of his riches. Sarat's mother had died when he was a year old. So, he was his father's precious treasure. To Dhirendra Babu, Sarat was equal to the wealth and splendor of the entire world. With his son beside him, Dhirendra could not imagine anything of greater value in the whole world.

For two years, Sarat had been suffering from pernicious diseases like malaria and an enlarged spleen. Dhirendra had lost faith in doctors and healers. No women lived in poor Dhirendra's home. He had neither mother nor sister. As for distant female relatives, why would they bother to visit a poor man's home? The disasters that befall a man who has been cursed by fate are all the greater. Nursing Sarat tirelessly round the clock, Dhirendra was exhausted and in deep despair. Finally in the hope of getting better nursing care for his son, he had brought Sarat to the Tarini Home for the Ailing and the Needy. The residents of the ashram did their best to look after him. Finally, they brought him to Kurseong for a change of air.

Eight days after Tarini arrived there with Sarat, Latif was brought in. He gradually recovered. Latif improved a great deal. He could now walk about, though slowly. He would at times come and sit by Sarat's bed. Sarat was now very frail. One day, turning to Saudamini with his typical child's smile, he asked, "Aunty, when will Father come?"

Saudamini: "Your father has just left. Why do you want to

see him again so soon? No affection to spare for us? Father's everything to you, is he? What do you think will happen if Father comes?"

Sarat: "Father won't be able to do anything, but when he comes, I feel better. My fever subsides. So much else happens. It makes me so happy to see Father."

Siddika: "Then shall I send someone to fetch him?"

Sarat: "No. There is no need to bother my father now. If I bother him too much, God will be annoyed."

Latif (with a tiny smile): "You know that as well, do you? What else do you know?"

Sarat: "I know how to sing. Shall I sing for you?"

Saudamini: "No, be quiet now. If you talk too much, your cough will worsen and that will sadden God."

Sarat: "Then could I recite poems?"

Saudamini: "Not now."

Sarat: "Don't any of you like my singing?"

Nalini: "Yes, of course we do. But it hurts you to sing. Now I'd like to see you get some sleep."

Sarat: "If I am prepared to suffer, if by suffering pain I am able to sing for you and make you happy, then what reason do I have not to do so? Our lives are so short. If I do not suffer for others, then what is there to do?"

Who is this boy, Latif wondered. Love personified? What kind of prayers had Dhiren Babu devoted himself to in order to be rewarded with a treasure of this kind? Latif was moved by the boy's radiant, open countenance.

Sarat began to sing, but his body was racked by coughs before he could finish even a part of his song. Saudamini exclaimed, "You don't do as you're told! You're a very naughty boy! You have all the virtues except obedience."

Sarat: "Aunty, haven't I already taken enough punishment for disobedience? Do I need more?" He coughed.

Weakened considerably by his illness, Sarat could no longer sing his very dear song "All that adorns this great world." Yet, at times he would practice the scales of the Bhairavi or Behag ragas. Only those who had heard him could appreciate how sweet those very ordinary scales could sound in the deep silence of the night, when they were sung in Sarat's mellifluous voice. Could celestial music have been any sweeter?

Gradually, Sarat became so weak that he had little interest in music. When the same Saudamini, who had once forbidden him to sing, entreated him now with the words, "Child, do give us a song," the boy would reply, "No, I just don't feel like it anymore." Saudamini would avert her face from him to shed silent tears.

Since the Tarini School vacation ended on the first of the Bengali month of *Asadh*, Tarini went back to Calcutta with her staff, leaving behind only Saudamini, Nalini, and Sakina to nurse Sarat and Latif. Since Siddika herself was not keeping well, Tarini left her behind too. Ishan Babu also remained. It was decided that those who stayed back would, depending on Sarat's state of health, leave for Calcutta sometime in the middle of the Bengali month of *Sravana*.

After dusk had fallen, Latif visited Sarat once more. There was something so appealing about the boy that everyone was drawn to him. Dhirendra was there too. Sarat wound his wasted little arms round his father's neck and asked, "How are you, Father? It seems that you've not eaten all day. You look worn out."

Dhirendra kissed his son and replied: "I am fine. Don't worry about me. All you need to do is get well and I will get a new lease on life."

Sarat: "Father, death is inevitable, so why does the very thought of it make you all so fearful? Life is short, death eternal. If you gave God all the love you have reserved for me—"

Dhirendra: "Son, please! Put an end to your speeches! Those very same words—again and again! Isn't there anything else to talk about?"

Sarat: "There may be other things to talk about, but I wouldn't know about them." (With a slight smile) "Wasn't it you who told me that one should love God more than anything else? Then why do you love Sarat, your little Sarat, more than you love God?"

Dhirendra: "So, you're not going to stop, are you? And you won't take a short nap, will you? Then I might as well leave."

When he realized that Dhirendra was about to leave, Sarat called out to him: "Father! Father! There you go again! Why lose your temper? Why feel such indignation, when it is a matter of just one more day?" Dhirendra had failed at the time to comprehend the significance of the words "just one more day." He did, the day after.

Sarat's condition was grave. Drained by his endless bouts of coughing, he was almost on the verge of losing consciousness. Everyone was distraught. Saudamini was gripped by a profound feeling of despair. It was as if she could hardly bear to look at that face, now shadowed by death. Sarat was anxious to see his father—as if holding on to life, just to bid him farewell. Then his poor father arrived. Sarat exclaimed impatiently, "Father! I can't hold on any longer!"

Dhirendra: "Child, please! If you carry on in this vein, I shall renounce the world and become a recluse. You are all I have! Without you, my life will lose all meaning, son! Don't you understand that?"

Sarat did not allow himself to utter a single groan after that. He knew what great anguish he was causing his father. So he kept the intensity of his own suffering to himself and endured his death throes in silence. When he could bear it no longer, he would lie in bed, thrashing around in pain. But not a moan escaped his lips. What fortitude! Was this humanly possible? Where would a human get such reserves of patience?

And then? Then what? Motioning his father to hold him in his arms, Sarat left his earthly father's home for eternal rest in the arms of the Divine Father. The clouds of Sravana roared and burst into a shower of tears. Alas! shrieked the wind. Neither moon nor stars lit up the sky—only an impenetrable darkness hung over the earth.

Saudamini was asleep. She dreamed that Sarat lay dying. With his dying breath he seemed to say, "Aunty! I am not yet dead—I am just waiting for you." The moment Saudamini woke up, she ran to Sarat's bedside like a crazed woman, her hair loose and flying behind her. She called out to him. Sarat opened his eyes slightly but did not utter a word. He had lost the power of speech. His eyes closed again. Go away, Saudamini! What is left for you to see? This is not the Sarat you knew; it is only a shadow of the boy. Your Sarat is gone—gone!

*

Dhirendra was Saudamini's younger brother. Saudamini had recognized him, but he had failed to recognize his sister. He had not seen her from the time she was seventeen years old; so it was impossible for him to recognize her so many years later. The exceptionally intelligent and perceptive Saudamini had, in the course of their conversations, managed to recognize her brother, but she had kept her own identity from him. In Sarat she thought she had, at last, found someone to call her own and seek the balm for her wounded heart. But her accursed fate would not allow her even that respite. This turn of events discouraged her from disclosing her identity to her brother. Who could tell what might happen if she did? What if God grew jealous at her happiness from being allowed to address her brother as "brother"? What if her brother was snatched away from her if she divulged her identity? So what good would it do? It would be quite futile to try to alleviate, even in an infinitesimal way, the anguish of a wounded heart. Let it hurt. Oh, let it hurt!

After Saratkumar's death, Dhirendra disappeared. No one knew where he had gone. Go, Dhiren! Go away and lead a hermit's life, traveling to the depths of the forests and the caves of the Himalayas in quest of Sarat—or rather, of Sarat's Creator. In no time at all, the cruel world will have forgotten you.

NINE

BENEVOLENCE

People occasionally find themselves at a loss to explain why they are attracted to something or someone. What could possibly be the mysterious reason underlying that attraction? When Latif was ill, he always longed for Siddika's presence at his bedside. The other sisters would try to ease his pain with their jokes and anecdotes, whereas Siddika would sit by him, immersed in silence. Latif loved that silence. Now that Latif was much better, Siddika no longer sat by him.

Latif experienced a pang of regret at having to leave this paradise of tranquillity, but go he would have to. The sisters had planned to stay on until fifteenth Sravana for Sarat, but this early autumn bloom had perished in the very first week of the month. The sisters now prepared to leave for Calcutta; all they would wait for was for Latif to return home. Latif calculated that for his fare home and so on, he would need no less than two hundred and fifty rupees. He needed some clothes. It was also proper that he reimburse the ashram for the expenses they had incurred on his behalf. If a well-to-do man like him accepted charity from the ashram, who, then, would be left to offer it donations? He wrote home, asking for three hundred rupees to be sent over.

In due course, a reply to Latif's letter arrived. It was evidently written in a lady's elegant hand, but Latif failed to derive any satisfaction from its corresponding elegance of expression. In sum, the letter stated: "It seems from your letter that a band of brigands robbed you clean and that you were unable to write to us because you were ill for two months. But your companion has come back and informed us that you were killed by the brigands. He has brought back all your belongings. Your letter, therefore, arouses our suspicion that someone impelled by the greed for money has forged your handwriting and written to us. Unless we see you in person, we are not willing to believe that you are alive. I have written to my brother about this. He will visit you. Please return home with him."

Latif shredded the letter into pieces. This was insane! Who wouldn't be infuriated at reading something of this sort? Saleha lacked the ability to undertake any responsibility at all. Prone to suspicion she might be, but she certainly wasn't qualified to indulge her suspicion. Latif began to wonder what he should do. If the money was not forthcoming, how would he make his way home? At that moment, Saudamini made her silent appearance.

Seeing her, Latif experienced a faint stirring of joy. Noticing the shreds of paper in his hand, she asked, "A letter from home, Mr. Almas? What does it say? I hope everyone is fine back home?"

Latif: "Yes, they are certainly fine."

Saudamini: "Then what's there to worry about?"

Latif: "Why no, I'm not worried."

Saudamini: "But it's obvious that you haven't received good news. At least, not the response you had hoped for."

Latif: "You are absolutely right. But I am certainly not worried."

Saudamini: "Perhaps not, but you are certainly angry."

Latif (embarrassed): "You have divine insight. It is futile to keep anything from you. I am, indeed, angry. I had asked for money, but they won't send it. I can't lay my hands on my own money."

Saudamini: "Why be upset over it? You can borrow as much money as you need from us and repay it when it is convenient for you to do so."

Latif: "Who knows me well enough in this place to lend me money?"

Saudamini: "We shall. If what we sisters have with us is not enough to meet your needs, we shall write to Mrs. Sen at Tarini

Bhavan and have the money sent over. How much do you need?"

Latif was stunned. These strangers were prepared to entrust him with money—with such a thing as money! And his own wife would not run the risk of sending him even fifty rupees, let alone three hundred. Full of gratitude, Latif replied, "Sister! I am deeply indebted to you. In fact, such tender compassion as all of you have showered on me makes me feel awkward. I am unworthy of it. I am unable to go home without money to pay my way. For the moment, a hundred rupees should suffice."

That evening, the sisters sat out in the garden. The sky was relatively clear after the day's rain. The moon of the tenth lunar day, beaming from the sky, frolicked merrily with the stars, the earth awash in its silver glow. Seated in a corner of the garden, Siddika was absorbed in a discussion involving the play of light in the sky and the congregation of the moon and the stars, when Saudamini and Latif approached them.

"Well Siddika, are you counting the stars?" Saudamini teased.

Siddika suddenly rose to her feet. "Sister, is there something you wish to tell me?" she asked.

Saudamini: "Yes, Mr. Almas is ready to go home, but he hasn't been able to get the money he needs for his traveling expenses. So, we will have to raise the necessary funds and give him a loan for his fare. We need at least a hundred rupees. How much can you contribute?"

Siddika: "I don't have more than sixty rupees to offer."

Saudamini: "See, Mr. Almas? You have sixty rupees."

Latif's boundless gratitude was plain for all to see. Siddika and Saudamini comprehended the import of that unexpressed gratitude.

After breakfast the following day, Saudamini asked Siddika for the money. When the latter rose to fetch it, Latif accompanied her. Siddika counted out the money, rupee by rupee, and gave it to him. Latif was thinking that if ever there was a place called Heaven, this was it! These were such trusting people! It did not occur to them to worry unduly about whom they were entrusting their money to nor about whether they would get it back. Latif gazed in wonder at the hands of the woman who had given him the money. How free those hands were from the burden of distrust and anxiety! Siddika asked him with tender affection, "How much more will you need?"

Latif: "If you can manage it, I'll be grateful for just enough to make a total of one hundred rupees."

Siddika: "I have given all I had; the other sisters will give the rest."

The words "I have given all I had" touched Latif's heart. He felt that those words ought not to have touched him as deeply as they had, because after all, there was Saleha. He glanced at his interlocutor's face. He could read no particular meaning there. That face was one of celestial beauty, compassion, and innocence. Latif sighed inwardly. Getting a grip on himself, he asked, "Won't you keep some money for your own needs?"

Siddika: "That won't be a problem. Please don't worry about it."

Nalini entered.

"Nalini-di! Aren't you contributing your share to the fund?"

The playfully mischievous Nalini replied, "Of course, I certainly shall! But the 'brother' we picked up from the wayside is off home now. Who knows when we shall see him again?"

Latif: "If you are kind enough to remember me, there is every chance of our seeing each other again. Unfortunately, I do not practice in Calcutta." Latif was an up-and-coming lawyer and a prosperous zamindar.

Nalini summoned Sakina Khanum: "Please open my trunk and bring me ten rupees, sister. Here is the key."

Sakina returned and handed Nalini twenty rupees. The latter counted out the money and asked, "Why ten rupees more?"

Sakina: "Does no one else have the right to contribute to the fund? I am a poor woman; I couldn't give much."

Latif (gratefully): "I envy you your graciousness and wonder why I wasn't given a chance to become a 'sister' of Tarini Bhavan like you!"

Nalini: "For that, all you need is a pair of bangles and a saffron sari!"

Sakina: "You are a man, the most superior of beings in God's universe. What greater heights could you aspire to? Are the sari and bangles prescribed by Doctor Nalini more exalted than what you have?"

Ishan Babu came in.

Ishan: "What is this discussion going on about creation?"

Nalini: "Mr. Almas regrets that he was not born a woman."

Latif: "Not just any woman, but divine beings like you."

Ishan: "Of course." Pointing to the three sisters, he asked Latif, "But have you any idea as to where they have come from?"

Latif: "No."

Ishan: "Then listen:

> The sound of poor people weeping
> Once penetrated the gates of heaven.
> The Lord of the World took pity
> And rained flowers on them.
> The various and beautiful flowers of heaven
> Fell to the earth;
> Here and there, where they could,
> They flowered in the groves of humanity.
> People are so mired
> That they do not love to care for flowers.
> The flowers said to God,
> 'Why did you send us to man's abode?'
> So the Lord, the sea of compassion,
> Wove a garland with the flowers fallen from heaven.
> From then on in Tarini Bhavan are found
> Daughters of the gods, the 'sisters of the poor.'"

Latif: "Ishan-da, you are a poet par excellence. I used to believe that the mind that preoccupies itself with the difference between barium sulfate and barium sulfide has little leisure to reflect on other things; I now realize that among the various bottles of medicine, there is also one containing 'sulfate of poetry.'"

Ishan: "Of course, there has to be such a bottle! A compounder has to work with all kinds of medicine. Particularly, wherever our Mrs. Sen goes, the hospital follows suit. Nurse Nalini and I have been summoned here to care for you. A dispensary box has also arrived with us."

Saudamini came in at this moment and said, "What's being discussed?"

Ishan: "Nothing in particular, Didi. Today, I followed the doctor's prescription and gave Mr. Almas a dose of 'bicarbonate of poetry.'"

Saudamini: "Well done! Have you got the money, Mr. Almas?"

Latif: "Yes, I have received eighty rupees."

Saudamini: "Good. You will receive the remaining twenty rupees as well."

On the day of his departure, Latif rose at dawn. As soon as he was awake, the sound of music reached him from afar. Since he was a great lover of music, he identified the raga and the beat—it was the melodious raga Bhairavi. Powerfully drawn to the music being played on a harmonium, he could no longer remain in his room. He would be leaving that day.

Was that why the gods in the city of heaven were singing a song of farewell mournfully?

He stepped out of his room and was informed by a maid he spoke to that Siddika was playing the harmonium. He listened attentively, hoping that he would also hear her sing, but his luck was out. Gradually, the music died away. Was this music an expression of the deep anguish buried in the singer's heart, abandoned to the winds and poured into the infinite expanse of the sky? Was the essence of her being borne away on the waves of that music? Or was this merely their regular morning song?

Latif bade farewell to everyone at noon. Each of them affectionately urged him to write to them. Only Siddika did not utter a word. Latif thought, "She is as unfeeling as an idol carved from stone."

TEN

DOMESTIC LIFE

Latif was unhappy at the thought of going home. He had not been elated in the way people were when they were returning home from distant lands. On the contrary, he went back with a heavy heart. What was the reason for such sadness at the thought of going home? Was there no peace there? Yes, it was precisely because there was no peace there that he could derive little pleasure from this homecoming.

Latif had lost his father in childhood. Since his grandfather was living at the time, he and his sisters, Rashida and Rafika, were deprived of their share of the inheritance. After his grandfather died, his father's older brother, Haji Habib Alam, became heir to their landed estate and took on the responsibility of his widowed sister-in-law and her three children. Latif's mother was a very intelligent woman; she realized that although their basic needs were taken care of, no suitable provisions were being made for Latif's education. Demeaning herself to the point of serving her sister-in-law like a maid, she managed to prevail upon her to persuade her husband to send Latif to school.

Latif was promoted from one class to the next until, at the age of twenty-two, he had passed his MA exams. His mother now arranged to marry Latif off to her elder daughter, Rashida's sister-in-law. She also arranged Rafika's marriage elsewhere. Rafika's wedding took place, but Latif only went through the *Akdbast*. In common parlance, one could say that Latif's future wife became betrothed to him.

Later, his uncle was generous enough to send him to England

for higher studies. Having been admitted to the Bar, he returned home after three years.

Haji Habib Alam was hungry for property. He realized that Latif, the lawyer, represented an irresistible bait for fathers burdened with the responsibility of marrying off nubile daughters. A certain relative of his had been widowed with a single offspring, a daughter. If he could get this daughter into his clutches, the widow's inheritance would also be within his grasp. But that imbecile, Latif, was not one to consent to a second marriage. So Haji Saab played a trick on Rashida's husband. Despite being a zamindar, Muhammad Suleiman was an unusual sort of man. He was an upholder of justice, virtue, and religion.

Three years after the Akdbast, Haji wrote to his son-in-law, stating that they were ready for the marriage ceremony. However, the young woman's share of the inheritance would have to be bequeathed to her before the marriage took place.

Suleiman wrote back that according to the contract made three years earlier, they were prepared for the marriage to take place. The date of the wedding should be fixed accordingly. Moreover, when the young woman attained majority at the age of eighteen, she would come into her inheritance. He would not take it upon himself to hand over any of her property before that.

Haji replied that if the property were not made over to the young woman as he demanded, she would not be acceptable as a bride for his nephew, and he would have to marry the latter off to someone else. And then, he could hardly be held responsible for what had transpired!

Suleiman wrote back, telling him that he could do as he wished. That very day, he also wrote to Latif, asking him for his own views on the matter.

It would not be an exaggeration to claim that in rural areas, the post office is under the zamindar's control. Haji was vigilant enough to ensure that Suleiman did not exchange any correspondence with Latif. Forging Latif's signature, he stole the registered letter that came in his nephew's name from Suleiman.

So, Latif did not even receive Suleiman's letter. What reply could he possibly give him?

Suleiman was both bewildered and offended by Latif's silence. When he heard, a fortnight later, that Latif had remarried, his annoyance flared into fury.

Poor Latif was quite unwilling to marry a second time. But the pleas of his uncle, his mother, and of other relatives he deferred to left him with no options. His mother told him, "Son! The world is not going to end if you marry again. If, on the other hand, you don't, Haji Saab will be furious and cut you out of his will entirely."

Latif: "I don't want a penny from him. That he has been generous enough to give me a sound education should suffice."

Latif's mother: "It matters little that you do not want his property. Your disobedience toward Haji Saab will make everyone despise you as an ingrate."

Latif: "Then I might as well solve the problem by committing suicide."

Latif's mother: "Why suicide alone? Why not commit matricide too? Come, let's go to the pond, hand in hand, and drown ourselves."

One of Latif's aunts from his mother's side of the family, cried, "Son! You are all I have in this world! If both of you commit suicide, what will become of me?"

Another aunt, related to Latif through his father, emerged from a room and exclaimed angrily, "Good Lord! The way young people talk these days would get on a dead man's nerves! What heinous crime has Haji Saab committed by asking for the property to be made over to you? If the property is acquired, it will be yours to enjoy. The doddering old Haji Saab is not going to carry it to his grave! Suleiman ought to be taught a lesson. That is why Haji Saab is asking you to remarry."

Latif: "It is not Suleiman who will suffer, but an innocent creature."

The aunt muttered silently, "He hasn't even laid eyes on her yet, and already he harbors such tender feelings for her!" She said aloud, "Pray what great harm will befall that 'innocent creature'? And, of course, no other wife has ever had to co-habit with her husband's second spouse? Listening to all this, people will wonder what terrible misdeeds Haji Saab must have committed to have driven mother and son to suicide! Look! Rafika's eyes are swollen from weeping. She hasn't touched food or water since yesterday."

Latif saw that Rafika was, indeed, sobbing. He snapped, "What, then, do you expect me to do?"

His aunt replied, "Really!" She joined her hands in a gesture of supplication and said, "All I am saying is, don't rock the boat and do respect the wishes of your elders and betters."

Without further ado, Latif presented himself like a sacrificial lamb for marriage.

The avaricious Haji Saab ended up being taken for a ride, however. Latif's mother-in-law, it turned out, was not the heiress to as vast a fortune as he had imagined her to be. All her landed property was heavily mortgaged. Far from profiting from it, members of Latif's family were obliged to squander their own money on futile lawsuits that fetched them nothing.

Latif's wife, Saleha, was well aware that she had been chosen as a bride because of her inheritance. She felt no obligation, therefore, to acquire any other qualities. Loud and sharp-tongued, her daily chore involved thrashing her maids. Latif, too, remained constantly on edge.

When he returned home after a day out, Latif would first go and see his mother. There he would find out about Saleha's doings before he ventured into his own part of the house. And if he heard from his mother that Saleha was on the rampage or thrashing a maid with all the enthusiasm of a prison guard, he would go out again right away. If Saleha happened to see him leave, however, there was no escaping her wrath.

This time, too, when Latif returned from Kurseong, he first went to meet his mother. Having presumed him dead, she was overjoyed to see her precious son again and could not contain her tears. Latif had hoped this time that Saleha, too, would demonstrate, if not wholeheartedly, at least to some extent, a measure of happiness at his homecoming. His expectations had been unrealistic. A few words between them had escalated into a quarrel.

Latif: "It wasn't as if your failure to send me money prevented me from doing what I needed to do. In this rotten world, too, there are divine beings who are only too willing to give. But to get down to brass tacks, if you didn't send me money, how was I expected to return home? I was really furious—I would not have come back here again."

Saleha: "Then why did you? Who begged you to come?"

Latif: "I came back because of my mother and Hamid (Latif's baby son)."

Saleha: "I was fine all this while. Now, you're back and those endless speeches have started."

The words, "I was fine all this while" hurt Latif deeply. "All this while"—the period during which Latif had been absent, during which she had received news of his death, during which she had presumed him dead—she had been fine all that while! Concealing his wounded feelings beneath a veneer of cheerfulness, Latif remarked, "You have long ears; so the speeches, too, seem longer."

Saleha: "What! I have long ears, do I? Fine! The long-eared ass won't remain here anymore—I'm off." She made as if to leave.

Latif: "No, wait!" He ran up and caught the free end of her sari. "I didn't say anything that could hurt you unduly, did I? I had endured such suffering and all I did was tell you about it. Well, I won't mention it if it upsets you."

Saleha: "What suffering? You were in seventh heaven with the divine daughters! They paid your fare home. Pray where was the suffering?"

Latif: "I was exiled far from home for lack of money."

Saleha: "Now that you have left your exile, what more do you want?"

Latif: "I need five hundred rupees. Send the money to Mrs. Dina-Tarini Sen right away."

Saleha: "It cost you five hundred rupees to come home? Then you must have undertaken a royal voyage!"

Latif: "How does it concern you whether I spent a hundred rupees or five hundred on my fare? The day I spend your money, I shall submit an account for it."

Saleha came in, handed over the money, and stomped off, muttering furiously. Rafika, who had come in at that moment to intervene and put an end to their quarrel, asked him about the money. Latif replied, "It cost a hundred rupees to come home. Around two hundred rupees was spent on my medicine and nursing for the two months I was ill and I shall donate another two hundred to Tarini Bhavan as a mark of my gratitude—so that they can help ill-fated and homeless people like me."

The news of Latif's arrival had brought Rafika to their house. She lived nearby with her in-laws; so, she was able to visit whenever she wished to. With Rafika there, Saleha roundly criticized Latif. This was nothing new. Rafika knew only too well that the moment she went to her sister-in-law's place, she would have to put up with a shower of abuse flung at her brother. Why Rafika alone? Whoever crossed Saleha's path was treated to a round of abuse directed at Latif.

Latif had taken it for granted that there was no such thing as happiness in this world. In his every word and deed, Saleha found nothing but cause for complaint. For two years now, he and Saleha had been traveling along the same path like the two wheels of a carriage, but they were poles apart in their views. If Latif said, "Winter is a pleasant season," Saleha would retort, "Summer is a pleasant season." When Latif fondled little Hamid, Saleha would do her level best to make him cry. Latif would endure such torment in silence. His heart remained untethered, wandering aimlessly in a vacuum.

To escape from this unhappy domestic situation, Latif would, for the most part, stay in town to carry on his law practice. Unlike other barristers, he did not live there *en famille*. He had come home after two years, having spent them here and there. But six months was as long as his wife would tolerate his presence. As I had mentioned earlier, this time, too, he had returned home disheartened.

Latif had become deeply embittered about life. He would think, "Either let me die, or let Saleha die—the two of us just can't make a home together." Sometimes, he was drawn to the idea of becoming a hermit. But his stern devotion to duty would prevent him from pursuing this train of thought.

ELEVEN

A DEEP HEART

If there is depth to an individual's personality, it is difficult to fathom the workings of her mind by reading her expression. Even those who are able to gauge a person's mind from her expression find themselves at a loss when confronted by such people. Siddika was the kind of person who was difficult to read. Exceptionally dedicated and unafraid of hard work, she did not reveal her feelings. After Latif's departure, it was apparent that Siddika's enthusiasm for her work had waned. Now she preferred to be alone, lost in contemplation of the wonderful change sweeping over her life. How could anyone else be aware of it? She was always so engrossed in her thoughts, the very image of melancholy, as immovable as a mountain, as unfeeling as a stone idol. Could that immovable mountain ever be shaken by storms? Impossible! Or perhaps, the surface of that stone now bore scratches?

If her pillow could speak, it would have told how many tears had fallen on it every night. It would also have revealed the number of sighs she expelled. But there were none to keep track of the joys and sorrows that set Siddika's little heart in turmoil. She had no close friends at all, this solitary creature. So the lightning flashes of hope and the turbulent waves of despair remained locked within the confining walls of her heart.

People usually long for their dear ones to be with them. Far from longing for the presence of her dear one by her side, Siddika fled from the very thought of his name. Her heart had now been burdened with an additional task. One by one, she would sift through the memories of Latif's words and deeds and mentally engage in a debate over them, analyzing them in detail. Her feelings would choose the very course down which she tried to stop them from flowing and gush along it in innumerable streams. She would exhaust herself from endless combat with the demands of her heart. Having observed Siddika's thoughtful ways, Sakina named her Sufiya or Wisdom. Ishan Babu, too, called her "the female hermit." But was anyone aware of the object of her devotion?

After Latif returned home, he had, out of courtesy, written letters to Tarini and the other sisters, expressing his deep gratitude. Along with the letter, he had sent a hundred rupees toward repayment of his debt as well as a donation of four hundred to Tarini Bhavan. Siddika, too, had received a similar letter of thanks.

Noticing the address "Rasulpur Village, District . . ." at the top of the letter along with Latif's monogram, Siddika's entire body quivered. So, he was Latif of Rasulpur, was he? To calm her mind, she said to herself, "So many people have the same name. So many villages are known by the same name. This Rasulpur, this Latif, are not the ones I know of. Even if it was the same person, how would it matter? Why would the rose care if the moon came up? He is Saleha's husband—what is he to you?" But if the mind always bowed to reason and logic, much of the world's suffering would have been alleviated.

*

One day, while Siddika was cleaning and tidying her trunk, Saudamini came in on some errand. Her curiosity was aroused by a small cardboard box in the trunk. She picked it up and saw that there was a delicate, gold necklace inside with a priceless pendant at its center studded with rubies, diamonds, and pearls. She snapped open the pendant. Inside was a photograph of Latif. She looked at Siddika inquiringly.

Poor Siddika hadn't the faintest notion that this photograph was inside the pendant. Realizing, however, that with the evidence that now lay in Saudamini's hands, nothing she said could absolve her of guilt, Siddika stood there, blushing and sweating. Saudamini left the room without saying anything further.

Whatever doubts Siddika had harbored about Rasulpur and

its inhabitants were dispelled when she saw the photograph.
Overcome by emotion, she reflected:

> The world is now his field of work,
> His hope fills the universe,
> Why, pray tell me, would he
> Remember a girl's love?

Have I gone mad? In this case, he did not know the "girl" at
all, so how was he expected to remember her? What a tortur-
ous game God was playing! The person who had been cruelly
indifferent to Siddika for no fault of hers, the person she had
never given a thought to, even in her dreams, had now become
her obsession. He would quite happily live out his days with
his wife and son, while her own life would be consumed by
sorrow. Siddika could not contain her tears. Fate, however
cruel, was inevitable. So, all my life I shall weep for him, and
close my eyes in grief over him.

Late in the evening, Saudamini called Siddika over for a game
of cards. Siddika gently demurred. "Sister," she said. "I do not
enjoy laughter, entertainment, or games. The spring from which
my laughter welled has dried up. I envy you your cheerfulness
and your humor. I feel like borrowing the poet's words to say:

> Could my heart be as light as thine,
> I'd gladly change with thee."

Saudamini smiled in reply, "Oh! You'd exchange your heart
with mine, would you? Now that would be a blessing for me!
You cannot imagine how traumatized it is, sister! Do you really think that Saudamini is free from all anguish? See how
beautiful is the lightning that streaks the clouds. That does not
make it less terrifying! I laugh so that you may laugh too. Even
this has now become a habit with me."

Siddika gazed at her in amazement. She saw that Saudamini was no longer smiling. Her expression was grave and
melancholy. She asked with trepidation, "Will you share your
anguish with me?"

Saudamini remained silent.

Siddika gently repeated, "Sister, please share your sorrow with me. I have a taste for sad tales."

Saudamini: "So, you do understand the meaning of sorrow?"

Siddika: "Please start narrating your story."

Saudamini: "I will. But Padmarag, everything is subject to the law of exchange. I hope you will reciprocate?"

Siddika: "I shall, provided that no one but you hears my story."

Saudamini: "Very well. I shall share my pain with you, while you tell me the story of your pendant."

The game of cards was forgotten. When Nalini came to summon them, Saudamini packed her off to bed. Nalini, on her way out, turned back to remark, "You look like you're going to discuss something in private. Can't I stay?"

Saudamini: "No, off to bed now. Sleep is far healthier than playing cards."

Nalini: "And for you?"

Saudamini: "Today, staying awake has been decreed. Go off to sleep and I shall join you."

After Nalini had left, Saudamini asked Siddika, "Are you really keen on hearing my story? If you are, what reward will you offer me?"

Siddika: "A few tears."

Saudamini: "That is precisely what I want. Alas! The cruel world—including my mother—has not deigned to shed a single tear for me. How miserly the world has been toward me!"

Siddika: "Good Heavens! Even your mother did not sympathize with you?"

Saudamini: "Not even my mother. She was above it all. She never quite understood how rotten the world could be."

TWELVE

SAUDAMINI'S FIRE

Saudamini said, "My parents' home was on Gorasthan Lane. At the time, we lived in a rented house in Calcutta. I was the daughter of a *Kulin* Brahmin. Since my father had died and I had no older brother to take an interest in my welfare, I was married off rather late—when I was almost seventeen years old. That the woman I had presumed to be my mother had not given birth to me, was something I discovered after my marriage. I was very naïve. My mother had died when I was seven years old. Yet, it never occurred to me that she was no more. I thought my stepmother was my own mother.

"Shortly after the wedding, some women from the neighbor's were doing my hair and my mother was sitting nearby. The women remarked to each other, 'The way the hair grows on her head indicates that her husband will have another spouse.'

"To set our minds at rest, my mother said quickly, 'Well, even if he did, the other wife is probably dead. So, why fret over it?'

"But little did they know that I was fated to contend with a rival, my husband's other spouse. When I was leaving for my husband's home, my mother advised me to be careful and especially stressed the importance of taking good care of my husband's offspring. Since I, too, had been brought up by a stepmother, it never occurred to me that being one could be a curse.

"My husband's son and daughter from his previous marriage were called Nagendra and Jahnavi, respectively. When I first went to my husband's home, they were living with their maternal grandmother. So I had not seen them. It was five years later that I met them.

"The moment I stepped into my husband's home, I was showered with poisonous barbs. It was the very people who had come to welcome the new bride who now poured ambrosia into her heart with their honeyed words.

"A said, 'From now on, Nagendra and Jahnavi won't be treated like family.'

"B: 'You're so right! Will the poor mites ever come here again?'

"C: 'How will their grandparents have the heart to send the little ones here?'

"D: 'Now they have been robbed of a father as well.'

"E: 'Who could have predicted that this house, these rooms, this courtyard was not meant to be enjoyed by them?'

"F: 'Those who have lost their mother have lost everything.'

"My two sisters-in-law had, meanwhile, begun to weep. The gist of their lament was as follows: 'Lakshmi, the goddess of prosperity, has forsaken us; in her place, a witch has installed herself,' and so on and so forth.

"Like the accused in a murder trial, I was beset by fear and anxiety. As though I had been the cause of all sorrow. As if I had slaughtered our Lakshmi, who was now in her heavenly abode.

"Gradually, five years went by. Motherhood eluded me. I was lonely, left to my own devices. My husband was often away on work. My two sisters-in-law would sometimes come to visit, but I did not look forward to their company.

"The fact that God had failed to give us children was somehow regarded as my fault too. Lalita (my younger sister-in-law) would say, 'In all fairness, should this be allowed to happen? Should fate allow the one who evicts those poor, motherless children from their own home to usurp and enjoy what should have been their just due? God is watching over them. Why would He allow anyone to lay claim to their share?'

"Five years later, the children came home. The brother and sister were twins. Their maternal aunt also accompanied them. From that very moment onward, Shyama Didi set about preparing a beautiful pyre for me where she contrived to immolate me, inch by agonizing inch. I am now ashamed to confess that I failed to attain the level of happiness I had expected to enjoy by having the children in my care. I admit that some lack in me must have been responsible for my failure. But what could I possibly do? I was not able to get a grip on my feelings. The emptiness within me that I had sought to vanquish by accepting Nagendra and Jahnavi as my own seemed to increase manifold. My mother-in-law had never said a harsh word to me. Now, Shyama Didi kept telling her, 'Nobody takes pains over the children's meals; the children don't have anything to wear,' and so on. Consequently, my mother-in-law, too, began to reproach me.

"My husband was extremely fond of me; he believed me to be a simple soul. He was the only certainty for me in those terrible times. In the desert I had been banished to, he was my only oasis. Having poisoned everyone against me, Shyama Didi started on my husband as well. At first, he refused to believe her; in fact, he requested her to leave. Didi burst into tears. How could she leave Nagen and Jahnavi in the hands of a witch? And where could she have gone anyway? She was a widow without a home to call her own.

"Didi would steal the children's clothes and send them off to her mother. To the master of the household, she would say, 'Your wife does not buy the children clothes.' The missing clothes would blatantly reappear as 'gifts' for Didi's son. I would hear, 'Khagu's aunt has sent this. Khagu's grandmother has sent that,' and so on.

"Food was always being siphoned off; I could not figure out where it went, so I ended up not being able to provide proper meals for the children. If I kept the food locked up, Didi and the neighbors would strike their foreheads in a gesture of lamentation and exclaim, 'It is mealtime for the children; yet, they're not given anything to eat!'

"Finally, a day came when even my husband asked, 'Pray tell, if the children don't get to eat, who will?' They remained blind to the fact that I was, indeed, taking pains to see that the children were properly fed.

"It often happened that *sandesh* and other tasty sweetmeats would be found discarded on the floor in the corner of a room. Didi stole them and threw them there. She would point them out to everyone with the words, 'See, she would rather throw them away than serve them to the children.' No one would believe me when I tried to explain myself. Didi's words were taken to be the gospel truth.

"How much more do you want to hear? These were daily occurrences. One winter, I had caught a terrible cold. A fire was lit in my room and it would burn day and night. I had dozed off one day and awoke to a foul smell pervading the room—the smell of burning silk! I noticed Didi hurrying from the room. My husband, too, arrived at that moment. He was put off by the offensive odor and asked for the fire to be taken out of the room. Didi appeared again and said, 'Let me see what's in there? What is causing this stink?' She extricated a burned fragment of fabric and exclaimed, 'Look! This is the velvet from which the children's clothes were to be tailored! She wasn't given a sari for herself; so, why would she allow the little ones to wear clothes made out of this material? No wonder I've been so baffled about what happens to all their clothes!' Simultaneously, the tears would flow. My husband would focus his silent gaze on me—not a single word did he utter. How could you possibly imagine the amount of venom contained in that silent reproach, Padmarag?"

Siddika dammed the flow of words and asked, "Why didn't you tell your husband that it was Didi who had set the fabric on fire?"

Saudamini: "Had I done so, who would have believed me? She was their aunt, while I was their stepmother. If my jealousy had not been the reason for setting the clothes aflame, how could their mother's own sister do such a thing? She was bound to them by the ties of blood and of untrammeled love. Who was I? Had I said anything in my defense, the situation would have escalated into a huge conflict, and I would have ended up antagonizing all the women in the neighborhood. How could I have single-handedly held my ground against Didi's army of soldiers? Moreover, misfortune seemed to dog my every step at the time. So, whatever measures I took then would have led to quite the opposite of what I had hoped for.

"On one occasion, Nagen ran in and climbed into my lap. The moment I wrapped my arms around him in a gesture of affection, he yelled out loudly, 'Oh my God! I'm going to die!'

"I was stunned. Was this a lovely, innocent child? The answer resonated in my heart: 'No, this is the other wife's form of revenge!'

"Lalita came running in. She gave Nagen a tight slap and exclaimed, 'You stupid fellow! What made you go to her, of all people? Your mother is dead! How could you expect to regain your mother's love?'

"I admit that I had not been able to give Nagen 'a mother's love.' But that certainly did not mean that I would strangle him to death! Real-life incidents involving maternal cruelty are rife. The 'step' relationship is a dangerous one. The world is ready to crucify a stepmother for the same gesture that would be perfectly acceptable in a mother.

"One day, I had unlocked a large cupboard in the pantry to hand out provisions for a meal to a guest. I had shut the cupboard door without locking it and had gone off to the kitchen to check whether there was any cooking oil there. When I returned to the room, I found the cupboard the way I had left it. Without a second thought, I locked it and went off. A few minutes later, the maid, Golap's mother, came in and said, 'Come and have a look, Madam! There are thudding noises coming from your cupboard!'

"'Nonsense!' I replied, 'I just locked the cupboard.'"

"Out of curiosity, my husband came along with me to check the cupboard. I unlocked it. There, inside, was Nagendra! I was flabbergasted. Shyama quickly picked Nagendra up in her arms. You can imagine the storm that ensued thereafter."

At this point, Saudamini fell silent. It was as if she were reliving the past. After a long silence, Siddika asked, "Were you able to find out how Nagendra managed to get locked in the cupboard?"

Saudamini: "No. From that day onward, my husband just stopped speaking to me. Could I blame him for that? What could he possibly have done? All these days, I had endured people's stinging barbs and poison arrows and had managed to withstand it. But now his neglect and indifference seemed unbearable. After suffering a week of anguish, I asked to be allowed to visit my mother. My request was granted.

"I went back with a sigh of relief to my mother's soothing arms. Unfortunately, I failed to win any sympathy for my woes. Not a soul commiserated with me. Even my mother, who happened to be the light of my life in spite of being my stepmother, felt no empathy for my plight. She would say, 'Daughter! I can't quite understand what you're trying to say. Do you mean you weren't able to tame those two children and have them eating out of your hands? How, then, did I manage to bring you up when I was younger than you are today? I am a mere five years older than you are!' That was my tragic fate. How could I explain why I hadn't succeeded in endearing myself to my stepchildren? That was the day I came to know how blind the world could be. That it lacked the vision to witness my pain. Not a soul was sensitive enough to notice my anguish, to probe its depths. If my beloved mother was incapable of understanding it, who would? It was as if the strings of my heart were playing a particular tune:

> Day and night, I think, how will the days go by
> In this abode of demons, in this desert?
> Here, there is no soothing shade, no sympathy for others' pain,
> How, alas, shall I spend my days in this prison?

"Nearly a year later, I went back to my husband. Once again, I tried to build a happy home with Nagen and Jahnavi. Now, a new form of slander was directed at me. Some expensive pieces of jewelry belonging to Jahnavi had been stolen. I could have sworn by the sacred waters of the Ganga that Shyama had stolen them, but I could not come out and say so. Shyama and Lalita heaped false accusations of theft on me. I could only say, 'Lord, you are my sole truth.'"

Siddika: "Such unspeakable torture!"

Saudamini: "Oh, this is not the end of it! There's more. A

rumor had circulated round the neighborhood that I had twice tried to kill Nagen. After the second attempt had supposedly taken place, I was nicknamed the 'She-Demon.' Ten years of life in my husband's home went by. My children were, by then, twelve years old. At around this time, yet another strange incident occurred. I was standing near the brick-walled well in the courtyard. For a moment, I was overcome by the desire to drown myself in it. Instantly, a voice seemed to say, 'Don't even think of such a thing! Just wait for a few days.' Perhaps, it was the same voice that had once told me, 'This is the other wife's form of revenge.'

"Jahnavi ran in from somewhere and hoisted herself onto the edge of the well. I thought of fleeing from that place in sheer terror; but the girl put her arms around my neck. 'Don't, child!' I protested. 'You'll fall in!'

"She retorted, 'Then pick me up and put me down on the ground.' The moment I held her, she shouted, 'Aunty! Look! Mother is trying to throw me down the well!'

"I could not make up my mind what to do then. I felt dazed. Before Shyama could make her way to the courtyard, my husband arrived. He witnessed what he believed was my attempt to murder Jahnavi. 'Well, I have seen your antics with my own eyes!' he said. I was about to reply, but he did not wait to hear me out. He left me abruptly, with Jahnavi in tow.

"There was no way out of this nightmare, no sanctuary where I could pause for even a moment without being beset by apprehensions. Fate would not even tolerate my lingering by the well! Every single instant of every single day made me conscious of the fact that while one's own children served as the binding factor in the relationship between man and wife, stepchildren drove a wedge between them. I was well aware that I had alienated my husband and that he was moving further and further away from me. And there was no one who could heal the rift between us. Perhaps, I was the one at fault."

Siddika: "I do not think it was your fault, since Koresha-bi has endured similar suffering. Why did she leave Patna and come to Tarini Bhavan? For respite from the same kind of anguish! For eight long years, she bore her husband's indifference.

After her stepson, the ten-year-old Kamrazzaman, died of cholera, this indifference became so intolerable that she left home to enroll herself in a teacher's training institute. Subsequently, she taught in girls' schools in Gaya, Muzaffarpur, and so on, before arriving in Calcutta."

Saudamini: "Even her working here and there, especially here in Calcutta, was done without her husband's consent. The reason he did not object to it was because of his supreme indifference toward his wife. For Koresha-bi, this turned out to be a blessing in disguise."

Siddika: "Koresha-bi's brothers-in-law, both the older and the younger one, their wives, and Kamru's sister conspired to convince her husband, who lived in another city, that Kamru had died from negligence and lack of medical care after being afflicted by cholera. Even though the poor woman had summoned Patna's most renowned doctor at three a.m. and had him examine Kamru, she was accused of depriving the boy of medical treatment."

Saudamini: "What's more, it was Koresha-bi herself who had given Kamru the money he had chosen to spend on the tasty snacks he shared with other boys that afternoon. Besides, the doctor, too, was a friend of her father's. I cannot bring myself to blame Koresha-bi's husband for what happened—what could the poor man do? If a sufficient number of people conspire together, even God can be proved to be a villain. The fact remains that he is civil to his wife. He comes here often to see her. Even Koresha-bi had gone home to visit him during the vacation."

Siddika: "I suspect the reason for this development is that she herself has, subsequently, given birth to a son. So, eleven years later, the tide has turned in her favor. Anyway, sister, let's carry on with your story."

Saudamini: "As I have already told you, for me the world was now a desert enveloped in darkness. The only person who was like a drop of nectar in that desert, the lone flickering star in that gloom, had moved away—far, far away. So I was suffering the torments of hell on earth."

Siddika: "Your Nagen and Jahnavi were mere children; what could be your grievance against them?"

Saudamini: "Quite true. That is why I had not shared these experiences with anyone for years; since you seemed genuinely interested in hearing about them, I have opened my heart to you. Otherwise, are these things fit to be laid bare? These torments are meant to be borne in silence and consumed slowly by the flames of bitterness. The children were completely innocent; they were not responsible for their actions. It was my responsibility that was unbearably heavy. I had to suffer the consequences of their actions. All you need is some imagination to visualize how terrible those consequences were."

Siddika: "Was your 'sister' the root of all problems? Had you been able to get rid of her, you could have lived in peace."

Saudamini: "Good Lord! Are you in your right mind! That would have been quite impossible. Who would have dared get rid of her? She was the mistress of the household; she was indispensable. In fact, I should consider myself lucky that she was kind enough not to get rid of me! If Shyama could have been packed off, then the house, the property, the children, and everything else would have been mine!"

Siddika: "Now I want to know how you got rid of the curse. I've had enough of the curse."

Saudamini: "Now are you convinced that I, too, have suffered? When human beings are utterly vulnerable, when they are in the grip of pain more acute than the throes of death, the Compassionate One takes pity on them and extends a helping hand.

> When the heat of summer becomes unbearable,
> It is then that the clouds rain water.

"God, the redeemer of the fallen, rescues the man who is desperately in need of succor. For some, death is ordained; for others, something else. God offers a way out. I, too, was offered a way out.

"We embarked on a pilgrimage. Lalita had made a vow to

offer prayers at the temple of some deity in Mathura to ensure her son's well-being. The temple where she was to offer her prayers was some distance from the place where we had put up. So, we had to make the journey by boat. Lalita had hired a small barge. There were several other passengers traveling with us. Having undertaken the responsibility of looking after Nagendra himself, my husband took pains to impress on Shyama that she should take good care of Jahnavi. Observing his concern for his daughter, I felt my heart turn over. What if Jahnavi drowned here, I wondered.

"That day, my husband seemed well disposed even toward me. He took me by the hand and led me onto the barge. He also indicated where I should sit. My eyes strayed to his face. That particular day, his face looked beautiful to me. I could not turn my gaze away from it. I wondered if I was looking at that face for the last time. Suppose I never saw it again? Let me have my fill of it, I thought. I could not derive any pleasure from the moment. My heart was heavy."

Saudamini stopped. Siddika thought that, perhaps, Saudamini was weeping. But no—she was dry-eyed. Having expended many tears, their very source had dried up. Calm and collected, she took up her story again.

"Lulled by the cool breeze blowing over the Yamuna, Shyama had dozed off. It was I who tried to keep the restless Jahnavi in check by saying, 'Come here,' 'Don't go there,' and so on. That day, she was in a contrary mood and prone to arguing with me over every trifle. Finally, she lost interest in me and attacked Lalita. They began to quarrel. I gazed through the open window at the dark waters of the Yamuna and thought:

> Mother of the world!
> To embrace the earth in tender compassion
> You rule as the Yamuna over the world.

"Suddenly, Jahnavi came up, stepped right over me, and sat at the extreme edge of the window. Agitated, I protested, 'Dear, you mustn't!'

"'Why?' she shrieked, '*You're* doing it! An old hag like you can enjoy the spectacle, but you can't abide my doing so! Am I a small child, that you're so anxious?' She burst into loud laughter. A little later, she said, 'Watch! I'll move further—' Before she could complete her sentence, she had fallen into the river. I fainted.

"When I came to, I saw that Jahnavi and I were lying on the ground, side by side. A handful of people were tending to us. Thanks to their ministrations, I survived. Jahnavi did not. When they saw that I had regained consciousness, they wished to take me elsewhere. But I could not wrench away my stricken gaze from Jahnavi. I could only cry my eyes out. How could I abandon the person I had been with at the moment of her death? Fishermen had caught us in their nets while out for their daily catch."

Siddika: "Well, that was quite a catch! But sister, how did they get you and Jahnavi together?"

Saudamini: "I, too, had gone under at the same time, so, I was somehow able to catch hold of her. I had held her firmly to my breast, thinking that if we were to drown, we might as well do so together. If we survived, we would survive together. But fate willed otherwise. Even though we both came up in the net, she and I were parted forever." Tears glistened in Saudamini's eyes. Her heart swelled.

She continued, "The fishermen took me along with them. I followed them in a daze. Soon after, I lost my sanity. They placed me in a lunatic asylum. It took me nearly a year to be myself again. I am referring to an episode that took place almost eighteen years ago.

"When I recovered, the authorities at the asylum found me the job of a governess with a respectable family. A year after I had been there, my pupil got married. Sarayu's family asked me to accompany her to Calcutta. Soon afterward, when Sarayu visited Tarini School to enroll her younger sister-in-law there, she took me along with her. That was the first occasion on which I met Mrs. Sen. And that is how I came to Tarini Workshop. I have been here for nearly sixteen years now. Now I find that my heart is big enough to embrace the whole world.

It is no longer upset by minor setbacks. Nor does a little neglect or indifference affect it."

Siddika: "In that case, you should be able to live peacefully in that household with the same people. Then what prevents you from going back there?"

Saudamini: "Oh, dear! How do I explain to you how poisonous and unhealthy the atmosphere in that house had become because of Shyama Didi? None of you can understand it, nor even believe it."

Siddika: "Nothing is impossible in God's kingdom. Why should it be impossible for a tender child to hurt an adult woman? The little creatures on this earth, rather than the large ones, tend to inflict greater pain. That is why, when you are out to rob a beehive of its honey, the sting of the bee is exceedingly sharp! It does not attack you without provocation. The tiny mosquito, on the other hand, attacks you when you are defenseless in sleep. Mosquito nets have had to be invented as protection against the torture inflicted by mosquitoes. But it has not been necessary to erect a fort against the pain inflicted by bees!"

Seeing that the night was nearly over, both women went to bed with heavy hearts. I do not know whether Saudamini fell asleep or not. Siddika, however, did not close her eyes for even an instant. The flames of Saudamini's anguish licked her all over. Her mind burned with the intensity of Saudamini's pain.

THIRTEEN

ANOTHER MEETING

Latif had gone to Munger. On his doctor's advice, he had gone there with his mother for a change of air. Accompanying him were his aunt (the woman who had no one to fall back on, but him) and Rafika. Almost a year had passed since Rafika was widowed.

Since Rafika had been eager to see Sitakunda, Latif had set out with them one evening, just before dusk fell, to visit the place. The sun was about to set in the west and there was a faint light to see by. While they were strolling around, they noticed some women in the distance near Sitakunda. When the group approached, Latif realized that it was Siddika and her "sisters." Noticing Latif, Siddika pretended not to have seen them at all and rapidly overtook them. Helen was following them. She called out, "How are you, Mr.—"

Latif stopped. After the usual exchange of greetings, he said, "Mrs. Horace has even forgotten my name!"

Saudamini: "But she remembers your face!"

Helen: "I cannot pronounce the second part of your name correctly. Won't you introduce us to your companions?"

Latif: "Isn't it enough to call them companions?"

Helen: "No, how can that be? But if you don't wish to introduce us, I won't insist."

Latif: "This is my sister and that is my aunt." Turning to the latter, he said, "These are my saviors, the 'poor sisters' of Tarini Bhavan."

Rafika: "We are glad to have met you."

Helen: "We feel equally honored."

Rafika: "Ever since my brother told us about your kindness,

I have been keen to meet you. That wish has now been granted."

Saudamini: "It does happen, sometimes, that pilgrims' prayers are answered. I, too, had attained my quest during a pilgrimage. Today," she said, turning to Rafika, "you, too, have had a wish fulfilled. You have met us." Observing Latif's eyes on Siddika in the distance, she asked, "Mr. Almas, have you also found something you desired? We, of course, have found your sister. What about you?"

Latif: "I met you, that is reward enough—what more could I hope for?"

But the person with whom it would have given him great pleasure to speak, was still far away. He had not exchanged a word with her.

Seeing Usha in the distance, Saudamini hailed her, whereupon she and Siddika came back to join them.

Usha: "We noticed Mr. Almas trying to elude us. So we, too, pretended not to see him and went our way."

Latif: "In fact, I fell back when I saw you overtaking us and going ahead. Well, now. I do hope you are fine?"

Usha: "I am fine, thank you. But Siddika is often indisposed."

Rafika (to Siddika): "My brother speaks highly of you. What kind of health problem is it that you are suffering from?"

The silent Siddika was perturbed that a question had been directed at her. "It's nothing of consequence," was her brief reply before she averted her gaze.

Usha: "Come, let us go and sit there."

The group went over to a boulder and settled itself there. Saudamini had inspired respect in Rafika from the very first glance. It was only in her husband that Saudamini had, apparently, failed to inspire respect.

Rafika: "The other sisters I have heard of—Koresha, Bibha—where are they?"

Saudamini: "They are all in Calcutta now. During the Puja vacation, only a few of us from the workshop came here. From the school, there's only Usha. She took leave to come here, because she was not keeping well."

Rafika (gesturing toward Helen): "Does that white woman live in Tarini Bhavan too?"

Saudamini: "Yes, she teaches English at the workshop. Since she does not have any accommodation of her own in Calcutta, she lives in Tarini Bhavan."

Learning that Latif's mother was unwell, Saudamini promised to visit her.

Rafika said to Siddika, "You are also welcome."

Siddika: "Please excuse me, but I shan't go."

Rafika: "If I can visit you, why won't you do the same? Isn't an exchange of visits the norm?"

Siddika: "It is people like you who have sealed off the path for people like us."

Rafika: "I haven't quite understood you—how have we sealed off the path?"

Siddika: "We do not belong to the material world. The norm does not, therefore, apply to us."

Now that dusk had descended, everyone made to leave. The four-year-old child accompanying Rafika, particularly, was overcome by drowsiness. Gathering him up in her arms, Rafika said, "This is my brother's son. It has been nearly a year since his mother passed away; since then he has been with me."

When she heard those words, a lightning ray of hope flashed for an instant through Siddika's heart. In the glow of that light, she visualized Latif for a second—liberated from all bonds. The next moment, a cloud of despair had obscured that light. No one was aware of the play of hope and despair in Siddika's heart. Latif and Saudamini alone observed the momentary change in her expression.

Rafika had noticed nothing. She was saying, "I have left my own children at home—I could not bear to leave him."

Latif: "You are spoiling Hamid rotten. Such indulgence isn't healthy for him. One only hopes that he doesn't turn out to be as cussed as his mother."

Sakina now spoke up. She said, "The boy looks just like Mr. Almas! I am meeting you again after one and a half years—you haven't changed!"

Latif said: "Was I a child to begin with, that you'd see me all grown up?"

Saudamini: "You used to be underweight. You should have grown hale and hearty by now."

Usha: "He should have, but he had suffered a serious injury."

Saudamini (whispering into Siddika's ear): "You're not putting on any weight either—did you also suffer part of that injury?"

At this, Siddika rose in a huff and moved away.

Noticing Siddika alone, some distance from the other sisters, Latif strolled down to where she was standing and paused by her. He thought of saying something to her. But unable to make up his mind about what he ought to say, he merely contented himself with gazing at her and drinking his fill of her presence. But even this happiness was short-lived, for Rafika and Saudamini soon joined them.

On their way home, Rafika caught hold of Siddika's hand and said, "You are coming to visit us and no excuses, please."

Siddika: "Very well, but you will have to become a member of our Society for the Upliftment of Downtrodden Women. The annual subscription is only twelve rupees."

Rafika burst out laughing. "Society for the Upliftment of Downtrodden Women? Never have I heard such a name! I knew that there was a Society for the Prevention of Cruelty to Animals. Fine! I shall certainly become a member. All women should have a positive attitude toward a society like this." To Siddika, she said, "Make my mother a member too. Here is the money for her subscription."

Latif: "Saudamini Didi is the society's Secretary. Hand the money over to her."

Saudamini: "No, Sakina-bu is the Treasurer; it is she who will collect the money."

Latif: "It appears that the society's activities are carried out in conformity with the rules and regulations!"

Saudamini: "Of course. This is no child's play. The eighteenth annual assembly of the society is being held this time. Please do participate along with the new members."

Usha: "Yes, Mr. Almas, please do come to Calcutta with your family. The twentieth jubilee celebrations of Tarini School and the prize distribution ceremony will be taking place at the time."

Latif: "Thank you so much! God willing, I shall certainly try to be there."

FOURTEEN

THE BEAUTY OF FIRE

Siddika no longer went out. She was reluctant to go anywhere for fear of meeting Latif. For some time, a storm had been raging in her heart. Her disobedient heart impelled her to follow a certain path. She tried to curb the impulse.

But how did it matter whether Siddika went out or not? Nearly every week, Latif would come to visit the sisters' tent, accompanied by his aunt and his sister. Over a period of time, they had become close friends. Rafiya and Sakina were relatives of his. Rafiya was a cousin, the daughter of an aunt from his mother's side of the family, and the spouse of one of his brothers-in-law. Sakina was a cousin, on the one hand, and a sister-in-law on the other. He had "adopted" Usha and Saudamini as his elder sisters and they had agreed to use the familiar form of address with him, the way they would have had he been their own brother. Siddika alone remained immune to the charm of his personality. But he would not give up trying to win her over.

Poor Siddika would wonder why, when everyone else in Tarini Bhavan seemed quite contented, she herself should be denied peace of mind. Even Saudamini had attained peace after enduring hell. When would Siddika's own torment come to an end? She would also imagine that the English sisters suffered no anguish of their own. They were supremely happy.

Helen was sitting out on the verandah one morning, absorbed in a newspaper, when she exclaimed distractedly, "Oh poor thing!"

"What's wrong, sister? What made you say that?"

Helen had not noticed that anyone was around. Siddika's

question made her instantly turn around and say, "Ah! Siddika, what good will it do you to hear it?"

Siddika: "Please do tell whom you referred to as a 'poor thing.'"

Helen: "Just suppose it was you I was referring to."

Siddika: "Why would you describe me as such? In what respect am I an object of pity?"

Helen: "Look, Miss Star has got married after remaining a spinster all these years."

Siddika: "Why does that make her an object of pity?"

Helen: "God willing, may she be happy. My long-suffering heart is beset by tremors of anxiety whenever there is news of someone's marriage."

Siddika: "Why, sister, what is there to be afraid of? A marriage is a happy event, after all."

Rafiya, Sakina, and Usha were sitting around and chatting at the other end. Helen pointed to them and said, "Look—all of them are married . . ."

Noticing Helen pointing to them, Rafiya joked, "Are you speaking ill of us, Helen Didi?"

Taking Siddika by the hand, Helen approached them and said, "See, every one of them has a failed marriage behind her. Rafiya Begum here comes from a wealthy family. She is the wife of an even wealthier man. But despite the dictates of your native customs, she does not wear the bangles that declare her identity as a married woman. Sakina Khanum there is also the daughter of a very distinguished family and the spouse of a certain Mr. Khan, a famous lawyer in Noakhali—I can't remember his full name; but observe: she wears no jewelry at all. Only Usharani has been unable to discard her white conch-shell bangle—'I won't take off my conch-shell bangle; it is the mark of a married woman.'"

Usha: "Helen-di, why, pray, have you got down to discussing our failed marriages today?"

Sakina: "Perhaps, she is warning Siddika-bu. I, too, advise you, dear Padmarag, not to marry. There's danger there!"

Rafiya: "But when Almas lands up, she won't remember a word of yours on this subject."

Usha: "When Mr. Almas comes, greet him from afar—don't give in to him, Padmarag."

In her haste to protest, Siddika said, "Usha-di! You misunderstood Sakina's words. The word 'almas' means diamond. Since Sakina-bu called me 'padmarag' (ruby), Rafiya-bu jokingly used the word 'almas.'"

Usha: "Yes, that is precisely what I'm saying—if the diamond arrives, the ruby should salute it from a distance and make itself scarce!"

Helen: "Siddika, I hope you have now realized that marriage is not a happy event. Otherwise, these women would not have become nuns and dressed in saffron and blue."

Siddika: "I haven't heard how their marriages failed."

Usha: "She wants firsthand evidence! Padmarag is not one to retreat easily."

Helen: "Then, listen. Rafiya Begum is the wife of a famous lawyer. Three years after their wedding, he traveled to England, leaving her behind with her two baby daughters. Usually, it takes people three years to qualify for the Bar. But her beloved stayed on in England for a full ten years. Utterly devoted to her husband, she counted out the days of that long separation. During these ten years, she abstained from mangoes and the creamy topping of milk, because those were the two items of food not available to her beloved in England—"

Rafiya: "Come on, Helen-di! What utter nonsense!"

Helen: "I am narrating the truth—not fiction. During his first year in England, her beloved would send her seven letters a week. During his second year there, he sent her three letters a week. The following year, one a week. Gradually, the letters dwindled to one every two months. Even this did not dampen Rafiya Begum's ardor. When her older daughter was around five years old, she hired a tutor for the child's schooling. At the same time, she devoted herself to studying the piano, the sitar, and so on, and began taking lessons in English, so that she could become a fit partner for a husband who bore the cachet of having lived in England and exchange words of endearment with her husband in English."

Rafiya: "Oh, come on, Helen-di! Won't you be quiet?"

Helen: "I will, soon enough—there isn't much more to say, is there? To give her husband a pleasant surprise, she wrote him a letter in polished English. Two months later, her husband gratified her with a cursory reply. Even this could not discourage her. Gradually, the time for her husband's homecoming drew near. He would be coming home two years later. Then, only a year remained. Now six months would go by without a letter arriving from him. Once he came back, he could repay her for all these lapses with interest! Her patience had to be seen to be believed! Only fifteen days remained before her dearest was due!

"It was around this time that her brother-in-law forbade her to accept any registered letters from the postman. Twelve days before her husband was due, an insured letter arrived from him. After six long months, such a thick insured letter! How could she possibly refuse to accept it? Perhaps, her brother-in-law had asked her to refuse letters from other people. How could a woman not accept her husband's letter? Even so, she returned it and asked the postman to come back the next day. When she met her brother-in-law that afternoon, she told him about the letter. In reply, he said, 'No, don't accept my brother's letter. Hah! Sir has deigned to write after six months! If you return the letter, it will teach him a lesson. He will understand that you, too, are capable of anger.'

"The poor postman turned up again at the same time the following day, when no male member of the family was present. Rafiya Begum thought—a letter has come after ages; have I the heart to refuse it? Her husband was due a mere ten days later; then surely, he could explain it all to her. She had imagined that here was a letter with his message of love. Perhaps, it contained an explanation for his long silence. So, she signed on the dotted line and accepted the letter. With the desperate eagerness of a starved creature, she began to read it . . ."

Unable to endure the situation any further, Rafiya got up and left. Helen, too, could not contain her tears. Siddika was amazed to notice that Usha and Sakina were also wiping their eyes on the free ends of their saris. Dismayed, she said, "Let it be. I don't need to hear any more of the story."

Helen wept and said, "This bit is the core of the story! Listen. She tore open the envelope and saw that it contained divorce papers. He had given her a divorce; she had accepted it. Therefore, their marriage was dissolved! All it took was a signature to end a marriage of thirteen years. Then he came back from England with a white woman in tow. Rafiya lost her sanity."

Sakina: "The assassin did not turn once to see how the half-dead victim writhed in pain."

Helen: "With proper medical treatment, Rafiya took nearly three years to recover. Later, she and Sakina somehow managed to make their way together to Tarini Bhavan. They have been here for five years. Rafiya has become Mrs. Sen's private secretary. Sakina has acquired nursing skills."

Siddika: "And Rafiya's two daughters?"

Helen: "Both of them were married off at the appropriate time."

Sakina: "Mrs. Horace, you have narrated Rafiya's story, but what about the tale of your own madman?"

Usha: "Yes, do tell us that story; you have even kept the cuttings of newspaper reports."

Helen: "In that case, Sakina, I shall also divulge the secret of your marriage."

Sakina: "Yes, do. After all, it is not a love story! Then listen:

> The compassionate damsel listens to the pained Sakina
> As she tells the story of Helen's marriage."

And, indeed, Siddika, the very image of compassion and tenderness, began devouring the story like a starved creature.

Sakina: "Helen-di had known Joseph Horace for three years before she married him. Having known him for so long, she had trusted him completely and had married him. They spent a year together in utter bliss. She did not know at the time that all that glittered was not gold, but merely a temporary semblance of it.

From the second year of their marriage, Horace took to drink and other related vices. He would return home after midnight and seize on Helen as the butt of his drunken rages.

Subjecting her to his wrath and abuse was an everyday occur-
rence. At times, beatings would also ensue. Even today, she
bears those scars on her person. She endured this physical and
mental torture silently and tried her utmost to put his life back
on track. Whenever he got the chance, he would escape. She
would search high and low for him and bring him back home."

Siddika: "Why did he escape?"

Sakina: "To seek his own hell. He would drink himself
unconscious. She would bring him back in that state. When
he finally escaped from Hazaribagh, she could find no trace
of him.

"Years later, a rumor made the rounds that he had killed a
man in Kanpur and had been arrested by the police. Didi made
her way there. When she arrived, she heard that a man named
Horace, proven to be incurably insane, had been shipped off
to England. Helen-di, too, sold off all her worldly goods in
desperation and followed in her insane husband's wake.

"When she arrived in England, she learned that Horace had
been caught in flagrante delicto with a young woman by the
name of Riva Sanders and that after killing another man, had
been locked up in Broadmoor Lunatic Asylum. Helen's mother
was still living at the time. She took this opportunity to have a
formal complaint lodged against Horace and got the court to
grant Helen a *decree nisi*. But Riva appealed against the
charges leveled at her, was declared innocent and released.
With Riva exonerated, Helen's *decree nisi* was deemed null
and void. God help the English and their wonderful laws!
Helen appealed again. The result was that the four Lords of
Appeal were united in their ruling that 'Mrs. Helen Mary
Horace could not be granted a separation from her husband,
Lieutenant Colonel Cecil Joseph Horace.'

"You might recall that nearly three years ago, a report had
come out in foreign newspapers under the headline, 'Tied for
Life to a Lunatic.' See, I have preserved that piece of paper
with care. Certain judges do have feelings. Therefore, Lord
Birkenhead had pronounced his verdict and added, 'Certainly,
your sympathy will be with this unfortunate sacrifice to our
marriage laws . . . It is most unfortunate, that this poor woman

should remain tied for life to a cruel, tyrannical, insane murderer. Many will consider our legal system to be harsh and inhuman—but this is the law of England. Any redressal in a case like this lies beyond the scope of law.'

"In other words, English law was unable to release Helen-di from the embrace of a lunatic. Helen would have to endure the terrible consequences of living with a madman. What greater injustice or oppression could one possibly think of? This England—this noxious, putrid England—claims to be civilized!"

Helen: "Why does this hurt you so, Sakina? You, too, were sacrificed in the interest of your country's laws and customs!"

Sakina: "Our country is, after all, a land of uncivilized, bonded slaves—it has shame written all over it. Your country, on the contrary, is as pure as the driven snow! Now, I shall come to the conclusion. In this way did Helen's days of happiness come to a swift end. 'Before the garland could be strung, the flowers withered.' Before one could enjoy the beauty of sunrise, the sun had set. The vine of hope was uprooted just when it had begun to flower."

Helen: "Sister! I have pondered over this and concluded that nothing is purified unless it is scorched by the fire of anguish. Thorny is the path of virtue. True love does not, therefore, offer any momentary pleasures. All beautiful things are rendered beautiful because of the fire of torment that burns within them. Had I not been alienated from Joseph, I would not have known about this cosmic love at all. Now, the torment which has sublimated my love seems beautiful in my eyes. That torment seems to be my source of happiness. The whole world is aflame with torment."

Siddika (absentmindedly): "That is why a fire burns even in Saudamini."

Helen: "Why only in Saudamini—there is fire even in the cheerful lotus, Nalini."

Siddika gazed at Helen's face in amazement. What was Helen trying to imply? Was this supposed to be a metaphor? Had she probed into Siddika's heart?

Helen: "What are you brooding about?"

Siddika: "I was absorbed in the thought that even a wonderful person like you could be so tormented inside."

Helen: "Is there no such torment within you?"

Siddika (fearfully): "No!"

The force with which this "no" was expelled seemed to imply a hundred replies in the affirmative. Everyone laughed. Siddika was embarrassed.

At this point, the maid entered with the words, "My ladies, have you no intention of taking your baths or your meals today? Saudamini Ma'am is sitting all alone in the kitchen."

Usha: "She's right! It's noon! But 'they have driven hunger away by quenching their thirst with the nectar of love'! Come, let's go."

Helen: "Yes, let's, but Sakina's and Usha's tales remain untold."

Siddika: "I shall hear those stories tonight."

After the evening meal, Siddika prevailed upon Helen, Usha, and Sakina to tell her the stories.

Helen: "Rafiya knows all about Sakina, since she is a relative of hers. Ask her."

Rafiya Begum began: "This happened nearly seventeen years ago. Sakina was married off at the age of fifteen. She is my sister-in-law and also my niece. Abdul Gafur Khan was then an up-and-coming lawyer in Khulna. Early in life, he had picked up immoral habits. His older brother went to great efforts to reform him but had to concede defeat. Finally, he hit upon a possible solution—marriage. People who knew the family refused to give their daughter in marriage to Abdul. His older brother then proceeded to hunt for prey further afield. Meanwhile, Abdul Gafur declared himself adamantly averse to marriage. After much cajoling, he agreed to marry, provided they could find him an impeccably beautiful bride."

Those listening to the story all trained their eyes on Sakina. She was certainly impeccably beautiful, like an angel descended from the heavens.

"Gafur's older brother now said that it was time his sibling changed his ways. He himself was a morally upright man; it pained him a great deal to witness his younger sibling's nefarious activities. Gafur's heart softened a little. Like a good little boy, he gave up alcohol and his other vices. Soon afterward, his brother went to Burdwan and arranged his marriage with Sakina. No one knew, however, that one of the housemaids was actually Gafur's mistress.

"At the appointed time, we accompanied the groom's group to the wedding. Bela, the maid, also went along. After the marriage ceremony was over, when bride and groom were sitting together in the inner quarters of the house for the ritual involving the couple's first look at each other's faces, Bela whispered something into Gafur's ear.

"It embarrasses me to say this—he is my cousin, after all, no matter how distant—but would you believe it? The groom got up at once, refusing to even glance at the bride's face, because Bela had claimed, 'Why, Madam is not bootifool, after all!' Stunned, the bride's family was left staring at the groom. Infuriated, the groom's brother declared that he was ready to commit murder. The people present suggested, 'See for yourself whether the bride is beautiful or not.'

"The ritual of the auspicious exchange of glances between bride and groom did take place. The next day, the groom disappeared with the new bride's jewelry. Once home, he threatened his brother with a lawsuit and said he would claim damages for having married him off to a hideously ugly woman. Fate never gave Sakina a chance to enter her husband's home.

"Gafur's brother cut him out of his life altogether. Soon afterward, Bela died. Gafur married a widow. Nearly three years later, Sakina's three brothers raised the issue of Sakina's bride price and succeeded in creating a great deal of trouble for Gafur. This went on for another two years. Realizing that he was cornered, Gafur proposed a truce with his brothers-in-law, which they accepted.

"Gafur set off to bring his bride back home, taking some female relatives and me along. We carried clothes and jewels and all kinds of gifts to appease the bride: 'I have brought a mirror and a comb and ribbons for your hair.'

"But who was there to appreciate it all? Sakina was down with a high fever!

"Gafur took it upon himself to nurse his wife. He massaged her head, fanned her face, and generally ministered to her needs. But do you know how the ungracious Sakina responded to all that attention? We had prepared to leave with the bride once her fever abated. Gafur's wife wrote him a letter the day before her anticipated departure for her husband's home. He gave me that letter to read. Every word of it is etched in my mind, even today. This is what it said:

MY SALUTATIONS—

It was not my intention to hurt you. But the bitter truth is this: it is impossible for us to share a life together. Had it slipped your mind that you had spurned me on the say-so of a maid? It seemed that she whom your Bela certified as "bootifool" would be deemed "bootifool"! I could not be "promoted" to the status of a wife because she had refused to issue me a certificate for being "bootifool." To this day, I have not been able to forget that humiliation—in my opinion, the humiliation of all womankind. That is all I have to convey.

YOUR DOORMAT,
SAKINA.

"When Sakina's brothers came to know of that letter, they were furious with her. They swore that they would gag her, truss her up like a parcel, and send her along with us. Poor Sakina realized that the whole world was against her. Finding no way out, she waited for dusk to descend before jumping into a well. Death does not come easily to ill-fated women, however! A maid spied her and raised a hue and cry, leading to Sakina's rescue.

*

"It took some effort to convince Sakina's three brothers that they should allow some more time to elapse. When Sakina was in a better frame of mind, she would willingly go to her husband's home.

"So, we had little option but to leave her behind when we set off for home.

"Seven years after that incident, Sakina came to Calcutta, accompanied by her sisters-in-law. At the time, I was also recovering from my nervous breakdown. The two of us, fellow-sufferers, became good friends. She showed me a newspaper report on Tarini Workshop. As a result, we both made our way there. Our relatives fiercely opposed our decision, but we did not heed them."

When Sakina's tale was over, Saudamini looked at Usha and said, "Now it is Usha's turn."

Usha: "Mine is not a love story. It does not tell of the pangs of separation. There is neither union in it nor separation."

Saudamini: "Why, then, do 'you roam this lonely forest in the garb of a hermit'?"

Usha: "Rafiya-di's husband was a scoundrel, Helen-di's was insane, and Sakina-di's was dissolute, but mine could not even lay claim to any one of these attributes."

Saudamini: "He who has no qualities at all to recommend him, deserves death and cremation—"

Sakina: "Oh, don't! Let's not be quite so harsh. Even twenty years of separation have not persuaded the poor thing to discard her symbols of marriage—her conch-shell bangles. Now, do away with the preliminaries, Usha-di, and sing praises of your 'man.'"

Usha: "My 'man' is a coward."

Saudamini: "Bravo! Otherwise, would 'a Brahmin housewife be roaming in Tarini Bhavan'?"

Usha: "Robbers had entered our house. They were 'sophisticated' robbers, armed with pistols. My husband and I were alone in our bedroom. The robbers kicked in our door and entered the room. At this, my husband vaulted over the windowsill and escaped! I was a mere girl then, only seventeen years old—and in the clutches of robbers! In spite of that, I showed presence of mind. I untied my key ring from the free end of my sari and handed it over to them. I took off all the jewelry I was wearing, except the conch-shell bangles, and handed it over as well. At first, they spoke to me with great deference, addressing me as Ma (mother); one of them said: 'Ma, do tell us where you keep your other valuables.' Another remarked, 'You are a good little girl.' Later, perhaps because I was all alone, they had a discussion among themselves in English. At the time, I had no knowledge whatsoever of English, so I was unable to decipher what they were discussing.

"The robbers gagged me, bound my hands, and dragged me out of the house. Not a soul did I set eyes on, although we had my four brothers-in-law living with us! I summoned up all my courage and prayed to God, God who is the Savior of the help-less, the One who protects us from all danger. I have never ever called on God with such fervor.

"The robbers dragged me along with them all through that dark night over overgrown forest paths, where thorns and net-tles pricked the soles of my feet and made them bleed pro-fusely. Then three men who were walking that way carrying hurricane lamps, caught sight of me. The robbers then aban-doned me and fled. Hurrying down to help me, the newcomers untied my bonds with words of reassurance: 'Ma! Don't be afraid of us. We are volunteers of the Congress Committee. Tell us where you live, and we will escort you home.'

"Those three men took me home. Firstly, I was not used to walking long distances. Secondly, the soles of my feet were badly scratched and bruised by thorns. So, it was daybreak by the time I reached home.

"The first person I saw was my mother-in-law. The moment she laid eyes on me, she began to wail loudly. My elder sister-in-law said, 'What possessed you to come back home?' My second sister-in-law exclaimed, 'Oh she had a gala time! Four men took her away. Three others have brought her back!' It was then that I understood the reason for my mother-in-law's lamentations. All day long, there was neither sight nor sound of my husband. My sisters-in-law had nothing to offer, but taunts and derisive remarks. My mother-in-law carried on with her weeping. My mind was in turmoil: what should I do? I could see no way out except suicide. Resolving to immolate myself, I waited for nightfall."

Helen: "Is no punishment meted out by your society to a coward who, instead of defending his wife, leaps out of the window to save his own neck?"

Saudamini: "No, not in this life; I can only hope that justice will be done in the afterlife."

Usha: "That evening, the servant Keshta's mother said to me, 'Madam, come with me.'

"I asked her, 'Why should I?'

"Keshta's mother replied, 'You went away with those robbers; the family is, therefore, going to ostracize you.' When I told her of my resolve to commit suicide, she said, 'You poor woman, why should *you* die and allow your unhappy spirit to roam restlessly? Embarrass them by taking up a job as a cook with another family.'

"The maid's words gave me courage. Of course, she was right! Why should *I* die? Those who were responsible for my plight should be shamed. Finding nothing else at hand, I took the bangles off Minnie, my sleeping seven-year-old sister-in-law, and followed the servant out of the house with nothing but the clothes on my back.

"A few days later, the maid told me that she had fixed up a cook's job for me. She would take me to meet the family a couple of days later. Keshta's wife confided to me, however, that her mother-in-law had actually sold me off to a prostitute. I was thunderstruck. It took me a while to compose myself. Then gazing at her helplessly, I asked, 'What will become of me, my friend?' She began to weep. Later, she promised me that she and her husband would take me along with them when they went to Calcutta.

"The next day, Keshta was to go to Calcutta with his wife in connection with a job. I secretly accompanied them. Keshta's mother-in-law worked in a school as a maid; I went to that girls' school looking for a cook's job. I discovered later, that this school was Tarini Workshop. I had left home with just the clothes on my back and they had become soiled. I had had no chance of buying myself a change of clothes. The fact that Keshta's wife had agreed to bring me to Calcutta in exchange for those two bangles was favor enough. I could not have asked for more.

"When I was brought before Mrs. Sen by Keshta's mother-in-law, the former rose from her seat to embrace me. I was amazed! So much affection, and for me! I was overwhelmed by a rush of joy and gratitude. Mrs. Sen immediately sent me off for a bath. After nearly a fortnight, I could change my clothes.

*

"Mrs. Sen paid for my higher education herself. I failed my BA exam by only three marks. Later, I would pass my teacher-training exams. And now, I am the head teacher of Tarini School."

Siddika: "Is there no treatment for these suppurating sores of society? You either have to remain tied for life to a raving madman or endure being abandoned for no fault of your own. If after being humiliated by a drunkard of a husband, you refuse to live with him and his concubine, your own brothers want to truss you up and pack you off to him. If a man runs for his life by leaping out of a window, abandoning his spouse to her fate, she is expected to beg strangers for shelter—is there no redress for these injustices?"

Saudamini: "There is! That redress is the Society for the Upliftment of Downtrodden Women at Tarini Bhavan. Come, all you abandoned, destitute, neglected, helpless, oppressed women—come together. Then we will declare war on society! And Tarini Bhavan will serve as our fortress."

Helen: "Why is there no law that protects women against the kind of divorce on flimsy grounds that was given to Rafiya?"

Rafiya: "Even if there was, I would not deign to take recourse to it. Why should I even cast a second glance at the person who spat me out?"

Sakina: "That is also why I have come to Tarini Bhavan. I want to prove that other choices are available to us. The essence of a woman's life does not lie in keeping house for her husband. A human life is a most valuable gift from God—it is not something to be wasted by merely devoting yourself to keeping the home fires burning. We have to declare war on society."

Usha: "Oh, dear! In that case, won't the fires of discontent heat up the homes of peace-loving Bengalis?"

Rafiya: "Away with peace! Away with a peace that is as inert and emasculated as death. We must smash the core of this custom of seclusion.* It is the root cause of all evil! No more putting up with abuse to preserve the dignity of seclusion!"

Helen: "I, too, shall move heaven and earth to ensure that these despicable English laws are abolished."

Since it was late, everyone went off to bed. Sleep overcame Siddika, while she was pondering over the beauty of a woman's inner turmoil.

---

*Gentle reader, please do not flinch when you read the words "smash the core of this custom of seclusion." The inner quarters as prescribed by our Shariat and the Indian custom of *abarodh*, or seclusion, are two completely different things. Six years ago, a remarkable essay appeared in the journal *Al-Islam*, complete with documentation from the Koran Sharif and the Hadith. It clearly proves that purdah has nothing to do with the custom of seclusion. The Shariat advises us to remain in purdah; it never directs us to remain imprisoned in seclusion. The wise old man, Maulana Syed Mumtaz Ali of Lahore, reiterates this. Anyway, there is no scope here for discussion on this subject.

FIFTEEN

A POEM HERSELF

Usha, Rafiya, Siddika, and Saudamini were out for an afternoon walk on Pir Hill. Saudamini and Siddika sat down on a boulder; Rafiya and Usha went off in the other direction.

Saudamini: "How much longer do you want to remain sitting here?"

Siddika: "Today, I would like to see what the sun looks like when it is about to set. Our tour of the hills ends today, after all."

Saudamini: "Then, I suppose, it will be for quite a while. Well, I don't mind. Meanwhile, I'll find out in which direction Usha and the others have gone."

Siddika: "Sister, if you could fetch me some water to drink— I am terribly thirsty."

Saudamini: "Keep sitting here, then. I'll go and find out where I can get water from."

After Saudamini had left, Siddika drank in the beauty of nature and found herself enraptured by it. The sky was adorned with multicolored garlands of light; in the west, the golden sun blazed down on the majestic Pir Hill with its varied plants and creepers. Lost in contemplation of nature's poetry, could one help lauding God's artistry? That day, Siddika was at her melancholy best. Her endlessly gloomy thoughts swirled around her. She sighed deeply over some reflection or the other and her eyes welled up with tears. She felt worn out and thirst seemed to be getting the better of her. She looked down the road wondering when Saudamini would return.

She heard faint footsteps—perhaps, Saudamini was approaching. Without looking up, Siddika said in a tone of reproach, "So, you've arrived at last! I thought you wouldn't come back at all! I had to wait for so long, I almost expired!" Having uttered those words, she looked up and realized that it was not Saudamini she was addressing, but Latif!

Latif was stunned. What had he just discovered! Siddika, whom he had presumed to be impervious to all emotion, was actually waiting for him? But what for? Surely, it was too much to hope for. He hastened to inquire, "Siddika! Were you waiting for me? Is this true or are my ears deceiving me?"

Siddika fell silent. She cursed herself a hundred times for having spoken without ascertaining the identity of the person she was addressing. If only the hill would split into two! Then, Siddika could bury herself in it! But the mountain was a mass of impenetrable rock. If only Latif went away without waiting for an answer. But that did not happen. Latif sat down on a rock facing her.

Siddika (softly): "I wasn't addressing you."

Latif: "Then whom were you speaking to? There is no one here except me."

Siddika: "I had been waiting for Saudamini-di. I addressed those words to you by mistake—do forgive me. In any case, why did you address me by my first name? And what makes you use the familiar form of address with me?"

Latif: "In your Tarini Bhavan, everyone addresses each other by their first names and uses the familiar form of address. Are you beyond the purview of these rules?"

Siddika: "It is true that I am bound by the same rules, but then, you are not a 'sister' of Tarini Bhavan."

Latif: "The sisters have honored me with the status of an adopted brother."

Siddika: "I have never claimed that you were an adopted brother. So please excuse me."

Latif: "Instead of protesting, why not retaliate? That is, you should call me Latif and use the familiar form of address with me."

For a long time, neither spoke. Not a word did they utter, although they had so much to say. A little later, Latif broke the silence and asked, "What is there in the western corner of the sky that captivates you so?"

Siddika: "The setting sun."

Latif (with a faint smile): "The sun rises and sets every day. Where is the novelty in that?"

Siddika: "True, there is no novelty to it; but see what a lovely sight it is today! The sun is departing, as though it were making its way home, utterly exhausted. And the melancholy earth is gazing at it with mournful eyes, as though it were saying, 'Where are you off to, abandoning me to the dark? Spare a glance for me at least!' The moon, on the other hand, reassures the earth with a gentle smile, 'Why worry? I am here, offering you pure, soothing moonlight.'"

Latif: "I wasn't aware that you were such a talented poet. I only knew you to be a poem unto yourself. Do narrate a lyrical tale like this about yourself."

Siddika: "Tell me about some episode from your life—I shall be only too happy to listen to that."

Latif: "You yourselves are, in fact, the heroines of one such episode in my life. Nothing else is of much consequence. You are poetry personified. Your story would be an enchanting one."

Siddika: "You travel to so many places in the course of your work as a lawyer. Why not recount some of your experiences from your travels?" Seeing Saudamini approach, she said, "Sister! You've turned up far too early—I haven't yet managed to expire!"

Saudamini: "God forbid that you should die! It is true that I took a long while to fetch water. But then, you were not alone, which might have been a reason for finding the delay intolerable."

Latif: "She was, in fact, alone; I have just arrived."

At that moment, Rafiya and Usha approached.

Latif (joining his palms together in greeting and addressing Rafiya): "The other day, I failed to recognize you at first glance, Begum Sahiba. Later, I heard about it all from my mother and Rafika."

Rafiya: "What of it?"

Latif: "Oh, nothing at all; I have now met you."

Rafiya: "Was anyone at all desperately keen to meet you?"

Latif: "Good God! Why should anyone be desperately keen to meet me? I am one ill-fated fellow!"

Rafiya: "Oh, don't feign such lack of interest! It should, indeed, be a matter for rejoicing that a vacuum exists in your home, because a new mistress of the house will arrive to fill it."

Latif (to Siddika): "In that case, listen to this—I have just remembered a story. Once upon a time, a young girl was the accused in a lawsuit."

Noticing that Saudamini had gone down to find out about their carriage, Siddika said, "We are about to return to the camp; let us keep it for another occasion."

Rafiya: "I'm sure the story will be quite interesting. Let us hear it today."

Meanwhile, their adolescent male servant came in with the missive that the coachman was unwilling to tarry any longer.

Siddika (to Latif): "We shall hear your story some other time."

As she approached them, Saudamini called out, "Come, Padmarag."

Latif: "Who is 'Padmarag'?"

Saudamini: "We call Siddika 'Padmarag.'"

Latif (gazing at Siddika's blushing face and bashful expression): "The name is appropriate as far as her beauty is concerned; but one hopes that her nature is devoid of the hard, stony quality of a padmarag, a ruby."

Saudamini: "I have heard that the word 'almas' means 'diamond.' Isn't a diamond a hard stone too?"

Usha: "Yes, sister, it takes one stone to challenge another."

After they had left, Latif gazed intently at the receding figures. He pondered over Siddika's words, "I have never claimed that you were an adopted brother." She was right. She had never addressed him the way one would an adopted brother. Why not? He also remembered how Siddika's expression had changed, the other day, when she had heard that he was a

widower. Latif had wanted to use the narration of his anec-
dote to detain Siddika a little longer.

> Worship and devotion are nothing but a mirage—
> Appear, O goddesses, using this occasion!

Meanwhile, Siddika was content that the promise of Latif's
untold story would provide an opportunity of seeing him
again. Had she heard the story today, there would be no hope
for the future.

SIXTEEN

VALIANT YOUNG WOMAN

Latif had specially come over that day to escort Rafiya, Sakina, and Saudamini to his house. Latif's mother had expressed a desire to see them. Because of work commitments, they had been delayed. Rafiya's typing assignment, in particular, seemed interminable. So, Latif was kept waiting for nearly an hour and a half. All the sisters were busy with their respective duties. Only Usha came in once to tell him in one breath, "We are terribly busy at the moment. Could you come tomorrow, brother? We are not going to be staying here for long. We will be off to Calcutta next Friday."

When they were on their way to his house, Latif remarked, "I notice that Begum Sahiba has learned to type with expertise!"

Rafiya: "Thanks to the abuse heaped on me by members of your sex!"

Latif: "Aha! Not only typing—you are adept at wielding the scalpel or the sugar-coated knife!"

Sakina: "For that, too, we have to thank your brethren!"

Latif: "Very well—thanks to us, Sakina Khanum has become a civil surgeon, Rafiya Begum has become a typist and—" (with a glance at Siddika, walking some distance behind them) "what has Siddika Khatun become?"

Rafiya: "A poet."

Saudamini: "Siddika writes wonderful poetry. She has participated in poetry competitions and thrice wrested the prize from the Englishwomen who were her rivals. Haven't you ever come across her writings?"

Latif: "No, I haven't had the pleasure."

Meanwhile, Siddika was musing that perhaps, she and Latif would never meet again. They would be leaving in a couple of days, after all. That day, she had not addressed a single word to Latif. She should have said something to him, at least! Latif, too, had not addressed her, thereby depriving her of the chance to say something to him in reply. Perhaps Latif was upset that she had turned down his request to be allowed to use the familiar form of address with her. Siddika was looking around for a way to begin a conversation. Meanwhile, Latif had gone ahead with Saudamini and the others. Then, with no other option but to hail them from behind, she began to follow them

Latif had instinctively realized that Siddika wished to say something to him. He had, therefore, feigned greater indifference to her presence than he actually felt. Now, observing that Siddika had followed them all this way, he turned to her.

Siddika: "Won't you tell us the story you had promised us the other day?"

Latif: "Are you really keen on hearing it?"

Siddika: "Yes, of course I am."

Latif: "I shall narrate it tomorrow."

Saudamini: "No, please! This very evening. We don't have any particular work to do. Do come, if it is not too much effort."

*

That evening, Latif began his story. He had only four listeners—Siddika, Usha, Rafiya, and Saudamini.

Latif: "Nearly two and a half years ago, I had gone to Chuadanga. At the time, a white man called Mr. Robinson had an indigo plantation there."

Siddika shivered at the name of Mr. Robinson, but immediately covered up her response. Latif noticed her change of expression without understanding the reason for it. He continued with his narration: "Robinson had quarreled with a certain distinguished Muslim zamindar. The quarrel gradually escalated. At the time, the zamindar in question, Muhammad Suleiman, was suddenly murdered. His only surviving relatives were his wife, an infant son, and his unmarried younger sister. His nineteen-year-old son had also been murdered along with him."

Saudamini: "Good lord! A double murder! No less!"

Latif: "That is exactly what had happened. Neighbors report that the robbers who attacked their house that night were the ones who killed them. And his helpless widow and sister said that the robbers were none other than Mr. Robinson and his henchmen, because nothing had been stolen from the house—merely destroyed. So, who else could the robbers be?

"Robinson had visited Mr. Suleiman a few times at his house; so, the servants knew him. Robinson was furious and sued Mrs. Suleiman for libel. He spread the rumor that Suleiman, apprehensive about his sister laying claim to her share in the family inheritance, had forced her into a nominal marriage. But since he had made her lead the life of a spinster, refusing to allow her to live with her husband, relations between the siblings were strained. That is why Suleiman's sister had rid herself of the obstacle in her path by murdering him and her nephew.

"Robinson left no stone unturned in his bid to frame the helpless young woman for her brother's murder. As a white man, he could get away with anything. My acquaintance with Robinson predated this incident. He had considerable regard for me and sought my help in this matter. Acting as Robinson's lawyer at a daily fee of two hundred rupees, I made my way to Chuadanga."

Saudamini asked, "How old was the girl?"

Latif: "According to Robinson, she was twenty-eight years old; the local people had claimed that she was around eighteen or nineteen."

Saudamini: "Lovely! He commits the murder himself and calmly foists the blame on the bereaved sister who has just lost her brother!" (To Siddika) "What do you say, Padmarag, do you believe that a sister would kill her brother?"

Siddika: "Let us hear the rest of the story. Even if you don't believe it, white folks can hardly be criminals, can they?"

Usha: "But what evidence was there against the sister?"

Latif: "Robinson had collected the evidence. The knife with

which Suleiman's son had been murdered belonged to Madam Zainab. Robinson had bought over Zainab's servants with bribes. The police were also in his pay. The police were duty bound to arrest the murderer; if a hapless young woman could serve their purpose, why would they bother to look for the accused elsewhere?"

At that moment, noticing that Sakina had arrived, Latif looked at her and said in an amused tone, "You remember, don't you, that 'she whom Bela certified as 'bootifool'" would be deemed 'bootifool'?" In this case, too, 'she whom the police would certify as the accused, would be the accused'!"

Sakina: "Yes, and I also remember that although the person whom the police framed as the accused was completely exonerated of the charges, the police received a reward of ten thousand rupees!"

Latif: "Robinson realized, moreover, that while Zainab was alive, he would not be able to cultivate indigo on their land. This was because Zainab was exceptionally intelligent and highly educated. Suleiman had educated his sister well, because he had loved her dearly. So, cheating Zainab was not going to be child's play. Robinson decided to adopt a course of action which would force Zainab into exile, leaving her home and property behind.

"As Robinson's lawyer, I was privy to his plans. I visited Zainab's house in disguise. After overcoming many obstacles, I succeeded in meeting her brother's widow and advised the family to escape. Not only did I offer them advice, I secretly helped them to get away by arranging for a palanquin and a boat. I had planned on the family leaving before Robinson could alert the police; later, when the warrant was out, I would tackle the situation. I was also careful about keeping Robinson completely under my thumb so that I could curb any attempt at mischief."

Usha: "Why did you betray your client in this way?"

Latif: "There were sufficient grounds for that; I would rather you did not ask me this question."

Rafiya: "That is Mr. Latif's secret."

Sakina: "Or the source of his heartache." She and Rafiya, unnoticed by the others, exchanged meaningful glances.

"The following day, when I went over again to inform Mrs. Suleiman that everything was ready and that they would have to leave that very night, under cover of darkness, she told me that Zainab had decided not to leave. She would commit suicide. I replied, 'No religion sanctions suicide. A Muslim, especially, can never commit suicide. So persuade her to put this evil thought out of her mind. Be ready; I shall come at midnight with the palanquin. Bring no more than a couple of maids with you.'

"At the appointed time, I escorted the group to the riverbank. It was then that I learned that Zainab had stayed back. I was extremely upset, but there was no time to reason things out. I put Mrs. Suleiman on the boat and raced back to the house, the palanquin in tow, in search of Zainab. It was the rainy season, the end of the Bengali month of *Bhadra*, and the roads were awash with slush. Even though it was early autumn, and the moon was in its waxing phase, the night was even darker than it would be at new moon. I had not been able to arrange for a vehicle for myself, so I had had to follow Mrs. Suleiman's palanquin on foot. You can imagine the spectacle I presented, plastered with mud!

"When I reached the house, I saw that all the doors and windows were bolted from within; nothing was visible from outside. There was no way of knowing what Madam Zainab was up to inside. I felt impotent, like a man who had been trussed up. I felt that all my efforts had been in vain. So, I concluded, Robinson's wishes have finally come true. Zainab has been removed!

"With the help of a trusted servant, I climbed over the wall and entered the courtyard. At that moment, the moon came out from its cloud cover; in the faint moonlight, I made out a door opening. A woman emerged, carrying a large pile of clothes. I decided to follow her, but the clouds moved in again and I could see nothing further. Unfamiliar with the layout of the house, I could not follow her in the pitch darkness and stood there, nonplussed. It could well be that Zainab's devotion to her self-imposed duty was steely, her intentions noble. And all my efforts would have been in vain.

"All of a sudden, I noticed a light and started. The light was burning inside a room fashioned from straw. I felt my head reel. With great difficulty, I climbed over a fence and entered the room. The sight that met my eyes still sends a shiver down my spine. It was a truly terrifying spectacle! I saw the bundles of clothes going up in flames. Standing resolutely within the circle of fire was the valiant Zainab!"

Saudamini: "What courage that chit of a girl had! If suicide had been her intention, she could have taken poison or hanged herself. But self-immolation! What a horrible death!"

Without seeming in the least bit surprised, Siddika asked with her usual composure, "Why, sister, is death by burning not to your liking?"

Saudamini: "No, I object to so cruel an end. She could have drowned herself."

Latif: "In retrospect, I believe that the path she chose was the right one."

Saudamini: "Give us the reasons."

Latif: "Perhaps, she had thought that if she did it any other way, her body would not perish. It was intolerable to her that the police or a doctor should examine her corpse."

Saudamini: "Right—you are absolutely right! This possibility had not occurred to me!"

Latif: "I cannot explain how I brought her out of that ring of fire. When I became aware of my surroundings again, I saw that Zainab and I were standing in the courtyard, her hand gripped in mine. 'Let go of my hand!' she snapped at me. 'Let me go!' As if I were her obedient slave!

"I replied agitatedly, 'I cannot let you go, you are my—' Before I could finish my sentence, the order came again, 'Release me!'

"I repeated, 'Release you? That's absurd! Let's be on our way! I have brought a palanquin for you. Your sister-in-law is waiting for you—we should not delay any further.' But with a sharp tug, she freed her hand and fled. I chased her and caught the free end of her sari. The scorched edge (the border had been burned) tore off in my hand. She ran inside the house and shut the door.

"Stunned, I stood there for a while. A little later, drawn by the light, some people turned up to put out the fire blazing inside the house. The time they took to do so must have given Zainab the chance of accomplishing whatever she was about. I had no way of knowing what she was up to.

"I came out and discovered that the palanquin I had brought with me had disappeared. The palanquin bearers, too, were nowhere to be found. Instead of going in search of it, I returned home and had a bath. It was probably four a.m. by then. I was exhausted and fell asleep.

"The next day, while searching the woods and forests on my own, I came upon a deep well in the heart of the forest. Perhaps, jumping into that well had enabled Zainab to soothe her agony.

"This is the most notable of the tragic tales in my career as a lawyer."

Usha (sadly): "To this day, you do not know whether Zainab is dead or alive?"

Latif: "No, but I still think that Zainab went off somewhere in that palanquin. Perhaps, she is still alive."

Rafiya: "The poet says that 'the lover's heart is like a mirror—it is aware of the beloved's state of being.'"

Latif: "If the lady does not sheathe her sugar-coated knife, it won't be possible for me to continue with my story."

Saudamini: "Please, brother, carry on. Rafiya-bu, pay attention." (To Latif) "And the sister-in-law?"

Latif: "She is now leading a peaceful life. Robinson's intention had been to remove Zainab. Once Zainab went, the act was over. This kind of self-sacrifice is in no way less praiseworthy than your charitable calling. Like a civil surgeon, Khanum Sahiba brings peace to people; that is, she heals them by cutting and carving them up. Zainab brought peace to Chuadanga by destroying herself."

Sakina: "See how he's managed to turn everything on its head? The reality is that I apply ointment on and bind the incisions of those whom the civil surgeon cuts up—cutting and carving is not my job."

Usha: "A woman is taught the principle of self-sacrifice from

birth. When she is a spinster, she sacrifices her own interests
for the sake of her father and her brothers. When she marries,
her husband's needs take precedence. And, finally, she sacrifices her own needs to those of her children. The self-sacrifice
of certain women remains confined to domestic life; that of
others encompasses the whole world."

SEVENTEEN

THE JUBILEE AND
THE PRIZE DISTRIBUTION

Tarini Bhavan was bustling with activity. This year, nearly five different ceremonies would be taking place almost simultaneously. The twentieth jubilee of the school would be celebrated on the first day. Scheduled for the following day was the eighteenth annual meeting of the Society for the Upliftment of Downtrodden Women. On the third day, the Muslim sisters of Tarini Workshop would read and listen to the *Milad Sharif*. The prize distribution for the school's students had been organized on the fourth day. Scheduled for the fifth day was the Evergreen Association of the alumni of Tarini School. After an interval of two days, a weeklong exhibition of artifacts crafted in Tarini Bhavan would be held. Here on display would be handicrafts made by women including seven-year-old students of Tarini School and all classes of women from Tarini Workshop.

The Evergreen Association was a society comprising only former students of Tarini Bhavan; none, apart from the school's alumni, had any connection with the society. Tarini had named it Evergreen so that, in time, both mothers and daughters could participate in its activities. On the day of the assembly, they would be expected to forget that they shared any bond other than as alumni of the same school.

Starting from the head teacher to the servants, each bore an expression of festive joy. Each was intent on completing her respective duties. Each wished to finish her work before anyone else. It was as if preparations for a wedding were in full swing!

Latif had undertaken the responsibility of buying toys and other sundry items and of decorating the rooms. Apart from this, he would also have to find the lady who would do the honor of distributing the prizes. He was, therefore, busy corresponding with the maharanis of the country's various principalities.

Let us enter the house for a moment to find out who was preoccupied with which task. Miss Charubala Datta had opened a cupboard and was busy directing the maids to take out the things stored inside it.

Maid: "Where shall I keep the books, Madam? Please tell us."

Charu: "Follow me."

A teacher: "Why, where is Miss Datta? Ah, there she is! Miss Datta, look—how about dressing up these two girls like wood nymphs?"

Charu: "Excellent idea. Find three more girls."

Another teacher: "Just listen to this, Miss Datta! These girls say they won't come to school on prize-distribution day. Someone has apparently told them that they won't be getting prizes."

Charu: "What nonsense is this! Of course, they'll come on prize-distribution day."

The girls: "No, our mother has forbidden us to do so."

Charu: "Very well, don't, then."

The teacher: "It won't do to say 'don't,' Miss Datta. They are supposed to perform in *The Sign*."

Charu: "Get hold of some other girls, then."

Usha: "Amiya! When will you allow me to go through that poem by the resident scholars?"

Amiya: "You will get it tomorrow."

Usha: "Bearer, call Jafri Khanum."

Jafri Khanum came in.

"Well, Khanum Sahiba, what news of the poem your Muslim girls were composing?"

Jafri: "Oh, don't ask! Is it possible for the girls of Calcutta to speak Urdu? Every word is laced with a Bengali accent! I'm fed up."

Bibha: "Miss Datta dear! Do come and listen to the Muslim girls reciting Bengali poetry. They sound as though they're in deep distress!"

Charu: "I'm coming! Let me shut this cupboard first."

Usha: "Charu-di! When will you be vacating your room?"

Charu: "In a couple of days."

Usha: "You've been telling me 'in a couple of days' for the past four days."

Charu: "What do I do, sister? I'm not getting the chance to sit in peace for two seconds, so that I can sort out all the stuff. All day, it's 'Look, Miss Datta,' and 'Listen, Miss Datta.' I wish I could be everywhere at the same time like Durga, the ten-armed goddess!"

Usha: "I, on the contrary, would prefer to be Ravana, the ten-headed demon—that way I could entrust each of the heads with the responsibility of pondering over a different problem!"

The office room of Tarini Bhavan was noisy with the clickety-clack of typing. Tarini asked a teacher called Nirupama, "Niru! Have you finished writing out your history of the jubilee?"

Niru: "Yes, I have. Let me read it through once before handing it in."

Tarini: "You're already lagging behind. It has to be sent to the printer today. Rafiya! How far has your typing progressed?"

Rafiya: "Still a long way to go."

The mason's apprentice said from the doorway, "Ma'am, the slaked lime for the whitewash has run out."

Tarini: "How many rooms left to be done?"

Mason's apprentice: "Five more. Could I have the money to buy the quicklime?"

Tarini: "Ask the purchase-and-collection clerk for it."

From the doorway, the Sikh coachman said: "Madam, a wheel of Bus No. 7 has to be changed."

Tarini: "Well, go and change it, then."

Coachman: "Please give me money to buy brass polish."

Tarini: "Ask the purchase-and-collection clerk for it."

The gardener from Orissa, a broad grin lighting up his face, said from the doorway: "Ma'am, give me money to buy paint."

"Well, go ask the purchase-and-collection clerk for the money."

Gardener: "The purchase-and-collection clerk is refusing to hand it over. How am I supposed to paint the flowerpots? And so many flowerpots, at that!"

Tarini: "What a pest you are! Summon the purchase-and-collection clerk."

Gardener (noticing the purchase-and-collection clerk approach): "He's coming."

Tarini: "Why have you set all these people on me today?"

Clerk: "No, Madam, these fellows are real troublemakers! I said to them, wait, I'll fetch the money from Madam upstairs. But they wouldn't listen and came right up. Here, these are the accounts for the money you had given me earlier. Now, I need some more money."

Tarini: "Padmarag, put this account book away for now; we can go through it some other time. And bring a hundred rupees to give our purchase-and-collection clerk."

The bearer came in with a visiting card.

Tarini, reading the card, said, "Mr. Almas. Very well, bring the gentleman in."

Latif had brought with him a whole lot of toys and other knickknacks. With the help of the other teachers, Usha put them away and said, "We need to buy another forty-odd dolls."

Bibha: "True. The majority of the students are little girls."

Koresha: "Please do buy whistles and rattles too."

Latif: "Very well, prepare a list for me, will you?"

Tarini: "Mr. Almas, are you leaving right away? Why not sit for a while and relax?"

Saudamini gestured to the maid to bring tea for Latif.

Tarini: "Saudamini, I hope everything is ready at your end?"

Saudamini: "Oh, don't ask! A lot of the sewing still needs to be done."

Tarini: "Usha-di, are you going to end up embarrassing me? How far have your girls progressed with their tasks? I hear the

Muslim girls are having difficulties with their Bengali pronunciation?"

Usha: "They can't enunciate Urdu words properly either. Anyway, don't worry—with time, things will be fine. It seems that you still haven't settled on the lady who is to distribute the prizes either."

Tarini, offering a plate of sweets to Latif, who was drinking his tea: "Well, Mr. Almas? Any news of that maharani of yours?"

Latif: "I had gone to see her this morning, but in vain. I shall be visiting her again, day after tomorrow. These maharanis can be tiresome. Shall I try getting in touch with some notable Englishman's wife instead?"

Tarini: "We are poor, humble women. We don't need any notable Englishman's wife. The wife of any other government servant will do. Such as Lady Chatterjee or someone of her ilk . . ."

Latif: "Lady Chatterjee is, at the moment, in Delhi."

Usha: "Bibha dear, go and tell the constable at the nearest crossing to ask his wife to come and distribute the prizes in our school."

Bibha: "But his salary is only eight rupees. It's true he is a government servant, but his pay is meager."

Usha: "So what? This constable, who now earns eight rupees, may, in time, become an inspector with the honorific title of 'Ray Bahadur' and earn eight hundred rupees. Why not honor him in advance."

Saudamini: "Why not wait for him to become a Ray Bahadur first?"

Tarini: "Aha! But at that point in time, won't his dignity be compromised if he comes to distribute prizes in our school? And his health, too, will be frail then."

Bibha: "Come, Padmarag, come and listen to the girls singing."

Siddika: "I don't know the basics of singing."

Bibha: "How, then, will I train them on my own to sing tunefully?"

Koresha: "They can't be trained—they have toads croaking in their throats."

Siddika: "What's this, Koresha! We are talking about devotional songs—I don't think it's right to make fun of them."

Koresha: "Didn't you just say that you didn't know the basics of singing?"

Siddika: "I may not be conversant with beat or rhythm, but I do understand lyrics. You are twisting the word 'tone' into 'toad.'"

Bibha: "Come, Usha! We don't have much time to waste. If Rahila is quite incapable of singing in tune, we shall have to drop her."

Usha: "Come, we must get on with our work. But none of you bother to help with my share of the responsibilities. I continue to struggle alone with the English songs."

Koresha: "No, Usha! You're going to watch the rehearsal for my drill first. Mrs. Sen has given me such inexperienced little girls to train, that they can neither march in step nor coordinate their arm movements. You can just as well listen to the songs at night."

Bibha: "Absolutely not! It's far more difficult to teach people how to sing, because its intricacies can't be taught manually."

Tarini: "Bibha, why are you getting so agitated? Let Usha supervise the drill. And arrange for your singing rehearsals to take place here in Mr. Almas's presence; he is a connoisseur."

Bibha: "The Muslim girls won't agree to make an appearance in his presence."

Latif: "That's right. There is no need to bring the girls here." Turning to Siddika: "Siddika, sing to them yourself and help them polish up the songs they are supposed to perform."

Siddika: "That's all very well, but I haven't a clue about the basics of singing."

Latif: "When I was in Kurseong, I heard you playing the harmonium."

Siddika, embarrassed: "It's true that I know something of melody and rhythm. But since I don't have a sweet voice, I cannot sing."

Latif to Rafiya: "Sing a song, why don't you?"

Rafiya: "I'm good at shouting, but my knowledge of melody and rhythm is nil."

Latif: "Fine. Combine your voice with Siddika's knowledge of melody and rhythm and sing in tandem. And I beg of you, don't come up with any more excuses! I'm not about to accept them. Miss Chakrabarti! Get hold of these two, and your songs will shape up fine."

Latif himself had contributed a thousand rupees to the Prize Fund that year. And he had managed to raise another two thousand rupees. He had also donated five hundred rupees to the Society for the Upliftment of Downtrodden Women.

EIGHTEEN

MIRAGE

The jubilee, exhibition, and other sundry events of Tarini Bhavan had taken place on schedule. But Latif's mother, sister, and aunt had remained in Calcutta. His mother had recovered her health and grown quite robust. She visited Tarini Bhavan quite often and had won everyone over with her unreserved affection. Perhaps, she came to Tarini Bhavan in quest of something she had lost; perhaps, to pursue a mirage. She was especially drawn to Siddika. The latter, however, avoided her as far as possible. One day, she caught hold of Siddika's hand and exclaimed, "Why, child, you don't even wear a pair of bangles! Your arms look so bare and unattractive!"

Tarini, present at the scene, said, "It would be unseemly for her to look attractive. Superstition has prevented certain Hindu women here from discarding their conch-shell bangles. Fortunately, your Muslim society is not burdened by such superstitions."

Latif's mother: "You have great regard for Muslims. Had there been two dozen more women like you, it would have been to Bengal's credit."

Nearly every day, Latif's mother would invite the sisters and teachers of Tarini Bhavan over for a meal in groups of six. Everyone, from Tarini to Koresha, Bibha, Jafri and so on had been invited. Now, only the last half a dozen remained—Rafiya, Sakina, Siddika, Saudamini, Usha, and Nalini.

Today, Rafika had asked them over for lunch. Everyone had happily accepted the invitation except Siddika, who begged to be excused. But when Rafika began pleading with her to accompany her, Siddika replied, "Just because you got your way once by shedding tears, are you hoping to do so again and again?"

Rafika: "The meaning of what you say eludes my grasp. How did I get my way by shedding tears? Some of your words are like riddles to me. That day, in Munger, you had said, 'It is you who have sealed off the path for me.' What did those words mean?"

Rafiya: "The Riddle of Padmarag—

> The learned can guess it in two to four days—
> The fool cannot guess it in forty years."

Rafika: "I beg you, my sweet sister, please explain it to me."

Rafiya: "I don't understand it myself."

Later, Siddika went to the school's boarding section to look into the nitty-gritty of cooking and shopping for provisions. Happily for the matron, Siddika had come to do her share of the work. Rafika also accompanied her.

Just as there were women in Tarini Bhavan who belonged to different races, religions, and classes, so, too, were there maids from various regions. There were Bhutiyas, Nepalis, Biharis, Santhals, Kols, South Indians, and so on. While an ayah from Ganjam set out the items that had been bought from the market, Siddika ticked them off on a list and checked the balance amount of cash. When she could not account for a particular item, she asked the ayah about it. Since the latter had some difficulty understanding her, Siddika said rather loudly, "Where is the Bengali *dumbal*?"

The ayah immediately replied, "I'll fetch it right away."

Rafiya (laughing uproariously): "Bengali dumbal! What's that?"

Siddika replied, "A potato. They call potatoes 'Bengali dumbal.' Do you know of an uncouth word for 'water'?"

Rafiya mused, "I don't think so. In all the synonyms for 'water' that I can think of in Indian languages—*jala, salila, ma-a, aab, bari*—there is a sense of softness and fluidity; only the English word, 'water' sounds a bit harsh."

Siddika: "Apart from these, you couldn't find a more un-couth equivalent?"

Rafiya: "No. You are widely traveled—you tell me."

Siddika: "*Maichredo*."

Rafiya: "Oh dear!"

At that moment, Saudamini and the others arrived, ready to set off for lunch with Latif's mother. Having failed to persuade Siddika, yet again, to accompany them, Rafika went off with the other women.

*

The meal over, everyone was busy chatting. Saudamini said to Latif's mother, "No, indeed! We know nothing of Siddika's true identity."

Latif's mother addressed Rafiya: "Rafu dear! Do you have any idea?"

Rafiya: "No, Aunty. Siddika hasn't told me anything about herself."

Latif's mother retorted: "You've been living together for three years, and yet you don't know who she really is!"

Usha: "It's true we live together, but we remain busy with our respective duties. Who asks another, 'Which sky does a star like you belong to, which garden does a flower like you bloom in'?"

Latif's mother said: "Around twelve or thirteen years ago, I had seen a nine-year-old girl; I find a strong resemblance between Siddika and her."

Sakina: "Can one person not resemble another?"

Rafika: "Is it possible for their features to be identical?"

Sakina: "One can't really tell. In our school, we have several pairs of twins. In each pair, the girls are nearly identical; I cannot tell Fazila apart from Mahmuda."

Latif's mother: "Very well! I accept that none of you know about Siddika's true identity. But I'd like you to help me make her my daughter-in-law."

Saudamini: "How can we help you in this matter?"

Latif's mother: "Persuade Mrs. Sen to arrange this match."

Usha: "Siddika is a member of your religious community. How can Mrs. Sen possibly marry her off?"

Latif's mother: "She is everyone's guardian."

Nalini: "That doesn't mean that she can get them married off."

Rafika: "Nor can she prohibit anyone to marry."

Nalini: "Of course not. But what do you expect her to do in this case?"

Rafika: "I would ask her to be present as the guardian of the bride and give the bride away."

Rafiya: "Come, Rafika dear, I shall give you away in marriage right now."

Rafika: "There's absolutely no need for you to take the trouble!"

Rafiya: "Then who dares give Siddika away in marriage? Unless Siddika gives her consent, no one can marry her off."

Sakina: "By the way, Aunty, can't you get hold of another prospective bride? Who wouldn't want to give away their daughter in marriage to such a handsome, upright, wealthy, and respected man as your son?"

Usha: "Absolutely. What would you want with this girl of unknown lineage? You should try for a family of equal wealth and status."

Latif's mother: "Latif doesn't wish to marry anywhere else."

Sakina: "Very well! In this benighted country, there are many widows. Let's have a few widowers too."

Rafiya: "Quite. Why coerce him into marrying? Hasn't your wish of getting him forcibly married off been fulfilled?"

Rafika: "Ah! Now I'm beginning to understand! It's taken me all this while to solve Siddika's riddle. She had reproached me for using my tears to persuade my brother to marry."

Latif's mother: "This time, I am not going to resort to coercion. Let him marry whomsoever he chooses to. I'll be happy enough to see him settle down."

Nalini: "Then why are you looking for a bride?"

Latif's mother: "All I am going to do is give him the particulars of potential brides, and say, 'Look, here is one family, and there is another. Marry wherever you choose to.'"

Rafiya: "But why does Siddika's name figure on your list of nominated families? She has neither landed property, nor cash, nor jewelry. She receives two hundred rupees every month as salary. From this, she spends a very small amount, between thirty and forty rupees, on food and clothing and donates the rest to the Tarini Bhavan treasury. How did a poor ascetic like her attract your attention?"

Latif's mother: "We are not interested in money."

Rafiya: "Since when did you rise to this level of detachment?"

Latif's mother: "We played no part in the issue of property raised by Haji Saab on the occasion of Latif's marriage with the girl from Chuadanga. Why reproach me for that?"

Saudamini: "Aunty, we'll have to take your leave now."

Rafika: "Do tell us how we can win over Siddika."

Sakina: "That's a request and a half! Are we supposed to trap Siddika for you? Perhaps, if she had had a guardian, he might have trussed her up and delivered her to you."

Saudamini: "For all you know, Siddika may have given her heart to someone. What then?"

Rafika: "In that case, we shall try to change her mind."

Sakina: "What audacity! Why are you so bent on pursuing Siddika? The poor girl has come to Tarini Bhavan, for reasons unknown, for a bit of peace."

Rafika: "We would bear her no grudges for seeking and finding peace. But the fact is, she has now started a fire in other people's hearts."

Rafiya: "That which is combustible is bound to burn—where's the problem, then? The moth will be doomed to burn, lured by the fatal flame!"

Rafika: "And won't we be able to win over Siddika?"

Saudamini: "Probably not. What's the good of pursuing a mirage?"

Latif's mother: "Child! How can you be sure that she is a mirage? Has she clearly said that she won't marry?"

Rafika: "She has made it especially clear that she won't marry my brother."

Usha: "Why don't you pursue her and find out, if that's what you want."

Latif was listening to their conversation from an adjacent room. He heaved a sigh and said to himself, "It is, indeed, a mirage! God gave me everything—except happiness! Happiness has become a mirage for me!"

NINETEEN

HOLDING COURT
IN SCHOOL

Tarini was busy in the office room, pouring over a pile of exercise books and other papers. Since Siddika was her personal assistant, she was also present. Rafiya and Siddika were Tarini's right-hand women. A little farther off, Rafiya, Sakina, Saudamini, and Usha were engaged in their own work. At that moment, the purchase-and-collection clerk came in to say, "I beg to be excused, Madam! I won't work here any longer."

Tarini: "Why not?"

Clerk: "Only someone who can endure being beaten up will stay on. Didn't you hear that din outside?"

Tarini: "Tell me, what is the matter? Who came to beat you up?"

Clerk: "The guardians of some of your students came to beat me up today. Sailabala's uncle asked, 'Why hasn't Saila been awarded a prize?'

"I replied, 'Perhaps because she hasn't been promoted.'

"He then shouted and swore at me with the words, 'Rascal! Scoundrel! What do you do sitting around all day? Can't you even get the girls promoted?'

"I tried to explain that I had no hand in the girls being promoted or not being promoted.

"Their response was to try to hit me. The fist that Harimati's father had raised to punch me on the nose—"

Male servant: "If I hadn't come on the scene, they would have broken his nose!"

Tarini: "Do you really believe that if you resigned from your job here, you wouldn't ever face similar situations in the future? You are a man. You'll have to tackle the vicissitudes of life by countering raised fists with kicks."

Usha: "The offspring of Bengalis amaze me! It seems that a man must resign from his job because someone tried to punch him on the nose!"

Clerk: "Why are you reproaching me? Is this an isolated incident? Sushila's father asked me, 'Is the horse carriage your personal property? Why didn't you send the carriage to pick up my daughters? My poor darlings couldn't get to school for the prize distribution.'"

Tarini: "Usha-di! Were Sushila's three sisters not present on the day of the prize-giving?"

Usha (examining the attendance register): "No, they were not present on that day. They haven't come to school for nearly a month."

Tarini: "Why haven't you been sending the carriage to pick them up?"

Clerk: "At the time they were enrolled, you had given express instructions that the carriage was not to be driven so far into the lane. So, the girls would come over to the house of Jahur, the tanner, on Gorachand Road, and wait there. Every morning, they would get into the carriage at that point and be let off there, as well in the afternoon. Now, Sushila's father is insisting that we drive the carriage right up to his doorstep. You had forbidden us to do so; therefore, the carriage is not sent to pick up the girls."

Tarini (while examining the register containing the students' addresses): "I had also forbidden the bus to go to Rasekha's house. But Rasekha and Jamila are coming. What's the reason for this?"

Clerk: "Since Rasekha's father had refused to tip the coachman and groom, they had lied to you about there being no way for the carriage to enter the driveway of the house. Later on, I visited the house on your orders and discovered that there was, on the contrary, a clear path for the carriage to go through. From that day onward, the carriage has been going to that house."

Tarini: "You may go now. We have a lot of work to do. We have to read and answer a stack of letters."

Usha handed over a long list to the purchase-and-collection clerk with the instruction, "Check out the houses of all these girls and hand in your report in three days."

Tarini: "Janaki, Nihar, stop typing for a while. Padmarag, do start reading the letters."

Siddika: "Here, listen to Letter Number One: 'A humble request to the honorable lady—'"*

Tarini: "Spare us, Padmarag! Leave aside the terms of address. Just read out parts of the letter and the name and address of the sender."

Siddika (suppressing her laughter with difficulty): "'Why did my daughter, Urmila, not receive a prize this time? Your stock answer is: "She hasn't come first or second in the exam." But whose fault is it that she didn't? You know how to extort money all year long but are unaware that there are attendant duties as well. I won't take this as far as I could, simply out of deference to your status as a woman.'

"Letter Number Two: 'My daughter, Zuleikha, has been a student of your school from the age of five. Every year, she would come first in the annual examination. Since she has been absent from school for around nine months this year, you have not given her a prize. What sort of judgment is this? With this kind of inferior intellect, only to be seen in women, how do you expect to make any progress? Now, had a man been a member of the school's executive committee, he could have shown you how a school ought to be run.'

"Letter Number Three: 'Please strike the name of my daughter, Nirupama, off the rolls. A teacher of yours called Bibha had glared at her on prize-distribution day because she had been talkative. If I could get hold of that teacher, I would put out her eyes.'"

Usha: "Is there anyone around? Call Bibha!"

---

*Many of the letters were written in various styles in English. These have been given in translation.

Tarini: "Not right away; let's hear Siddika read out a few more letters."

"Letter Number Four: 'Why set up a school if you don't know how to run it? Only to make a name for yourself? My daughter, Prabhati, has been a student there for three months. She has neither been promoted nor has she received anything from school except a doll.'

"Letter Number Five: 'My daughter, Abbasi, has been studying in your school for three months; she still hasn't learned how to spell correctly.'

"Letter Number Six: 'My daughter, Atifa Begum, still wets her bed. Can't you discipline her a bit? If not, what kind of education are you giving them at the school?'

"Letter Number Seven: 'It is unfortunate that the government has no authority over your school. Otherwise, I would really show you what's what. My daughter, Manorama, has been going to school for the last two months. To date, she hasn't learned how to dot her i's and cross her t's.'

"Letter Number Eight: 'My daughter, Prajnasundari, is disobedient. She abuses her mother. The state of her reading and writing, like her conduct, leaves much to be desired. It would be better if such famous schools as yours did not exist.'

"Letter Number Nine: 'My daughter, Saramasundari, is a student of the matric class in your school. A certain junior teacher of yours called Sarada struck her because she quarreled and fought with the other girls on the day of the prize distribution. Sarada could have reported the matter to you. Why did she take the law into her own hands, instead? Because of this serious criminal assault on Sarama, I am compelled to file a criminal case against Sarada and name you as witness.

"'PS: If you mete out appropriate punishment to Sarada and render your apologies to me, I may let you off.'

"Letter Number Ten: 'My darling child, Lila, has received nothing but a doll from your school. She has cried her eyes out. Your school does not come under the purview of government-run institutions. Otherwise, I would have exposed what kind of school you run! The uncle of the father-in-law of the second cousin of my uncle by marriage is the education minister's own brother-in-law.'"

Many letters of the kind were read out. Later, Usha summoned Koresha, Jafri, and Bibha to show them the letters of grievance written by the students' guardians. Bibha and Koresha then excused themselves and went back to the school.

A little later, Koresha came in, accompanied by a group of Muslim girls, while Bibha and Sarada arrived with girls from a variety of age groups belonging to different faiths.

Koresha: "Firstly, Abbasi enrolled in school last November. At the time, we were revising the lessons that had already been taught for the annual examination; no one was set any new lessons. While the first half of December was spent in holding examinations, the second was devoted to preparations for the prize distribution. The first week of January was taken up by the hectic activities of the prize distribution and the jubilee. Today is the twenty-first of January. Test Abbasi and see how much she has learned in these two weeks."

Tarini: "Rafiya, test her spelling by referring to the text of *Reading the Baghdadi Way*."

Rafiya did as she was told and concluded, "She is five years old. What she has learned in two weeks is well beyond what can be hoped for."

Koresha: "Secondly, Atifa is twelve years old. And it seems that the school is to be held responsible for her nocturnal bed-wetting! Thirdly, Zuleikha was absent from school for nine months this year. Yet, she must be promoted and be awarded a prize as well! Fourthly, Mariam is as belligerent as a bandit; she fights with her schoolmates all day and has to be forcibly restrained. So, when will she study? Fifth point: Aliya is a thoroughly eccentric girl; on her way to school, she would break the windowpanes of the school bus; she would scratch, beat, even bite the other girls! It took eight months and a great deal of effort on my part to set her right. She was picking up Mathematics and other subjects quite well. At that point, her family took her out of school and to their country home. After keeping her at home for two years and driving her mad again, they have enrolled her in school once more. Today, they send us a letter stating that their daughter has been in school for three years, yet has learned nothing. Sixth point: Amena is a Punjabi girl; no one understood the language she spoke; neither did she understand ours. It took a couple of months and much effort before she began to follow our language and read a little. At that point, they took her out of school with the excuse that 'no proper teaching was done' here. Seventh point: Zaheda is a girl from Kutch. In her case, too, we faced the problem of not understanding each other's language. When, after three months, we had, to a large extent, solved the problem, her parents put her into another school, claiming that 'no proper teaching was done' here."

Sarada: "Koresha, do leave off your excuses now. Listen to what I have to say. Firstly, Nirupama is a student of the middle section. She is unrivaled in the art of quarreling. Her clothes are filthy, her hair infested with lice, and her feet lacerated with cuts. In no way can I rectify this situation. If I write to her mother, she snarls at the maid and says, 'What use are the teachers then?' Look at Urmila. She has a fever of about one hundred and two degrees and her spleen is enlarged. Yet, she comes to school every day. We make her lie down on the bench in class. Sometimes, we take her to the Home for the Ailing and the Needy. Just explain to me how this girl is supposed to pass her exams and be promoted from one class to the next? Thirdly, Prabhabati is hardly four years old—how is she supposed to pass her tests? Fourthly, the moment the prize distribution ceremony ended, Sarama started a violent fight and quarreled with the other girls—Lady Chatterjee had still not left. The other girls heeded my warnings when I scolded them, but Sarama began answering me back. That's why I slapped her. At the time, Usha and you were lost in the crowd of eight hundred people. How could I have sought you out to report the matter? If a criminal case is filed against me, too bad! I shall also find out what a great son of a gun he is! Point Number Five: Manorama's father happens to be a veteran school-inspector. So, within two months (December, last year, and

January, this year) he wants his daughter to know how to cross her t's and dot her i's. He is oblivious to the fact that his daughter has neither book nor slate nor chalk, and that her body is covered with running sores."

Bibha: "Now, listen to what I have to say. Firstly, this Atifa surely suffers from some ailment which causes her to wet her bed. Miss Bose, the lady doctor, visits twice a week to give the boarders a health checkup. Two or three months ago, she had examined Atifa and declared that the girl needed immediate medical treatment. From then onward, we have repeatedly written to Atifa's mother about her need for medical treatment. But all her family can do is ask us to discipline her (see Letter Number Six). Secondly, this group of tiny tots, who are no more than four years old, have nothing better to do in class than soil their clothes. Thirdly, this is one class which seems to be completely insane. They create a ruckus, beat each other up, and are incorrigible. The fourth bunch has sores covering their bodies (make them take off their clothes if you want to check), lice in their hair, and are running temperatures that vary between one hundred and one and one hundred and two degrees Fahrenheit. They spend almost all their time in the Home for the Ailing and the Needy. They are served meals and administered doses of medicine at regular intervals."

Tarini: "Usha, why do you allow girls with fever and sores to attend classes?"

Usha: "I have forbidden them from attending school. But the bus goes to the same houses to pick up other students along with their sundry female relatives. It is then that their mothers forcibly put them on the school bus. If the female attendant on the bus refuses to bring them to school, the ladies pick fights with her and argue, "How the hell does it concern you? We pay the fees every month—and you refuse to take the girl? Is it any business of yours if the girl has fever?"

Saudamini: "Mrs. Sen, I suggest that you add two more sections to Tarini Bhavan: Tarini Nursery and Tarini Lunatic Asylum."

Bibha: "Why leave out Tarini Maternity Home?"

Usha: "Have no fears. By God's grace, may Mrs. Sen live long—in time, that, too, will come into being."

Tarini: "Usha-di, spare me from further curses! Now get your mates together and be off to the school. Meanwhile, I shall get these letters answered. Janaki and Nihar, finish your typing. Rafiya-bu, please come with me to the library. Padma-rag, bring the letters, will you, dear?"

TWENTY

THE SECRET OF
THE PENDANT

For a long time now, Siddika had been sharing a room with Sakina and Rafiya instead of staying with Koresha. It was around 9:30 p.m.; all the women had gone to bed, wrapped in blankets. But none had fallen asleep. When Saudamini knocked on the door, Siddika got up to let her in.

Saudamini: "Padmarag dear, I hope you don't mind my bothering you?"

Siddika: "No problem."

Saudamini: "You had promised, remember, that you would unveil the 'mystery' of your pendant? What with the frenetic activity surrounding the jubilee and so on, I never got a chance to hear about it all these days. I'm keen to listen to the story today."

Siddika: "Fine. Sit down, sister. I'll just go and switch off the light so that Sakina and Rafiya can sleep in peace."

Saudamini: "No, I won't sit here. Come, let's go to Mrs. Sen's room. She will also listen to the story."

Siddika: "That's not fair, sister! We had agreed that you would be the only one to hear it! I won't be able to narrate it in Mrs. Sen's presence."

Saudamini: "She, too, needs to hear it, since she keeps a particularly sharp eye on all of us, and that is part of her duty too. You do know about women being compared to earthen pots, since clay vessels are polluted very quickly."

Siddika: "But this story of mine—

No love purer than this
Has ever been, nor will ever be, in any country."

Saudamini: "Then why so much hesitation? Come, let's go. And bring that pendant along as well; you can show it to Mrs. Sen."

When Siddika brought it in its cardboard container and gave it to Saudamini, the latter fastened the chain holding the pendant around Siddika's neck.

Siddika (with tears in her eyes): "Oh, what have you done, sister! This is supposed to bring bad luck!"

Disconcerted by Siddika's tears, Saudamini reassured her with loving words. "Sister," she said. "It was not my intention to hurt your feelings. But this is, after all, a cherished object to be worn around the neck—held close to the bosom!"

Saudamini approached Tarini's room and knocked very gently on the door. Reclining on an armchair, Tarini was going through a book. At the sound of the knock, she called out, "Come in."

Saudamini: "We have to hear the story of Siddika's pendant today, but she is feeling shy about narrating it in your presence."

Tarini (in a voice tender with affection): "There's no need for you to feel shy in my presence. Rest assured that you have my heartfelt sympathy and a genuine, compassionate friend in me."

Tears still coursed down Siddika's cheeks, drop by drop.

Saudamini: "You amaze us, Padmarag! We have always known you to hold back your feelings. Why have you let yourself go today?

Tarini: "Let it be. There's no need for you to tell us anything, if it causes you so much grief."

Siddika (controlling her tears): "No, where's the grief? I'm fine. Here's my story: When I was only twelve years old, I was married off to my brother's brother-in-law. I had lost my father in early infancy. My elder brother was my sole guardian. He loved me dearly, because I was the same age as his older son. Thanks to him, I never felt the lack of a father. My brother did not wish to marry me off at such a tender age, but my mother argued that it would not be easy to find another bridegroom as eligible as this one. He should at least be bound to me by a contract. So, on the condition that I would be married to him after three years, my *akd*, or betrothal ceremony, took place. Akd is, in a sense, a proper wedding, except that the bride and groom do not meet. The official ceremony of giving away the bride would have taken place three years later."

Tarini: "'Would have taken place'? What is that supposed to mean?"

Siddika: "It hasn't taken place till today. Soon after the betrothal, my mother died. At that time, the only family I had was my brother, my sister-in-law, and their offspring.

"In due course, a letter arrived from the bridegroom's family, with a request for the wedding to go ahead. But the groom's eldest uncle wanted my share of the property to be handed over to me before the wedding. Upset by the proposal which had aroused his suspicion that he was being distrusted, my brother refused to comply. In reply, the groom's uncle wrote bluntly that if they did not get the property, the family would refuse to accept me as a bride and he would be forced to arrange his nephew's marriage elsewhere.

"My brother was thunderstruck. He had not been prepared for such humiliation. I, too, felt as though I had been kicked in the teeth and summarily rejected."

Tarini: "They refused to follow your social customs and welcome a priceless gem like you into the family? Was that how your fiancé felt about the situation as well?"

Siddika: "I cannot tell how my fiancé felt about it. My brother sent him a registered letter asking him for his personal opinion on the matter. My fiancé did not reply. A fortnight later, we heard that he had married again. As deeply hurt as I was by this news, my brother was a hundred times more grieved. For about two months, he virtually went off food and could hardly sleep. He would weep uncontrollably whenever he saw me.

"Getting a grip on himself later, my brother said to me, 'Come, Zainu'—my real name is Zainab—'get set for the battle that is life. I am bent on giving you the kind of education that will make you so self-reliant that never will you have to depend on some rascal for your daily bread. You must lead the life of a child-widow or a lifelong spinster. So, be firm of resolve.'"

Tarini: "Ah! Even before the body could fall,

It was cremated."

Siddika (tearfully): "My brother applied himself with utmost diligence to the task of teaching me everything he knew about the landed estate. He would always maintain that the main duty of a zamindar was to take care of the tenants, not to tyrannize them. He did his level best to give me a sound, comprehensive education.

"On my eighteenth birthday, my brother made over my share of the property to me and gave me all the official papers that pertained to it. He said, 'Let the fact of your coming into your inheritance remain a secret for the time being. I shall now try to liberate you legally from that heartless creature. If he gives you a divorce, it will be a blessing—your life will take an upward turn. If not, you have no option but to weep out your life for him. In other words, you will have to assume that you are a child-widow.'

"By then, my fiancé's uncle had died. So, he was independent. My brother would show me all the letters he wrote to him. He would also hand me all the letters my fiancé sent, so that I could read them. From then onward, I was able to recognize his monogram, his handwriting, and his signature."

Tarini: "But you have not seen him in person?"

Siddika (with her face averted): "I first saw him in Kurseong... at your place. But I did not know his identity at the time."

Tarini: "At my place . . . in Kurseong . . . Who is he?"

Saudamini: "Probably Mr. Almas. Don't you have his photo in your locket?"

Siddika: "Yes. But I did not get the locket and the photo directly from him."

Saudamini showed Tarini the pendant that hung on a chain round Siddika's neck.

Tarini: "What reply did Mr. Almas send your brother? Did he agree to give you a divorce?"

Siddika: "No. He proposed a reconciliation. After nearly six months of correspondence, his mother's uncle, Maulavi Jonab Ali, paid us a visit. One day, my sister-in-law caught me by the hand and drew me near the shuttered window of his room that faced out. We stood there in silence, listening to the conversation between my brother and Jonab Ali. Meekly acquiescing to all that my brother said to him in anger, Jonab Ali admitted, 'Yes, everything that you say is true. I abide by whatever you say. Grant this old man his wish. Bind Latif through the ties of matrimony and personally mete out to him whatever punishment you deem fit.'

"My brother picked up a five-barreled pistol and said, 'This is the punishment I deem fit. Look, there are only three bullets inside. I shall finish Latif Almas with the first, Zainab with the second, and commit suicide with the third.'

"Jonab Ali exclaimed, 'By God! Don't make such plans, please!'

*

"My sister-in-law took up for her own brother and adopting a gentle, self-effacing manner, began to explain to my brother that Latif was not to blame, that relentless pressure from his elders had forced him to marry again. 'How stubborn can you be?' she asked. 'Don't women ever set up house with their husband's other spouses? "She whom the lover desires is a fortunate woman." There is not an iota of doubt that our Zainu is a fortunate woman.'

"My brother retorted, 'While his other wife is living, I shall not, under any circumstances, give Zainu away in marriage to him. He once rejected my only sister, my most precious sister, Zainu! For this, Latif will have to shed tears all his life!'"

Saudamini: "The poor man is, indeed, shedding tears now."

At Saudamini's words, Siddika allowed herself a faint smile of triumph.

Tarini: "The curse has penetrated deep!"

Siddika: "One day, my sister-in-law summoned me to her room and showed me five valuable pieces of jewelry. 'A trader has come to sell them,' she said. 'I will buy you whichever one you like.'

"My brother said with a faint smile, 'And if Zainu likes them all?'

"My sister-in-law replied, 'No matter. I shall buy them all.' Assuming that this pendant was the least expensive, I pointed to it."

Saudamini: "Did you choose the locket because of the gem-studded workmanship outside or the photograph inside?"

Siddika: "I had not noticed the photograph at the time. With a smile, my sister-in-law immediately fastened the chain, on which the pendant hung, around my neck. I was about to unclasp the locket, but she caught hold of my hand and urged, 'Careful! You're not to open that now. The day your bridegroom arrives, you can open it.'

"My brother, too, said with a smile, 'No, don't open it.' It was a long time since I had seen my brother smile so spontaneously.

"Later, I came to know that no trader had actually come to sell those ornaments. It was Jonab Ali who had brought them for me. It is likely that reconciliation would have taken place between the two parties. But that night, a hair-raising incident took place. My brother and his elder son were murdered." Siddika's voice was choked.

After a while, Tarini asked, "And then?"

Siddika: "Later, circumstances forced me to leave home. I quite forgot about the locket I was wearing. I became aware of it again the day I arrived here and touched it, quite by chance, while I was taking a bath. Considering it to be unlucky, I took it off and tossed it carelessly into a box.

"A month after we returned from Kurseong, I was dusting and tidying the things in my trunk, when Saudamini Didi caught sight of the locket. Out of curiosity, she picked it up and saw what was inside. That was the first time I saw the photograph inside. Well, that is the mystery behind my locket."

TWENTY-ONE

WHAT SOCIETY
GAVE BACK

"Banu dear! Why didn't you come on prize-distribution day this time? And you didn't even attend our Evergreen Assembly afterward. I'm not about to forgive you for that. Since when have you turned into a shy bride all over again?" Having said these words, Shahida pinched Banu's cheek.

The two young women were sitting and chatting in Tarini's drawing room. They had been classmates at Tarini Bhavan. Six or seven years ago, they had left school to get married. Banu had come to enroll her eldest daughter, five-year-old Zarina, in school.

Picking Zarina up in her arms and cuddling her, Tarini said, "That certainly was quite a surprise! Rezia Banu was our first Muslim student—and that very Banu absent on the day of the all-important jubilee! Why, dear?"

Banu (tearfully): "Aunty! I am not responsible for this—my mother-in-law wouldn't allow me to come.

Shahida: "Oh, really! You come every year without fail for the prize distribution and the Evergreen Assembly. Now that you're the mother of three sons, she stopped you from coming! How had you managed to on the previous occasions?"

Banu: "Every year, why every month, when the time arrived for the meetings of the Society for the Upliftment of Downtrodden Women, there would be unpleasantness. Since my husband was out of town this time, my mother-in-law won. Amma has strong objections to my coming here; she says, 'The custom of purdah is not observed in Tarini Bhavan.'"

At the other end of the room, Sakina and Rafiya were chatting in low tones. Hearing Banu's last words, they turned their attention to the conversation taking place at this end. Rafiya said, "Well, Banu dear, it seems that your mother-in-law maintains purdah even though she bathes in the courtyard in front of the male servants; whereas we are without purdah, even though we are always well-covered."

Sakina: "You appear before servants who don't belong to your household. They, on the other hand, fraternize with their own servants!"

Rafiya: "We merely appear in front of servants; we do not get our feet massaged by them."

Shahida: "Oh! I had quite forgotten that even though male servants massage Banu's sister-in-law's head and body and rub her feet, that doesn't jeopardize her purdah!"

Banu: "And why not mention the way your sisters-in-law dress! Those net blouses and saris that are as diaphanous as air! In that attire, they appear before their brothers-in-law! The mother-in-law is stretched out on the bed, and the son-in-law comes and sits right there."

Sakina: "You really are stupid, my friends! Even if one is naked inside the four walls of one's house, purdah is respected!"

Usha: "Well, Banu, all right, you were not allowed to come because there is no purdah here. But your mother-in-law is very wealthy. Why didn't she donate a few hundred rupees to the Jubilee Fund?"

Banu: "It's precisely because I had asked for the money that the quarrel took an ugly turn. She said such vile things about Aunty that anyone hearing her would want to plug his ears!"

Shahida: "Really? What vile things did she say about Aunty?"

Banu: "I can't repeat them."

Shahida: "Whisper them in my ear, there's a good girl."

On hearing Banu's words, Shahida ground her teeth in anger and exclaimed, "Really! How low-down can they get? To say such a vile thing about Aunty! Banu has tolerated it because she is a timid person. Had it been me, blood would have flowed."

Saudamini: "Don't be a spoilsport! Do tell us what she said!"

Shahida: "I can't bring myself to say it. Ask Banu to do so."

Banu: "Write it down, *Baji*."*

Shahida wrote it down without the others being able to see what she wrote, folded the piece of paper and gave it to Usha. With an uproarious laugh, Usha spelt out the word: "W-h-o-r-e."

Saudamini took the piece of paper from her and said, "She has said that Mrs. Sen is like a . . . , but she hasn't called Mrs. Sen a prostitute, so why all the fuss?"

Tarini: "Members of the Brahmo community call me a . . . outright. Muslim society hasn't got around to loving me quite as much!"

Siddika came in carrying some letters and said, "Excuse me, please take these letters."

Seeing that Siddika was about to leave, Tarini said, "Sit, Padmarag! These are our old students. I'd like to introduce them to you."

Usha: "Padmarag, first read out the letters; then you can introduce yourselves to each other."

Banu: "Respected teacher! Why don't you read them yourself?"

Usha: "It is quite likely that most of these are love letters addressed to me. There is not much pleasure in reading such letters on one's own."

Tarini held out a dozen-odd letters to Usha and said, "These are your love letters." In other words, they were letters of complaint from the guardians of students.

When the letters were read out, Shahida remarked, "Many of them have threatened to withdraw their girls from the school. In what way is that likely to harm Mrs. Sen?"

Usha: "If the daughters of these Sanaullahs, Panaullahs, Ghoshes, and Boses leave Tarini School, generations of Mrs. Sen's ancestors will burn in hell."

Bibha came in carrying some sheets of paper and said, "I have come to personally deliver these priceless documents to you. I have also received one of them."

*In Persian, an elder sister is called *baji*. Banu was a Mughal.

Shahida: "I see that the documents look like a summons. A summons for what? Inspector Amulyadhan Bagchi has complained against Sarada, one of our teachers. Mrs. Sen and I are witnesses. These are summons for the witnesses."

Saudamini: "Indeed! Yes, I, too, have heard something about this. He has apparently written in his application that our teacher, Sarada, viciously attacked Sarama and struck her hard on her head and back. As a result, Sarama fainted and was unconscious for three hours. She went home and ran a high temperature, tossing and turning all night; she could not sleep a wink."

Banu: "Even I have heard that he has submitted medical certificates from three different doctors as evidence."

Saudamini: "Of course, he would! 'There is nothing in the whole wide world that the police cannot do.'"

Bibha: "Sarama has been coming to school right from the age of three. We have put up with so much of her mischief and troublemaking. Now, having reached the matriculation class, this is what she gives us in return!"

Tarini: "Why such regret over this, Bibha? What else did you expect?"

Shahida: "And here is Banu's mother-in-law who claims that Aunty has been embezzling money from everywhere, that she has opened a 'certain' kind of business called Tarini Bhavan, that she is luring wives and daughters from Bengali families out of their homes. She is extremely selfish and greedy for money. And . . . and . . . that her thirst for money is as acute as those of pros-ti-tutes. But then, if Aunty had not set up this business, where would that lady have found such a daughter-in-law graced with all the virtues as Banu is?"

Banu: "The slander which really hurts me is the one involving embezzlement of funds. Someone who has spent and continues to spend her entire personal fortune of four lakh rupees on activities that contribute to the welfare of the country is going to appropriate other people's money?"

Shahida: "Not only money. She has dedicated twenty-two years of her valuable life to the country and sacrificed her health, strength, and capabilities for its sake. Is this what she receives in return?"

Banu: "All my life, I have worshipped gods and sages,

And the result, child, is that you are leaving for the forest?"

At this juncture, the maid brought tea and snacks for everyone.

Tarini (pouring tea): "Why are you all so upset, my dears? People are in the habit of saying such things. They are not to be taken seriously. Now drink your tea. Why, Zarina, come here!"

Saudamini: "Well, it's true, isn't it, that the country and society did not come and fall at Mrs. Sen's feet, sobbing, 'Dina-Tarini, savior of the oppressed! Save us! Dedicate your wealth, health, and life to us'? Why did she go out of her way to serve the country? Does the country want her services?

You say that you have given your heart and soul to him;
Why do you give them? And to whom? He does not want them!"

Rafiya: "Saudamini, I accept your argument that 'he does not wish for your heart and soul,' but why does he come to take them? Does Mrs. Sen go from door to door like a peddler, offering her heart and soul? The truth is that we shall take, enjoy, and also abuse."

Picking up her teacup, Bibha said, "The higher a person goes, the heavier becomes her responsibility. And greater, too, is the abuse heaped on her. If Mrs. Sen didn't endure this torment, then who would?" (To Banu and Shahida) "Don't you remember that you had read in an English poem that a certain king of England had, out of despair, wished to exchange his crown for the cap of a miller?"*

*"Thy mealy cap is worth my crown,
Thy mill my kingdom's fee."

From *The Miller of Dee* by Charles Mackay.

TWENTY-TWO

GODDESS OF STONE

Latif was facing a great dilemma. He was unable to forget that he had been betrothed to Zainab nine years ago. It was his duty now to spend his life with her. But from deep within his heart, a voice seemed to say: once upon a time, you had married a woman you did not know and had suffered its bitter consequences for five years. Zainab, too, would be a stranger. Siddika, on the other hand, was desirable in every respect. Another point: Zainab was absent, while Siddika was very much there. His conscience protested, "Oh, no! It is wrong for your thoughts to stray to Siddika; you are honor bound to spend your conjugal life with Zainab."

Latif had left no stone unturned in his search for Zainab. But the moment his thoughts lingered on Zainab, the image of Siddika would come in the way so that Zainab and Siddika merged into one woman! Zainab, the valiant young woman described in chapter sixteen, whom Latif had tried to rescue from the fire, was his lost treasure. That night, his camouflage had been in vain—the trophy had eluded him. What a cruel fate! When even in these two and a half years he could not trace Zainab, he gave up all hope of finding her.

Even though Latif had not received any encouragement from Siddika, he could not bring himself to give up hope. He tried through hint and innuendo to make Siddika aware of the intensity of his feelings for her. She remained indifferent. As unmoving as a lighted lamp with a steady flame, she rejected him without uttering a word. There was no way he could express his regard for her in words, for her unresponsiveness was as impenetrable as a deaf-mute's.

This time, when Latif returned home from a six-month tour of Munger and Calcutta, he discovered that many essential duties pertaining to the estate had been left incomplete. All these years, Saleha's obnoxious behavior had driven him from his home. Now, he felt, he should devote himself to it. If he extended the garden adjoining the house a little farther toward the river, and if he had a small bungalow constructed on the spot from tin sheets, it would make a charming country house. But what was the point? Where was the woman in his life? Should he approach Siddika with another, more direct proposal of marriage couched in unequivocal language?

And that is what he did. He sent Siddika a long registered letter. Its language was so judiciously crafted, that Siddika would be obliged to commit herself to a reply—whether it was positive or negative. If she did not answer it, she ran the risk of having her silence interpreted as her unspoken consent. So, remaining mute would not work this time.

The bungalow had been constructed. With a pair of gardeners to help, Latif was beautifying the garden with vines and shrubs appropriate for its different nooks. He was wondering about naming the garden house Ruby Cottage. Just then, a postman brought him a registered letter. Not daring to read it in the garden in the presence of others, he took the letter into his room and shut the door. When Latif did not emerge even after quite some time had elapsed, the gardeners continued to wait for him, a trifle bewildered.

It was nearly three p.m. The master had neither had his bath nor eaten his lunch. Apprehensive, the servants would knock gently on his door. Not getting a response, they would retreat. Was he asleep? But no, he did not have the habit of napping at odd hours, as he seemed to be doing now. Finding no other way out, the servants led Rafika's seven-year-old son to the door of Latif's bedroom, stood him before it, and instructed him to cry and call out, "Uncle! Uncle!"

Latif was extremely fond of the boy. What a royal nuisance, he thought. It seemed that he was not even free to weep in the privacy of his room. Nor even to remain locked within it. His heart overflowed with feeling:

My heart weeps with terrible pain for my beloved.
I want to fleé where no man nor beast resides,
And prone upon the earth, unburden my heart of tears.

Latif flung the "cruel" letter into a box, opened the door silently, and ignoring the weeping boy, went out into the fields. Strolling along, he wondered whether Siddika was, indeed, as cold and unfeeling as she seemed to be. Forget about love, she did not even seem capable of normal human kindness, tenderness, or sympathy. A poet had once said:

With "no" as her answer, again the heartless lady said,
If this kills you, what can I do?

How was it possible for a human being to be so cold, so heartless? So be it! There was no reason why he should reserve a place for her in his heart. She had been quite explicit in her letter in which she had discouraged him from pursuing her. Then, what was the use? But merely dwelling on the thought broke his heart into a million pieces. If he put her out of his mind, what would be left in life? The poet had said: the lover revels in his anguish, so why does he weep? The joy lies in the tears. He who submerges himself in that ocean of joy is loath to rise from it.

Alas, alas! Why does the lover seek love?
If love is requited, the thirst for it ends.
Love wishes to love another; to wear the noose, not drape it on another,
Hoping neither for return nor response,
Fulfillment means loving alone.

Fine, if that's the way it had to be, "Siddika, I will love you all over again!"

Nothing was impossible in this benighted life. Perhaps Latif's tears would not be in vain. The cruel goddess just might, one day, turn into a goddess of mercy. Nothing was impossible in this curious theater of life. A couple of tears rolled down his cheeks again. This was disgraceful! Why couldn't he hold on to his manly fortitude today? Why was it so difficult for him to get a hold on himself? Man lived in hope; there was no need to despair. But

> Tell me how many more times I shall
> Build and destroy edifices of hope?

Latif had not realized that he had reached the riverbank. It was as if he had come to, revived by the bustle of activity around the fishing boats on the water. This time he wept in earnest. It was so embarrassing! What would people say if they saw him in this state? He stood there, intently counting the waves. Someone crept up behind him and covered his eyes with his hands.

"Great-Uncle Jonab Ali! What news?"

"He's fine. Death has not been Jonab Ali's fate. But what's wrong with you today? I was told that you had done without both bath and lunch and that the little darling had wept and not been comforted. Why, pray?"

Latif: "Are a man's moods always the same? And besides, don't I have even a wee bit of freedom to laugh or weep?"

Jonab Ali: "You've been mourning for the past eighteen months, ever since your wife, the lady of the house, passed away. But I don't remember seeing you red-eyed with grief as I do now. It's obvious that someone has infiltrated into our home and burgled it. Who is it? Do tell. I shall try and nab the burglar." Seeing Latif silent as ever, "You have loved your Great-Uncle Jonab from infancy. Don't hide anything from him. Or am I regarded as an 'outsider' today?"

Latif: "We have lost that case over the land formed by siltation. Haven't you heard about it?"

Jonab Ali: "I have. But I also happen to know that Latif is not the man to weep over a lost lawsuit."

Latif: "A lot of money has been squandered on this lawsuit."

Jonab: "There you go again, acting smart! I am not such a fool. Tell me honestly what has caused you such pain. As far as

I can tell, there was no love lost between your late wife and you. Then whom have you been pining for?"

Latif: "You have a fertile imagination—you're free to think what you want."

Jonab Ali: "We'll see, my boy, whether your secret is ever exposed or not."

Unfortunately, Latif's secret was exposed right away. The moment he brought out a handkerchief to wipe his eyes, a letter fell out of his pocket. Jonab Ali picked it up at once. He laughed triumphantly and asked, "Well?"

Latif: "Well what? What great secret have you unveiled?"

Jonab Ali: "I have unveiled 'Siddika.' Yes, indeed. I have heard that name from your mother and Rafiya."

Latif: "It is unwise to jump to conclusions from a mere signature. Read the letter from beginning to end. Then you can draw your inference."

Jonab Ali (having read the letter): "The handwriting seems familiar. It resembles Zainab's. When I had gone to Chuadanga to propose a reconciliation and had virtually set up camp there, I had the chance to see that lady's handwriting several times. She was, to all intents and purposes, the mistress of that house. The servants were more afraid of 'Madam' than of 'Sir.'"

An electric current shot through Latif's veins. Of course! Some letters written by Zainab were in his possession too! But he had remained oblivious to the possibility . . . not once had he compared those letters with Siddika's missive! He concealed his feelings and said to Jonab Ali, "Can you say for certain that the writer of this letter is the same person?"

Jonab: "No, I can't swear to it. And it was nearly three years ago that I saw her handwriting. But I think there are similarities in their script."

Latif: "Now do give back the letter."

Jonab: "But the letter hardly has any content! It begins with, 'my humble offering,' and ends with 'Yours sincerely, Siddika'; why have you preserved such a useless piece of paper with such care?"

Latif: "Somehow, it has been lying there."

Jonab: "In that case, it would have lain in a box or among a pile of papers. It would not have lain next to your heart on the pretext of being in your pocket!"

Latif: "Couldn't it have lain in my pocket by mistake?"

Jonab (looking once more at the date on the letter): "No, it couldn't have, since the letter is an old one. It was written at the time you returned from Darjeeling. If it had accidentally remained in your pocket from that time onward, the letter would have perished by now in the hands of the laundryman. You can't fool me anymore. I didn't go gray in a day. Once upon a time, I, too, was a young man in his early thirties."

Latif: "Is anyone casting aspersions on your seniority? You have lectured me endlessly; now do hand over the letter."

Jonab: "What will you do with such trash?"

Latif: "How does it matter? Is it going to harm you in any way?"

Jonab: "If you are absolutely unwilling to relinquish it, then is there a way out? All right, I am casting it into the water—catch it."

Latif: "This is a dangerous game. If I cannot catch it, I won't resurface from the water."

Jonab: "Such profound love! Such great sacrifice for just an ordinary letter?"

Latif: "Are you going to give it to me or not?"

Jonab Ali eventually returned the letter and gloomily pondered over Latif's plight.

Latif: "What are you thinking about, Great-Uncle?"

Jonab: "I was testing the depth of your love. If it had been a love letter, such terrible eagerness for it would have been appropriate."

Latif now felt rather embarrassed at having expressed such eagerness for the letter. But he had quite forgotten himself and was not in a position to differentiate between what was proper and what was not. He had been afraid that the insensitive Jonab Ali might destroy the letter. Face averted, he brooded on the fate of man who was so fettered by constraints that he couldn't hope for a moment of privacy during which he could be at peace with his thoughts, whether it was in his room or outdoors. And it wasn't even as if those thoughts were happy ones, centered as they were on a heartless image of a woman.

Jonab (pleadingly): "You're sure you won't tell your Great-Uncle Jonab about it? Even though Siddika Khatun lives in an ashram of ascetics, she hasn't renounced her thieving ways!"

Latif: "Now, why leave me alone just to relaunch your attack on her?"

Jonab: "Because of this morose expression, these tearful eyes, this despairing heart. You are hers to the core."

Latif thought again, what a trying situation! In spite of the care he had taken to conceal it, the pain hidden away in the most secret recesses of his heart had somehow made itself apparent. Now, his mother knew about it, as did Rafika, Jonab, and several others in Tarini Bhavan. Only that unfeeling woman failed to understand it.

TWENTY-THREE

REPAYING THE DEBT

"Let me see you climb up to that rock!" Pointing toward a boulder on Bariatu Hill, Tarini said to Siddika, "Let me see you climb up to that rock on the hill!"

It was the Puja vacation during the Bengali month of *Kartik*. Tarini had gone to Ranchi, accompanied by only four companions, to spend a fortnight there. This time they had not been able to bring a cook along with them and took turns to prepare their own meals. That day, Usha and Rafiya had stayed at home to do the cooking; Koresha had also been unable to go out because of a headache. Since they had managed to hire a *push-push** easily, Tarini had come to explore Bariatu Hill with only Siddika for company.

Hearing the sound of horses' hooves approach from the other direction, they looked up. An old Englishman was trying to climb the hill on horseback. The sight of him stunned Siddika. The setting sun was painting the sky with its bloodred rays. Siddika climbed down slowly and said, "Didi! Let's be on our way home now."

Tarini: "Yes, let's go. It'll probably be dark by the time we get home. There are only two coolies to draw the push-push."

While returning home in the push-push, Tarini and Siddika gazed at the landscape through the window. They observed the horseman, also on his way back. Oh, no! Colliding with something, the horse had fallen down! The animal got to its

---

Push-push: a kind of vehicle similar to a sampan. Two or more people draw it, one pushing it from the back, the other pulling it from the front. Most likely it has been termed *push-push* because it is pushed from behind.

feet again, but the rider did not. Meanwhile, Tarini's push-push had traveled on for some distance.

Glancing back, they saw that the white man was still lying on the ground. The horse, free of its reins, stood beside its fallen rider, as if apologetic about the accident. Not a soul could be seen nearby who might come to their aid. A solitary star had appeared in the evening sky. Tarini feared that if the man lay there in that state, jackals or dogs might get at him.

They turned the push-push around and headed back to where the man lay. Then, with the help of the coolies, they lifted him into the carriage. The push-push was not equipped with a seat. One could easily lie down on its level floor. Tarini and Siddika laid the apparently lifeless man on the floor of the push-push and covered the distance on foot.

Some distance away, evening prayers were being held in a small mosque. Fetching water from there, Tarini tried in vain to revive the injured man by sprinkling water on his face. Having said her evening prayers by the wayside, Siddika tore off the border of her sari to prepare bandages and tied them around the man's head and arms. Asking the push-push bearers to take the man to the hospital, they followed on foot. Soon, the push-push had left them behind and moved on rapidly.

The loyal horse followed the push-push. At the sight, Siddika remarked, "Did you see that, Didi! The horse is voluntarily accompanying the push-push!"

Tarini: "You're right! If man were able to reciprocate even one tenth of the love that animals are capable of giving back to their human masters—"

Siddika: "Then the guardians of your students would not have honored you with such a gem of a title."*

Tarini (laughing uproariously): "Oh! You still haven't been able to put out of your mind all the discussions that took place the other day? 'Let the dogs bark.' Idle gossip is no more than water off a duck's back, after all."

Siddika: "Off a duck's back, perhaps, but not off a human being's."

*Whore.

At ten p.m., after dinner, Usha asked, "Why did you have to put yourselves through so much strain by walking the three or four miles back from Bariatu? What happened to your push-push?"

Tarini then explained about the Englishman they had picked up from the road.

Koresha enjoyed conversing in Bengali. She said, "When the owner of the push-push comes to collect his fare, we will get to know whether they have put him in hospital or elsewhere."

Siddika: "We paid off the push-push bearers, both fare and tip, in advance. They won't be coming again."

Koresha: "Mrs. Sen, how could you do such a thing without thinking of the possible consequences? The coolies must have abandoned the injured man on the way and gone home."

Tarini: "Had they been hired coachmen in Calcutta or Patna, they would have done such a thing. The Kols and Santhals of Ranchi are not so 'civilized' yet. Anyway, the hospital is not very far from here; I shall send the gardener there right away for information."

The next morning, Tarini, Usha, and Siddika went off to inquire about the injured Englishman. Some money, notebooks and card cases had been found in his pocket. Siddika asked for one of his cards and looked at it. A shiver went through her again when she saw the card; the name and address on it were:

MR. CHARLES JAMES ROBINSON
PLANTER AND ZAMINDAR
CHUADANGA

With Tarini's permission, Siddika began to nurse Mr. Robinson in hospital. She did not stay overnight but spent the day there. Tarini and the other women took turns to stay at the hospital with her. One day, Rafiya said with annoyance, "Mrs. Sen, please put Siddika in charge of the Home for the Ailing and the Needy this time. Let her indulge herself by nursing patients."

Tarini: "What can I say, sister! 'Go to Nepal, and your destiny goes with you.' There is no one in the hospital here to provide proper nursing care. I do not wish to put obstacles before this great act of charity on Padmarag's part."

A day later, Robinson recovered consciousness. His head injury had not been that grievous. But the injuries on his arm and thigh were. He was screaming with pain, "Oh, why can't I die!"

A clergyman called Reverend Henry White came to see Robinson and sat by his bed. It was not so much the pain from his injuries that tormented Robinson, but the anguish of his polluted soul, scorched with the heat of sin. It was that which made him toss and turn. He grasped the clergyman's hand and said, "If I am dying, I must confess my sins. Oh, God! I am dying!! White! Father! Will you hear my confession?"

White tried to console him and failed. Robinson tried to sit up but could not. In a harsh voice he said, "Am I really dying? My death has come far too soon . . ."

Siddika brought a bowl of brandy and milk for the patient to drink. Robinson said, "Nurse! You do not know what a heartless rogue I am! I have survived by laying my burden of sin on the shoulders of an innocent girl and finishing her off."

Robinson had been in hospital for six days. His condition was gradually deteriorating; there was no possibility of recovery. In the afternoon, the white-haired Reverend White came to visit. Finding Robinson restless, he attempted to persuade him to try to sleep.

Robinson (loudly): "I can't sleep! I have no peace of mind! White, you have no idea of the kind of person I am! I have killed a man in a rage! Yes, see, his spirit haunts me. Oh, White! Save me!"

Having said this, the patient trembled with fear and fainted. Usha poured a little tonic into his mouth. Siddika fanned him.

When he regained consciousness, Robinson sat up. Humbly, he said to the clergyman, "Father, please show everyone out. I want to confess to you in private." White motioned everyone to leave.

Now, only the sinner and the clergyman remained. It was quite a virtue for this breed to confess their sins with their dying breath. God knew whether this brought salvation in the afterlife, but it was to our advantage that we got to know about the man's brief history.

Robinson: "I had cultivated indigo for a long time in Chuadanga. I have lost count of the number of men I tyrannized. I owe my present plight to the curse of those poor people. I destroyed innumerable fields of crops. My crimes became more atrocious by the day. Finally, I demanded fifty *bighas* of land from the local zamindar, Muhammad Suleiman. He refused. I tried threatening him, but it had no effect on him. He was an honorable man. I tried to incite the tenants to revolt against him, but even that attempt failed. When I could no longer contain my impatience, when I could not stand it anymore—"

White: "Don't get so excited, calm down."

The patient's head drooped. White brought another pillow and placed it under his head.

Robinson: "Don't stop me. Let me speak. I must say what I have to. I was tempted to call Suleiman over and shoot him like a dog. That did not happen then. I abused him roundly. He gave it right back to me. Not the slightest fear did he betray even though I was a white man. Could I tolerate this? Who did he think he was? Was he living in the Mughal era, that he could afford to flaunt his complete lack of fear?

"That night, I went to Suleiman's house with my gang. His throat was the first I slit. His eighteen-year-old son, Aziz, aimed a knife at me. It missed its mark. I stabbed him with that knife. I had not planned to kill him, but why did he come to fight us on his father's behalf? Why did he aim a knife at me? Father! See, there is Suleiman! Save me! Save—"

White: "Calm down. And do stop talking about such things. Now, relax and try to sleep."

Robinson: "No, there is nothing to fear anymore. Listen to what I am saying. When I was turning back, I heard a young girl's voice address me in English. Speaking in a tone of reprimand, she said, 'I have witnessed everything, Mr. Robinson! You will not get away with this.' I did not wish to turn back then and challenge the girl. Like a hero, I strode home."

White (aside): "What praise for such heroism!"

Robinson: "An investigation into the robbery was launched

from the following day. Suleiman's sister was well educated. It
was she who had reproached me. The knife with which I had
stabbed Aziz to death actually belonged to Zainab. Exploiting
that fact, I tried to frame Zainab as the culprit.

"I had a friend who was a lawyer; I called him in to collude
with me in this matter. Hearing my plan, the lawyer, Mr.
Almas, enthusiastically agreed to frame Zainab as the criminal.
When he visited Suleiman's house at night in disguise, he saw
that Zainab had lit her own pyre and was standing there, sur-
rounded by the flames! Mr. Almas saved her from death on that
occasion. The next day, however, there was no sign of her. Perhaps, she had committed suicide by drowning herself. Father—"

Robinson suddenly fell silent. He was trembling with fear.
Again, he screamed, "Father! Father! Save me! Do you truly
believe that I will be granted salvation? Alas, no! Where is my
salvation?"

White pacified him with great difficulty and said, "You will
certainly obtain salvation; God's compassion is infinite."

The patient said in a sad, hushed voice, "My guilt over
Zainab's fate is a thousand times more acute than my regret at
having committed murder. I drove her to suicide. Why did I
torture that innocent girl?"

White: "Then what do you wish to do now? What would
bring you peace?"

Robinson: "I wish I could hear that Zainab was alive and
well. Then I could die in peace."

White: "It might benefit Zainab if you wrote down all that
you have recounted to me. Will you?"

Robinson: "Certainly. Bring me a pen and paper."

Once writing materials were given to him, Robinson began
to write with a trembling hand. Unable to carry on, he instructed White, "You write. I shall dictate. Later, I will have it
attested."

So it was done. It was not possible to get it attested then, as
the day was over. The following day, two trusted lawyers and
magistrates were called in as witnesses and Robinson signed
the document he had dictated in their presence.

That day, Robinson's condition was grave. Imminent death

had cast its shadow over his face. Even if he was a sinner and a rogue, he was dying. Gradually, Robinson's restlessness increased. Tossing and turning, he muttered, "Zainab, where are you? I have been severely punished for the wrong I did you!" A little later, he cried out, "Can anyone hear me? Can any of you give me news of Zainab? Can you bring me peace in my final moments?"

Siddika: "You will get whatever you wish for. Now, you must concentrate on getting well."

Robinson (with a horrible laugh): "Get well? Not again. Will you really give me what I want? Well, let me see you bring me news of Zainab."

Siddika: "Listen, I know for certain that Zainab is alive. She is safe and sound and living happily."

Robinson (with the same laugh): "Ah, my tender-hearted little girl! Are you hoping to deceive me? Anyone can concoct a couple of lies like that."

Siddika: "What proof do you want? That Zainab is in Ranchi?"

Robinson: "I want to see her."

Siddika: "Would you recognize her if you saw her? Have you ever seen her?"

Robinson: "I had heard her speak; I believe I would recognize her voice."

Siddika: "There, too, you are mistaken. You heard her speak just once, nearly three years ago, and you expect to recognize her voice? Have you managed to recognize it?"

This time, the patient gazed, wide-eyed, at Siddika's face, as though he were trying to make out who she was. Later, he asked, "How did you know that I had heard her speak three years ago?"

Siddika: "Zainab told me."

Robinson (suddenly taking her hand): "Now, I understand! You—you are Zainab! Yes, I understand! Tell me, I want to hear in your own words that you are Zainab—only then will I let go of your hand."

Siddika: "If my words can bring you peace of mind, let me tell you that I am, indeed, the same, hapless Zainab!"

Robinson (releasing Siddika's hand): "You aren't lying to me, are you?"

Siddika: "Ask me whatever questions you feel like to allay your suspicions."

Robinson: "In that case, you are really Zainab. Tell me, how did you escape from there? And how did you manage to come here?"

Siddika: "I disguised myself in my brother's English garments and set out with a handbag containing a sari and a few hundred rupees. Fortunately, a palanquin was waiting outside in the compound of our house; I used it to get to the station quickly, where I boarded a train for Naihati. From there, I had planned to make my way to Hooghly, but I missed my train and was forced to spend the night at Naihati. Walking absent-mindedly along the road, I arrived at a spot near a mosque. Three teachers of Tarini School, Mrs. Usharani Chatterjee, Mrs. Harimati Ghosh, and Miss Bibha Chakrabarti were walking down that road. I pleaded with them to give refuge to my imaginary sister."

White was standing in a corner of that room and listening attentively to the conversation between the patient and the nurse. When he saw Siddika pause, he said, "Go on with your story; don't hesitate. The end is near."

Siddika: "When they agreed to take me in, I came to Calcutta by the evening train. In the carriage I hired, I changed out of my gent's outfit and put on a sari. This is how I came to Tarini Bhavan. All this while, they knew me as Siddika. Today, they have discovered my real identity."

On hearing Siddika's story, Tarini and her companions were both surprised and pleased. Now, they understood why no one at Tarini Bhavan had been able to catch a glimpse of Siddika's "brother."

Robinson: "Zainab! I have seen that you are alive. Now, I can die in peace. But you have repaid my debt beyond what I had hoped for. I had caused you much distress, whereas you have given me back my peace of mind—you have nursed me yourself. You are to be lauded! You are a valiant young woman. I shall give you a reward of one thousand rupees."

Siddika: "I shall not take a penny of yours. For me it is reward enough that I was able to nurse you during your final moments. Your debt has been repaid after all these years!"

Robinson (to the clergyman): "Father! White! Now, I have no more earthly worries. Father! Come close! Now, my sorrow is spent. Pray for me—"

Robinson could speak no more. He fell back on the bed and did not rise again. The end had come.

TWENTY-FOUR

THE SUBARNAREKHA RIVER

Tarini had come down with a whole group to the bridge on the river Subarnarekha. At four p.m., a train would pass over the bridge; they would watch that spectacle from below. The bearers of the push-push came around to tell them that they would pick up the women at six p.m.

Even though at this time of the year the Subarnarekha was not as fast-flowing as it was during the rainy season, its currents remained fierce. The river was not deep—the water would, at most, be knee-deep—but with what tremendous speed it coursed along! This river flowed over hills. The hills were not high, just huge boulders. The riverbed was full of mud and pebbles. Since no one could cross this shallow watercourse on foot, a bridge had been built across it. The train, too, passed over this bridge.

Tarini had spread out a large rug on the sand below the bridge and had installed herself there with everyone around her. A short while later, Usha, Koresha, and Siddika went down to the river's edge and stepped into the water. Siddika was no longer the melancholy, brooding person she used to be. This change for the better had come over her since Robinson's death. Now, she was a smiling young adolescent, full of good cheer, brimming over with good humor and happiness. She perched herself on a large boulder, not far from the bridge. The waves undulated over her outstretched feet. Usha and Koresha each sat down on a boulder a little way off.

When the muezzin's call for evening prayers was sounded,

Rafiya and Koresha knelt on Tarini's carpet and read the *namaz*, while Siddika completed her prayers on the boulder on which she had been seated. Tarini was watching out to ensure that the waves did not spill over and drench Siddika. The waves, seemingly on the verge of embracing her, failed to reach her. The coolies still had not arrived. The evening happened to be the first marking the waning phase of the moon. The moon would be late in rising. The thought made Tarini anxious. She noticed, then, that Latif had turned up from somewhere. Tarini welcomed him with a smile and invited him to be seated. It had hardly been five days since he had arrived in Ranchi. On learning that the push-push had not turned up, Latif reassured the women: "You need not worry on that score. You can make two trips in my car. Do remain for a while longer."

Having chatted for a while with Rafiya and Tarini, Latif, too, slipped off his shoes and socks and stepped into the water. He kept away from Siddika, since he had still not forgotten the cruel letter she had written him a few months back. He stood beside Usha and warned, "Sister! Be careful about the child!" (meaning Koresha's three-year-old son). "If he falls in, the current will be merciless."

Koresha: "There's no danger of drowning here."

Usha: "It's true that he won't drown, but the current is so fierce that he'll be smashed repeatedly against the boulders and perish."

Latif could not quite fathom how, while feeling his way with his cane to a convenient boulder to sit on, he had come to perch on the rock where Siddika was seated. Both were entranced by the melody of the running water and the beauty of its dancing movement. What a charming metaphor this river was of their unspoken love! Day and night, without pause, the river battered itself in vain against the foot of the hill; and the hill, eroded by the waves of love, wore away and broke off into countless pieces. How wonderfully moving this relationship was, marked by the dichotomy between their union and their separation!

No one quite noticed when evening had turned to night and

the moon had risen in the sky. A puff of dark cloud drifted in from somewhere and obscured the moon. A little later, Latif remarked, "Many fools perish by battering their heads against the rocks, just like this river!"

Siddika replied cheerfully, "And I don't suppose the rocks shatter?"

Latif: "But Padmarag, the ruby is tougher than ordinary stone."

"That is why the ruby lasts."

Latif turned around to locate the owner of the voice and saw Tarini! He was quite disconcerted and wondered what could have made Tarini say such a thing.

Siddika, too, was very embarrassed at the thought that Tarini might, perhaps, have overheard her as well.

The full moon suddenly emerged from its cloud cover and shone down brightly on everyone. Given the chance of studying Latif and Siddika's embarrassed expressions, Tarini was amused. She announced, "Come, Padmarag, the push-push has arrived!"

When Latif realized that they were all about to leave, he thought it would be rude of him not to exchange a few words, at least, with Tarini on this occasion. So he moved rapidly forward, splashing water as he went, and asked, "Mrs. Sen, I hear that you picked up another injured man the other day?"

Tarini: "Yes, Mr. Almas, we did. A porter must bear his burden, even in heaven."

Latif: "Ishan Babu says that the hospital follows you wherever you go."

Tarini: "This time, I didn't have a hospital with me. I had admitted that wounded Englishman in the local hospital. He died four days ago."

Latif: "All of you would visit him twice a day and your companions would go to the hospital to nurse him."

Tarini: "Where did you get so much news?"

Latif: "The news is all over Ranchi. Can the fragrance of a flower be kept hidden?"

Rafiya (in Siddika's ear): "That is why the naughty bumble-bee never leaves it alone!"

TWENTY-FIVE

LOVER OF THE WORLD

The Tarini Bhavan building had been repaired during the summer vacation. Now, things were being arranged and put back in their usual places. That afternoon, Siddika was in the library, arranging books in a cupboard with the help of two maids. The free end of her sari with which she had covered her head, had slipped off. The warm breeze from the electric fan ruffled her flowing hair, but she paid it no mind. She was engrossed in checking the books and ticking them off against a list.

Tarini was busy entertaining some female guests in the drawing room. At that moment, an errand boy came in with the news that some gentleman had called. Tarini told the boy, "The office room is very untidy. Take the gentleman to the library. I'll be with him shortly."

Adam Sharif* took the gentleman there accordingly. The latter stood there in silence, watching, enraptured, as Siddika went about her task of arranging the books. The two maids were about to alert her to the visitor's presence, but with a gesture, he forbade them to do so. So engrossed was Siddika, that she failed to notice their faint smiles and their exchange of meaningful glances. Finally, the visitor asked, "Siddika, are you learning yoga? You look very serious!"

Startled, Siddika hastened to cover her head with the free end of her sari and exclaimed, "Why, it's you! Do take a seat." Having said this, she went back to putting the books in order.

---

*The name of the errand boy was Adam Sharif. Muslims in Madras (Ganjam) usually bear such names. The names of fisherwomen there, like Dandasi, are just as strange.

Latif: "Is this how a guest is welcomed?"

Siddika (softly): "Do forgive me, but it won't be much longer before I finish my work. And you are not my guest, after all!"

Latif now knew Siddika's true identity. This Siddika—whom he loved more than life itself—was his lawfully betrothed Zainab. It was why he dared adopt a slightly more aggressive approach in his efforts to get closer to her. Consequently, Siddika consented to speak to him using the familiar form of address. Following this marginal victory, Latif said, "We are meeting after nearly eight months. Yet, you did not greet me with appropriate eagerness."

Siddika: "Why did you hope for so much? You are not, after all, my only object of affection or concern. A person whose heart has place for only one individual can give him or her full attention and care; whereas a person who has four friends will give each one a quarter of it. In this manner, the amount of love one can hope to get from a person is inversely proportional to the number of claimants to her love. The heart has its limits; it cannot expand. You cannot expect more than a penny's worth—no, less—of measured affection from this woman who loves the whole world. I have to think of so many people picked up from the streets!"

Latif: "I no longer belong to that category of people. What you just said is relevant for other people, not for me. From you, I hope for—no, I demand—if not full attention, at least more than the usual quota. And my response to your speech is, why should the heart have its limits? Particularly, if the heart of the woman who loves the whole world has its limits, how will the world find its place there?"

Siddika: "It will make a place for itself in the space that is already there. If ten people share five rooms in a house, it is possible to accommodate five hundred people in the same five rooms. As a result, there will be less space for each and less attention and care devoted to each."

Latif: "You were bent on arguing, but you couldn't sustain your argument. No, the heart has no limits. It is like fire—no matter how many lamps you light from it, it will glow just as fiercely. It is capable of burning all the insects you want to burn in it!"

Siddika (smiling): "One can't help pitying the burned insect; but I have to ask this as well: is the insect entirely blameless?"

Latif: "Of course it isn't! Its greatest fault is that it is drawn to beauty and craves for love. So its due reward is the humiliation that is heaped on the beggar. That is why it repents by sacrificing its life."

Siddika: "That is, undoubtedly, a matter of great sadness; but what is the way out?

> The Lord gave the *bulbul* a sweet voice,
> It is the fate of the insect to die by burning;
> To my portion He allotted sorrow and torment,
> Seeing that this was the most painful of all."

Latif: "And to my fate He has doled out the pursuit of a mirage."

Siddika: "If you know it to be a mirage, why pursue it? Don't you have anything else to do in life?"

Latif: "If the mind could be treated like an obedient little boy and tamed by reason and logic, this benighted world would be freed from half the torment that plagues it. Anyway, it is my firm conviction that there is no longer any obstacle to my winning Siddika."

Siddika: "There you go, hoping again in vain, building castles in the air! Carry on. Build as high a castle as you want—double-storied or triple-storied!"

Latif: "And if it is your sweet will, smash my precious mansion to pieces and grind it beneath your feet!"

TWENTY-SIX

AN ATTEMPT AT A TRUCE

"Listen, Padmarag, I'm not in the habit of joking with you. I am being utterly serious when I advise you to agree to a truce."

Usha, Siddika, and Saudamini were chatting in Tarini's room. It was Sunday, a day of rest, so they were chatting at leisure. Seated some distance away, Tarini was going through a daily newspaper, *The Mussalman*. Occasionally, she would intervene in their conversation. It was she who had made the above remark.

Siddika: "There is no war raging here, so why the need for a truce?"

Tarini: "All that had happened before—your marriage, the despicable behavior of the groom's family—put it out of your mind. Now marry a new man, Mr. Latif Almas, and settle down."

Siddika: "Old and new have become a tangled mess. Married life is not for me. How can I forget the humiliation of being cast aside because the property was not handed over? They had coveted my property—not me. Are we women puppets that men can reject us at will and take us back again when it suits them to do so? I wish to show the world that opportunity knocks but once in life. That era is over when men would trample on us and still have us licking their boots.* By dedicating my entire life to Tarini Bhavan, I shall try to further the welfare of women and eradicate the tradition of seclusion from the root itself."

*See footnote to the tale "The Creation of Woman" (*Narisrishti*) in *Motichur*, vol. 2.

Tarini: "No, no, no! Tarini Bhavan is undeserving of the sacrifice of so precious a life! It is not an all-consuming monster!"

Saudamini: "You will be able to serve Tarini Bhavan far better as a married woman. Here are the former students of Tarini School—Shahida, Reziya, Banu, Tarangini, Jnanada. They are all contributing wholeheartedly to the activities of Tarini Bhavan while leading fulfilled lives with their husbands and children. Only Banu's mother-in-law happens to be a bit ill-tempered; but then, her husband is a gem. We hope to receive the sponsorship of such a gem as Mr. Almas through you."

Tarini: "Yes, we shall consider that itself a major gain. Do fulfill our request, Padmarag!"

Siddika: "This is cause for immense regret, sister. You, too, dispense such advice? If I overlook the rejection and humiliation I faced and agree to adopt the average woman's way of life, future grandmothers will cite my case to independent-minded young women with the words, 'Damn your vows and your spirit! Look at Zainab! After enduring such tribulations, she ultimately made her devotion to her husband the be-all and end-all of her life.' And men will proudly boast, 'No matter how highly educated, noble, spirited, great, and honorable women may be, they are, ultimately, bound to humble themselves before us!' I wish to prove to society that married life alone is not a woman's ultimate quest; a housewife's responsibilities do not constitute life's essential duties. In other words, I hope this sacrifice of mine will in future contribute to the welfare of women."

Rising from her seat, Tarini patted Siddika on the back and said, "Bravo! It is precisely this kind of sacrifice that is necessary for the future welfare of womankind. The more valuable the desired object, the greater should be the sacrifice associated with it! Of course, God is neither blind nor deaf—the kind of life Sakina has lived or the way Siddika is sacrificing hers will never be in vain. Mother India! Who says that you are a poor beggar? When you have such gems for daughters, in what way are you impoverished?"

Usha: "The assumption that the husband is the supreme

master is fatal. Whatever extremes the man may go to, there seems to be no way for the weak, simpleminded woman to function other than with the help of her husband. Why, pray? Is this vast earth reserved exclusively for you men?"

Saudamini: "As a result of Siddika's great sacrifice, Muslim men will, in the future, at least hesitate a little before spurning a woman they have been betrothed to through the akd ceremony. And may marriages never take place on the basis of property and jewelry. A daughter is not a commodity, that motor cars and three-storied houses must be given with her as 'free gifts'! Very well, Padmarag, sister,

> Then this stream of tears
> Will flood the earth,
> It will make the Sahara fertile and bear just fruit!"

Siddika: "I shall ensure, however, that Tarini Bhavan does not acquire a reputation as a place where all disreputable women congregate. I shall return to Chuadanga. Until such time as my eight-year-old nephew attains majority, I shall look after him and the estate; in addition, I shall try my utmost to awaken the women of decadent Muslim society to their real purpose in life."

Saudamini: "But Mr. Almas loves you with his whole being. Will you cause him so much heartache?"

Siddika: "It cannot be helped." In a very low voice, "Very well—in return, I shall love him too."

At that moment, Adam Sharif came in with the news of Latif's arrival. Tarini laughed and said, "Mr. Almas has arrived. Now that you will be coming face-to-face, you can decide on victory or defeat in open combat!"

Usha: "What do you say, Padmarag? Will you be able to confront him?"

Siddika: "Siddika does not withdraw from open combat."

Tarini (to the servant): "Ask the gentleman to come in."

Saudamini: "I shall take Mr. Almas's side."

Usha: "I shall also support him!"

Tarini: "But in that case, poor Padmarag will be all alone."

Saudamini: "You take her side."

Tarini: "I cannot take sides—I am neutral."

Usha: "Then today is Padmarag's trial by fire."

Siddika: "If the whole world is on one side,

What can it do to one by whom God abides?"

Latif came in. After the usual exchange of greetings and a few remarks here and there, Tarini left the room. Latif had also been looking for this opportunity. He said to Usha, "Sister! I have heard that Zainab was present at Mr. Robinson's deathbed; do tell me where she went afterward."

Usha: "What do I know about Zainab's whereabouts?"

Latif: "That's not worthy of you, sister! Is it fair to deceive your adopted brother?"

Usha: "That is why, like a true younger brother, you pester me with unreasonable demands! Your latest demand is that the whereabouts of some Zainab Bibi or other be located!"

Latif: "I have become spoiled because you spoil me like an older sister. Please, sweet sister of mine! Do grant me this unreasonable request."

Saudamini: "But why are you so bothered about this Zainab?"

Latif: "Because she is my affianced wife."

Siddika: "Oh! That is why you have no idea of her whereabouts!"

Saudamini: "Listen, sister, even if the truth sounds harsh, I shall speak it. He is now busy pursuing you; that is why he has no news of his lawfully wedded wife's whereabouts."

Latif was embarrassed by her words and Siddika, too, blushed like a ruby. Latif entreated, "Sister, please do not reproach me anymore—I have now come to inquire about her."

Saudamini: "'Come to inquire about her'—why come here instead of going to Chuadanga?"

Latif: "She is not in Chuadanga now."

Usha: "But in Tarini School!"

Latif (glancing sideways at Siddika): "If not quite in Tarini School, certainly in Tarini Workshop."

Saudamini (with a hearty laugh): "This slander is rich! All

the men who lose their wives will come to Tarini Bhavan in search of them! Do we steal men's wives and daughters?"

Latif: "Great-Uncle Jonab Ali has told me, 'Gafur's wife, Sakina Khanum, is in Tarini Bhavan; Muzaffar's wife, Rafiya Begum, is there too. Go there—you'll see yours there as well.'"

Usha: "Why not try coming here with a gang and attacking Tarini Bhavan?"

Latif: "Swear by your faith and tell me—is Zainab really not here?"

Saudamini: "There are only a few Muslim women here like Koresha, Jafri—"

Latif: "Come on! Everyone knows who they are. The only person of unknown lineage and origin here is Siddika. People slander lawyers by claiming that they turn truth into falsehood and black into white—"

Usha: "Why slander, brother? It's absolutely true. Why, this very moment, you are trying to prove that Siddika is Zainab!"

Latif: "And all of you are opposing it with equal vehemence! Anyway, does Siddika refuse to acknowledge her betrothal to me? That is God's truth."

Usha: "I have something to say about this. Your betrothal to Zainab took place at the behest of your uncle. It was also aborted at his wish; you had no opinion of your own about it. Then why are you bothering yourself about this issue now?"

Latif: "Our betrothal was not aborted. It is also beyond someone else's authority to abort it."

Usha: "But your uncle was the supreme authority in this affair. You were merely a witness, a puppet. If he had wished, he could have made you annul the marriage."

Latif: "It is now futile to speak of what my uncle would or would not have done. The outcome of it all is that our betrothal remains intact."

Siddika: "Usha-di! My point is, if you have thrown your bangle far away so that it is bound to break, if you have ground it under your foot but find it intact because of its own resilience, why bother to try and pick it up again?"

Latif: "You are mistaken. The bangle was not thrown away on purpose; it had slipped off accidentally. But thanks to Usha

Didi's luck, it had not broken. It is only natural that she should now pick it up eagerly."

Saudamini looked at Siddika's face but noticed no change of expression. She then told her in a soft voice, "I hope you have no further retort to that. So, let us presume that silence implies agreement—"

Siddika: "I don't have time to waste by engaging in futile argument with a lawyer. I'm off."

Latif: "What do you mean, 'I'm off'? Either refuse to acknowledge the betrothal, or surrender!"

Siddika (smiling): "Does anyone surrender of her own free will?"

Saudamini: "Right. I am yours if you can catch me! Well, brother, why don't you take recourse to the courts? As a man, the law has always been in your favor."

Latif: "What use would that be? If the law ruled in my favor, I would be empowered to exercise my right over Siddika, but that does not mean I would be any closer to her. I want to win over her heart and soul."

Usha: "If you haven't been able to win over Siddika's heart and soul till now, then pray, what have you been doing all this while, brother?

Latif: "You know something, sister? The events ordained by providence are a little like our British system of justice. Shyam will have to suffer the consequences of Ram's crime, while the fruits of Shyam's virtue will be enjoyed by Kanai! That I am suffering is not because of sins I, personally, have committed."

Siddika: "Man's personal wishes are not of paramount importance. Circumstances often dictate the sacrifice of one's own wishes and self-interest."

Latif: "God bless you! I am delighted to hear you utter these words. Now you have realized that my marriage to Hamid's mother took place without my consent. And I was not the one who rejected you. I was waiting for an opportunity to win you over; unfortunately, those opportunities were accompanied by disasters."

Saudamini: "How so?"

Latif: "Following my uncle's demise, when I was on the

verge of writing a letter to my brother-in-law, that is Suleiman Saab, his letter to me arrived. He had written asking me to grant Zainab a divorce. The more I insisted on a reconciliation, the more incensed he became. At the same time, my sister (his wife) kept writing me long, abusive letters. My brother-in-law wrote that his sister was also keen on a divorce. I wrote to him that with his permission, I would like to correspond with Zainab herself and come to a decision about the matter. He gave me his consent and I wrote to Zainab. She replied that she had nothing to say for herself in this regard; she would fully abide by whatever decision her brother and her sister-in-law came to. I was in a great quandary. Here was my brother-in-law, sword in hand, ready to sever our marital bond, while Zainab expressed her willingness to submit to his will. Finally, I sent Jonab Ali to Chuadanga. For nearly two months, he badgered my brother-in-law and after much effort managed to persuade him to agree to a truce. When he agreed, that swine, Robinson, murdered him and his son, Aziz. I had narrated the subsequent events to you in the form of a story that day in Munger."

Usha: "Even when you went to Chuadanga in disguise to rescue Zainab, you ended up looking like a very foolish 'detective.' You got yourself plastered with mud in order to accompany the palanquin in which you planned to bring Zainab back with you, while she escaped in the very same palanquin."

Latif: "Absolutely, but am I responsible for those incidents?"

Usha: "Brother, I fail to understand your marriage customs. You remained in Rasulpur, while the bride remained in Chuadanga. And yet, you were married off to each other. Even if you were married off, it was without the bride and groom going through the auspicious ritual of setting eyes on each other for the first time."

Latif: "And even when that 'auspicious ritual' did take place, it was not followed by the couple setting up home together."

Saudamini: "When did your ritual exchange of glances take place?"

Latif: "In Kurseong. When I regained consciousness, it was on her that my eyes fell first."

Saudamini: "That sort of look does not count at all. What I really want to know is, on which particular day did you gaze upon Siddika with the same kind of expression that is typical of the ritual exchange?" Latif smiled but remained silent.

Saudamini: "Were no efforts made to arrest your brother-in-law's murderer? And Mr. Robinson was free to roam where he pleased?"

Latif: "Who said no such efforts were made? It is not, after all, an easy task to arrest white folks. Leaving my sister behind in Rasulpur, I went back to Chuadanga to collect evidence against Robinson. The atmosphere in Chuadanga was highly charged at the time. No one dared to say anything that might implicate Robinson. Anyway, after three years of painstaking effort, when I finally managed to have a warrant of arrest issued against him, I discovered that he had left for Ranchi the previous day. By the time the warrant reached Ranchi, Robinson was on his deathbed."

Saudamini: "What happened later to your problem regarding Siddika?"

Latif: "Perhaps, she has lost all respect for matrimony, having heard the tragic accounts of the failed marriages of Rafiya Begum, Sakina Khanum, and others like them. There is no doubt that their stories are heartrending; but does that mean that no one in this world should ever marry?"

Usha: "That's true. The number of child-widows in Hindu society is not negligible; yet, young girls continue to get married. Even Rafiya-bu's two daughters have gotten married."

Saudamini: "What do you have to say about it, Padmarag?"

Siddika: "On the day I was forced to leave Chuadanga, long before I heard the stories about failed marriages, I had decided on the path my life would take. In fact, on the very day that my brother was murdered, I realized that it was not God's will that I should marry."

Latif: "I am not prepared to accept this as your final answer. I am giving you some time to reconsider. If you have any complaints about me personally, I am willing to hear you out on that matter as well. I have committed but one crime—marrying Hamid's mother."

Siddika: "I have nothing against you personally. I genuinely respect you for sacrificing your own wishes and happiness for your elders. And Hamid's mother is alive no more either, so where's the need of bringing up that subject? God knows that I bear you no ill will."

Usha: "Then shake hands, both of you, and be friends."

Latif: "Siddika, tell me truly, will you be my wife?"

Siddika: "No. You find your way; I shall find mine."

TWENTY-SEVEN

FAREWELL

It was nearly four p.m. Siddika, lost in her own thoughts, was packing her suitcase. Early next morning, she would be leaving for her country home. Her sister-in-law had come down to escort her there. She had put up at the home of Rafiya's daughter, Gauhar Begum. One by one, Siddika had bade farewell to everyone except Tarini. The sisters who lived in the ashram had each given her a memento to remember them by and had pleaded with her to come back soon. Siddika's eyes were still damp with tears. At that moment, someone knocked on the door. Asking them to come in, Siddika looked up and saw that Tarini had arrived with Usha and her sister-in-law, Rashida.

Rashida (stroking Siddika's hair): "Let me see whether your hair is matted."

Tarini: "Is it really a woman with matted hair that you're looking for?"

Rashida: "From what I had recently heard about Zainu, I was under the impression that she was an ascetic with the typical matted hair that an ascetic sports. Zainu, are your bags packed? Shall I ask for the carriage to be brought around?"

Siddika: "Do stay awhile. Explore Tarini Bhavan at leisure."

Rashida: "I have explored it extensively for two hours and have worn out Mrs. Sen as well."

Tarini: "Oh, we are quite used to walking long distances. It is you who must be exhausted."

Rashida: "Then it's time we left, Zainu."

Siddika: "Early tomorrow morning, I will be at your place at the right time. I won't be able to accompany you now."

Rashida: "And who will come to pick you up at that hour?"

Tarini: "No one need come. We will arrange for Siddika to be escorted there. Bhalu Ayah knows your place. She and Ishan Babu will accompany her."

Usha: "I will also accompany her. I'll go right up to the station and put you on the train."

Rashida (to Siddika): "Your eyes are swollen with weeping like a new bride's! Mrs. Sen, you have all bound Zainu to you with such ties of affection and tenderness that she does not wish to leave you."

Tarini: "It is kind of you to think so. Rather, it is Siddika who has bound us all to her—"

Usha: "And is leaving us all tied up in knots."

When Rashida left, Siddika completed the work that remained to be done and went off to say good-bye to Tarini. She kissed Tarini's feet with deep respect and feeling, but her voice was too choked for her to utter a single word. Tarini kissed her on the forehead and said, "I am not sad about your departure, because even if you are leaving today, you will come back to us, whether it is in a couple of months or in six months' time. What makes me really sad is the fact of your having sacrificed your possibility of happiness in marriage for the collective welfare of society. This ingrate of a society will fail to grasp the full import of your priceless gift. If you have chosen to serve society, all your life will be spent fielding brickbats. There is still time—go back home, Padmarag!"

Siddika: "No, Elder Sister! There is no way I can, now. That day I had clearly told him, 'You find your way. I shall find mine.'"

Tarini: "Then, let my blessings go with you. May your noble purpose be fulfilled through your sacrifice. May you be happy always."

Later, Tarini kissed Siddika again on her forehead, just above her misty eyes, and bade her farewell.

It was true that Siddika had taken leave of everyone at Tarini Bhavan, but there was one person to whom she had yet to bid farewell. Who knew whether she would ever see him again in her lifetime? After reaching Chuadanga, Siddika would, for the time being, be imprisoned again by the practice of social seclusion. So even if Latif went to visit her there, she would not be allowed to see him. If, by chance, Latif had come here today, she could have seen him for the last, the very last time in her life.

Absorbed in such thoughts, Siddika absentmindedly made her way to the drawing room. She had done that room up herself—Tarini had placed the responsibility of decorating it on her shoulders. Dusk had descended by then, but Siddika did not switch on the electric light. This dark, isolated room seemed ideal for her hidden thoughts. She remembered that around four or five months ago, she had bidden Latif good-bye in this room with the words, "You find your way." Since then, she had not seen Latif. Perhaps they were never to meet again in this lifetime. Siddika could not hold back her tears. Her brother had said, "Zainu, prepare yourself for the life of a perpetual spinster or a child-widow."

Siddika would not consider herself a perpetual spinster, because a spinster possessed nothing. Her empty heart was bereft of an object of affection to focus on. To shoulder the burden of one so deprived, so helpless, was very hard. She would regard herself as a widow, because a widow had a treasure to bank on, namely, her husband's memory. Reminiscences of her husband would be her constant companions in life. If she did not have them, how would a widow survive? In a life that had thorns strewn all the way along the path, a husband's memory was a widow's only form of sustenance. When the world bloodied her soul with wounds, thoughts of her husband would act as a soothing balm. They would be her consolation. Brothers-in-law and sundry other relatives might use cunning ploys to wrest her property from her. But they could never rob her of the feeling that

The husband of the devoted wife is her lord and her life's essence,
So I crave to bow before him with my prayers.

That feeling could never be usurped. It was everything to a widow.

Suddenly, Adam Sharif came in and switched on the light. "Please sit down," he requested someone.

Siddika glanced at the doorway and saw that the visitor was Latif. Today, without warning, their eyes met.

"Sit down; Madam is still busy with her prayers. She will come soon, once her prayers are over," Adam Sharif reassured Latif before leaving the room.

Latif said in a tone of mild surprise: "Siddika, weren't you supposed to leave with my sister today?"

Siddika: "How did you get to know I was leaving?"

Latif: "Well, you may not be interested in anything that concerns me, but I happen to keep abreast of all that concerns you! I am not hard-hearted like you—I have feelings. Oh, that reminds me—you had said the other day that you would find your way. Very well, may I ask whether there are roads other than the one leading to Chuadanga?"

Siddika: "I haven't quite followed you."

Latif: "Then listen: I have no desire to make you suffer needlessly by keeping you locked up in the prison of marriage. Neither do I want to pollute your life by standing in your way. My aim in life is to do whatever makes you happy and fulfilled. That is why I wish to give you your freedom by offering you a legal divorce."

Siddika (agitated): "No, I don't want freedom. Why are you being so cruel to me?"

Latif (in a low voice): "Listen, forget your inhibitions and your concern for other people's opinions. Tell me what your real feelings are."

Siddika (holding back her feelings with difficulty): "It is the truth—I don't want a separation from you."

Latif: "Why, four or five years back, when my brother-in-law was begging me to give you a divorce, that was also what you had wanted."

Siddika (bashfully): "I did not know you then."

Latif: "Even after you got to know me, you refused, just the other day, to become my wife. You said you would find your own way in life."

Siddika: "But I hadn't asked you for a divorce, had I?"

Latif: "I don't understand your riddles. Then why did you object to becoming my life partner?" (Finding Siddika silent, in a voice, tender with affection): "I am not a low-down, self-ish man. I have already assured you that all I wish for are your happiness and good fortune. And for that noble purpose, I wish to liberate you from this bond."

Siddika: "If you desire my happiness and contentment, then my humble request is that you marry again and settle down. That is what will make me really happy."

Latif: "It is useless to tell me this. I have no other desire. I

Shall keep my heart for her whom I have given it to;
I shall surrender it to her when I see her in another life.
My happiness and peace are completely in your hands. You know
quite well that if I have you, then
No need have I of heaven, salvation, or piety—
From one life to another, you are my heart's desire."

Siddika: "To be your life partner is desirable not just a hundred times, but a hundred thousand times. But I am not destined for it." (With hands clasped in entreaty and tears in her eyes): "Don't say that to me again."

Latif (in a hurt voice): "Have I then, like an idol worshipper, devoted all these months to the worship of a stone image? My broken heart wishes to ask:

When my terrible pain comes to mind,
Does a single tear drop from your eyes?"

In reply, Siddika took off the pendant she had been wearing and gave it to Latif. He opened the pendant's clasp and discovered to his astonishment what was inside—his photograph!

Siddika: "Now are you convinced that there are others more idolatrous than you?"

Latif was about to reply, but at that moment, Tarini came in and nothing more could be said.

TWENTY-EIGHT

FELLOW TRAVELERS

Siddika was once again traveling in that vehicle which ran on steam. But today, it was not with the purpose of leaving her home to embrace the wide world. Today, she was returning to the embrace of her birthplace, as beloved as a mother's. On this journey, too, Siddika was gripped by a feeling of melancholy. It was she who had asked her sister-in-law to come and fetch her and was accompanying her home of her own free will. But she was leaving with a very heavy heart. It was as if Siddika were taking leave of paradise. Who knew when she would be able to visit Tarini Bhavan again? Her silent anguish defied description.

Rashida, her son, a maid, and Siddika were on the train. A compartment had been reserved for them. There was still some time left for the train to leave, so Usha was sitting with them in their compartment. A little later, Latif boarded the train. At first, Siddika could not believe her eyes—was this possible? Even if it was not, it was true! Siddika had completely forgotten that Latif was Rashida's brother. When Usha was getting off the train, she said, "Padmarag! Mr. Almas is your fellow traveler!"

After the train had started on its journey, Rashida started fussing over Siddika. She made the little boy lie down on the bench in the middle and made the ayah sit near him. Later, she said to Siddika, "Why do the sisters at Tarini Bhavan call you Padmarag? Is it because you are Almas's wife?"

Siddika: "Just as I am not responsible for the name Zainab, so also, I am not responsible for the name Padmarag."

Rashida: "Who named you Padmarag? Latif?"

Siddika: "Of course not! On the day that I was first brought in to see Mrs. Sen, she named me Padmarag right away."

Rashida: "But I still want to ask,

> How did the name-giver know
> The Tale of the Ruby and the Diamond?

By the way, instead of accompanying me on that fateful day, why did you prefer to endure so many tribulations?"

Siddika: "I did not dare accompany you because you escaped with a perfect stranger."

Rashida: "When I went off with that strange, masked man, I, at least, took two maids and one trusted male servant of ours along. You did not even bother to do that—you went off alone to conquer the world!"

Siddika: "My intention was not to conquer the world—it was quite different."

Rashida: "And what, pray, was it?"

Siddika: "To commit suicide."

Rashida: "It wouldn't have been a bad idea, if you had managed that: all traces of you would have been wiped out. I am not condoning such a sinful act, though. God willing, no one should be prey to such evil impulses. Anyway, when did the auspicious exchange of glances take place between you and Almas?"

Latif was about to say, "Last evening, in Mrs. Sen's drawing room," but refrained from doing so. With a faint smile, he restrained himself.

Then Rashida announced, "I am feeling awfully sleepy. Zainu! Go and sit on the bench over there; I would like to lie down for a bit."

Siddika: "Why, didn't you sleep last night?"

Rashida: "No, you know that I can't fall asleep easily in a new place."

Siddika: "And I suppose this bench on the train is comfortably familiar to you?"

Rashida (laughing): "Go on! Be off with you. Stop arguing with me! Get off this bench!"

As a result, Siddika went and sat on the same bench as Latif. Latif had pushed up the window shutter and was either contemplating the beauty of the world outside, or perhaps, merely staring out absentmindedly. He knew that, perhaps, he would never again get the opportunity to talk to Siddika. So, it would be a sin to waste this opportunity he had been given by his sympathetic sister. He began making good use of that time. He bent closer to Siddika and asked, "Siddika, have you ever traveled this way to Chuadanga?"

Siddika: "I don't recall going anywhere by this route ever before."

Latif: "Are you sorry to leave Calcutta?"

Siddika: "Not to leave Calcutta, but to leave Tarini Bhavan."

Latif: "Well, if you ever wish to go back to Tarini Bhavan, you can always do so. But—"

Latif's voice choked up. Making an effort to get a grip on his feelings, he hastily looked out of the window. His unspoken words took shape and appeared before Siddika's eyes: "But you will never see me again."

A time of distress seems everlasting, while happy moments disappear into the infinite void even as they are being savored. Latif felt that the train was moving exceptionally, inordinately fast. So, too, did Siddika. If the damn train traveled at a slower speed, she thought, would it have caused any harm?

Rashida had merely shut her eyes. She was not sleeping. She sat up and said to Siddika, "Listen, Zainu! I've suddenly remembered something else."

Siddika: "Yes?"

Rashida: "During that nightmarish period following your disappearance, when in great sadness and despair, I was returning the jewelry Great-Uncle Jonab Ali had brought with him, he had opened the case belonging to that pendant and chain and remarked, 'This is empty.'

"At the time, I had snapped at him, 'Then I must have swallowed the necklace.' Many days later, I remembered that I had put the pendant and chain around your neck. I can't recall what happened afterward—whether you kept it somewhere or whether I misplaced it in my absentmindedness. Can you tell me anything about it, Zainu?"

Ears pricked up and eyes gleaming with mischief, Latif waited eagerly to hear Siddika's reply. But Siddika remained silent. Moreover, when she recalled her moment of weakness, the previous evening, when she had impulsively shown the pendant to Latif, she was overcome by embarrassment. She just could not bring herself to look at Latif. After a while, his hopes of hearing Siddika's reply dashed, Latif leaned his head out of the open window. He gazed intently at the passing fields, occasionally stealing glances at Siddika's shy, blushing countenance. Perhaps, he was thinking:

> If reward there is for his love,
> If the lament of parting is heard by God,
> In another life shall this unfortunate one possess his precious woman.

Alas! "Another life" was far away. At this very moment, all meetings between them in this life were about to cease. The train was about to reach Chuadanga. Indeed, there was Chuadanga station!

Latif took Siddika's hand and helped her off the train. This would be their last meeting.

Essays

"GOD GIVES, MAN ROBS"

There is a saying, "Man proposes, God disposes," but my bitter experience shows that God gives, Man robs. That is, Allah has made no distinction in the general life of male and female—both are equally bound to seek food, drink, sleep, etc., necessary for animal life. Islam also teaches that male and female are equally bound to say their daily prayers five times, and so on.

Our great Prophet has said, "Talibul Ilm farizatu ala kulli Muslimeen-o-Muslimat" (i.e., it is the bounden duty of all Muslim males and females to acquire knowledge). But our brothers will not give us our proper share in education. About sixty years ago, they were opposed to the study of English even for males; now they are reaping the harvest of their bitter experience. In India almost all the doors to wealth, health, and wisdom are shut against Muslims on the plea of inefficiency. Some papers conducted by Muslims may or may not admit this—but fact is fact—the *Inefficiency* exists and stares us in the face! Let me also venture to say that it is so; for children born of educated mothers must necessarily be superior to Muslim children, who are born of illiterate and foolish mothers. The late Lady Shamsul Huda by way of conversation often used to say that the Muslim public abused her husband because he had given certain high posts to Hindus, ignoring Muslim claims, but they failed to see their own fault that such and such Muslim gentlemen were really unfit for the posts.

It is an irony of fate that the Hindus, who are bound by their cartload of *Shastras* to treat the women like slaves and cattle and to get their daughters married before they were hardly above their girlhood, i.e., within ten years of age, are, as a matter of fact, allowing the greatest liberty to their womenfolk and giving them high education. They are trying to get laws passed against child marriage, raising the age to sixteen years though their Pandits are loud in proclaiming the attempt as "unworthy of a Hindu"; and they are devising means to popularize widow marriage, heedless of their Pandits, who quote *Shastras* saying "not only should a woman refrain from marrying a second time but she should reduce her body by living only on fruits, roots, flowers, etc., after her husband's death."

On the other hand, while Islam allows every freedom to women (so much so that women cannot be given in marriage without her consent in free will, which indirectly prohibits child marriage), we see people giving away their daughters in marriage at tender ages or giving them in marriage without their consent. Many a time a bride bitterly bewails her fate on being compelled to marry a bridegroom whom she knows to be a drunkard or an old man of sixty, but the marriage celebration proceeds despite her silent protest. And so-called respectable families in our society take pride in preventing widow marriage, no matter whether the widow be a girl of thirteen or a child of seven years of age!

The worst crime which our brothers commit against us is to deprive us of education. There is always some grandfather or elderly uncle who stands in the way of any poor girl who might wish to be educated. From experience we find that mothers are generally willing to educate their girls, but they are quite helpless when their husbands and other male relations will not hear of girls attending school. May we challenge such grandfathers, fathers, or uncles to show the authority on which they prevent their girls from acquiring education? Can they quote from the Qur'an or Hadis any injunction prohibiting women from obtaining knowledge?

We know there are Mussalmans of advanced ideas who are anxious to give their daughters a good education, but for want of a suitable High School for Muslim girls they cannot have their wishes fulfilled, and so they groan under the wretched social system. Why cannot the public of Calcutta support one ideal school for Muslim girls? Such a High English School with boarding accommodation and hostel, which can supply the demands of all the different classes of people, high and low, is very badly needed in Calcutta. On our part we are willing to convert this school (we mean the Sakhawat Memorial Girls' School) to that ideal one, provided we get public support and money enough to meet the cost of upkeep.

"EDUCATIONAL IDEALS FOR THE MODERN INDIAN GIRLS"

From the most ancient times there has existed in India a system of education which, though distinct in its characteristics and ideals from the modern Western system, has produced great men and earnest seekers after truth. This ancient Indian education developed in the early period of history from the science of grammar and mathematics. It has enabled India to make a mark in the sphere of high philosophy and metaphysics. Conditions of life have changed considerably from those prevalent in those early days, and to work out without many essential modifications ancient theories and practices in education is by no means a practical proposition. Yet we must seek the elements of value in our ancient heritage. We must assimilate the old while holding to the now. Thus will we render our present educational system, the great defect of which is it is an exoteric in an alien soil. It is unsuited to our needs and requirements and incapable of developing the distinctive thread of our national thought and culture.

If education is described as the preparation for life or for complete living, the Indian educator had formed of it a true and valuable conception. The ancient curriculum was not confined to mere book learning. It included many more things. Physical development received its due share of attention. In those early days, little was known of our vast expenditure on costly buildings. The place of instruction was outdoors under the shade of a tree, in a natural environment, which impressed what was learnt all the more deeply on the mind. The student's life was, moreover, one of healthy activity, for he had to work for the teacher in his house and on the field, looking after his cattle and even collecting alms for him. Moral education was similarly not neglected. The period of studentship was a time for vigorous discipline. Rigid rules were laid down for the conduct of the pupils including hygienic, moral, and religious precepts and the regulation of good manners. Implicit obedience was expected and obtained from the student by the teacher and there were elaborate rules for the respect due to the latter.

The modern demand is for an education which develops all the faculties, physical, moral, and mental. From what we know of the ancient system of education in this country, methods were followed which conduced to the achievement of this aim. Those were days before science was known or had changed the possibilities of existence. Yet in this civilized and advanced generation we must acknowledge the value of Indian methods. The necessity for open-air schooling as far as practicable is emphasized by us today. Healthy outdoor sports are recommended to keep up the physique of the student, and the value of moral training is endorsed. We are thus advancing in a right direction. What we should recognize, however, is that our educational goal is age-old. We are not experimenting with new fancied ideas but are adopting traditions or our ancient system in introducing what we consider are twentieth-century educational reforms. Thus progress be accelerated, for the Indian mind is slow to accept innovation, but that which is traditional and of proved utility finds ready favor.

Religion is a tremendous force, and the chief concerns of all Asiatic people. From start to finish, all Eastern philosophy and literature is religious. In India religion has pervaded education as all things else. The very purpose of education in the early ages was religious, namely, to train young Brahmans for their duties in life as priests and teachers of others. Thus the spiritual side of education was greatly stressed. The idea of educational discipline was extended to the whole of life, and the theory of

Asrams or stages of those of student, householder, hermit, and wandering ascetic was developed. The student was first to acquire learning. He was next to enter upon the second stage of that of grihasta or householder. Then after having brought up a family and done his duty in the world he would enter upon the life of Vanprastha or forest hermit and later become a "Sannyasi" or wandering ascetic. The ancient Brahmanic education was therefore not only a preparation for the life but for a future existence as well.

In this utilitarian age when religion is treated as obsolete, and the all-engrossing objectives ordinarily are personal ambition and the advancement of material prosperity, it becomes all the more necessary for us to retain our ancient ideals. We should try as in the past to teach true values and give the students a guidance for all duties and relations of life [as well as in] the practical duties of life. At a later stage of history in India (as in the Middle Ages in Europe) a tendency arose to life. The current philosophy taught the unreality of the world, and that the highest wisdom was to [find] release from worldly fetters. But Islam has disapproved strongly of extreme other-worldliness. The Holy Qur'an has declared against the monastic life, for if all were to forsake the world the bonds of society would soon be broken. In our daily prayers we Muslims beseech Allah, saying, "Our Lord, grant us good in this world and good in the hereafter." Our aim should be to harmonize in due proportion the two purposes, spiritual and secular, in the education we impart. Much can be done in accomplishing this aim by impressing on the girls the excellence of our ancient ideals and of the life of great national heroes.

One of the most notable characteristics of Indian educational ideals is the relation between pupil and teacher. The Indian system knew nothing of a large institution or a large class of pupils taught together. There was usually one teacher for a few pupils from the beginning to the end of his period of studies. Thus individual attention was given. A family relationship sprang up between teacher and pupils which had a high moral effect. "In the West," writes an educationist, "it is the institution rather than the teacher which is emphasized and it is the school or college which a student regards as his 'Alma Mater.' In India it is the teacher rather than the institution that is prominent and the same affection and reverence which a Western student has for his 'Alma Mater' is in India bestowed with a lifelong devotion upon the teacher." It is not desirable or practicable in this democratic age, when a general spread of education should be our aim, to abolish large institutions. But we may with benefit require of the teacher the high responsibility of molding the character of the pupil by personal influence and example. We must require of our teachers a high intellectual, moral, and spiritual standard, and our aim should be to work for a condition which shall make such a class of teachers available. The teaching profession is one of the noblest in the world. Its responsibilities and opportunities both require to be increased.

The state of the education of women in India has for long centuries been deplorable. In the early Aryan period women held a position of authority and honor. We are told in *The Upanishads* of women who took part in deep discussion on philosophical truths, and the authorship of some Vedic hymn is ascribed to them. Yet even in the *Rig Veda* there are indications that women were coming to be looked down upon as inferior beings who should remain in subjection to men. Education for women has therefore become synonymous with us for breaking the barrier of ancient custom which shut them from learning. When we advocate the education of girls we generally imply the adoption of Western methods and ideals in their training to the exclusion of all that is Indian. This mistake on our part cannot be too strongly guarded against. We should not fail to set before the Indian girl the great and noble ideals of womanhood which our tradition has developed. This ideal was narrow and circumscribed in the past. We may enlarge and widen it, thus increasing its excellence, but what we should avoid is its total neglect and a tendency to slavish imitations of Western custom and tradition. In the past, with a few exceptions, our women were not noted for scholastic attainments. Their sphere was the domestic. Yet in the obscurity of their lives they conducted their duties with capacity and considerable amount of [love] and care. Their fingers were toil-worn. The cares of family, the effort to advance the happiness of others, these engrossed them. They were loyal and steadfast in times of endurance and hardship and proved to be, in the words of *The Mahabharata*, "A companion in solitude, a father in advice. A rest in passing through life's wilderness."

We should by all means broaden the outlook of our girls and teach them to modernize themselves. Yet they should be made to realize that the domestic duties entrusted to them cover a task on which the welfare of the country depends. They should not fall behind their illiterate sisters in splendid endurance, hero-ism, and discipline. We should teach our girls [that] if they are to fulfill their heavy duties commendably, [they should], above all . . . concentrate on desires and efforts which are not superfi-cial. We should teach them that the art of happiness lies . . . in discipline, that service should be their watchword, even though that service may not [bring more than a] transient sigh to the sum total of the world's unhappiness.

In ancient India the arts and crafts were not neglected. The caste system, with its many disadvantages, helped to foster them and keep up the standard of work. The dexterity and skill of each particular trade was handed down from father to son. The teaching was by handling and observing real things and unconsciously the boy picked up from his father many se-crets of the trade. The encouragement of kings and great nobles was also responsible for the production of really fine work. But in these days the tradition of vocational training has disap-peared in India. Parents give no thought to the career which their boy or girl [are driven] by temperament to adopt, all that they desire being that their child should obtain a hallmark of the university, a degree. I feel tempted to quote from a poem by Jus-tice Akbar, which runs thus:

How can the infant get any scent of its parents' character,
When it is fed on tinned milk and gets educated by the
Government?

The ancient tradition of vocational training (although this training must be given today under changed circumstances) must be revived by active propaganda.

The future of India lies in its girls. The development of its educational system on proper lines is therefore a question of permanent importance. Although India must learn many lessons from the West, to impose on it the Western system without modifications to make it suitable to us is a huge mistake. India must retain the elements of good in her age-old traditions of thought and methods. It must retain her social inheritance of ideas and emotions, while at the same time, by incorporating that which is useful from the West, a new educational practice and tradition may be evolved which will transcend both that of the East and the West.

In short, our girls would not only obtain university degrees, but must be ideal daughters, wives, and mothers—or I may say obedient daughters, loving sisters, dutiful wives, and instructive mothers.

Glossary

Babu: Used in Bengali as a suffix to a man's name. It marks the person referred to or addressed as being of the middle class.

Behag: A somber, dignified raga or mode in Indian classical music.

Bhadra: Fifth month of the Bengali calendar, extending from mid-August to mid-September.

Bhairavi: A raga with a wistful, plangent mood.

Bhavan: Residence or house. Used as the name of a building in the same way as the English "House" or "Hall." So, Tarini Bhavan is the equivalent of Tarini House or Tarini Hall.

Bi or bu: Short forms of Bubu, meaning elder sister. Commonly used by Bengali Muslims.

Bigha: Unit of measurement for land. The area signified by one bigha varies from state to state in South Asia. In Bengal, three bighas make one acre.

Da: Short form of Dada, meaning elder brother.

Di: Short form of Didi, meaning elder sister. Commonly used by Bengali Hindus.

Dina-Tarini: The name Dina-Tarini means one who, like a boatman, rows the distressed and deprived away from their suffering. The name may be translated as "the savior of the distressed."

Khanum, Khatun: Generic titles often used as surnames by Muslim women.

Kulin: A particularly elite subgroup of Brahmins; notorious because the male Kulins usually had numerous wives.

Milad Sharif: A festive occasion for Muslims celebrating the birth of Prophet Muhammad. An account of his life is usually recited and sung at such an event.

Puja: Durga Puja, the most important annual festival of Bengali Hindus, takes place in early autumn. Offices and educational institutions remain closed then, for a period ranging from a few days to one month.

Ray Bahadur: A title bestowed by the British Indian government on select men who had served them with loyalty and distinction.

Saab, Sahiba: As a suffix, the equivalent of Mister (Mr.) or Mistress (Mrs.); may be used with the first or last name, e.g., Suleiman Saab or Ali Saab.

Sandesh: Bengali dry-milk sweets.

Sarat: The season of early autumn, extending approximately from mid-September to early November.

Shankha: Conch-shell bangles that are emblems signifying that a married woman's husband is still living.

Sravana: Fourth month of the Bengali calendar, extending from mid-July to mid-August.

Suggestions for Further Reading

CRITICAL WORKS ON ROKEYA HOSSAIN

Azim, Firdous, and Perween Hasan. "Construction of Gender in the Late Nineteenth and Early Twentieth Century in Muslim Bengal: The Writings of Nawab Faizunessa Chaudhurani and Rokeya Sakhawat Hossain." In *Routledge Handbook of Gender in South Asia*, edited by Leela Fernandes, 28–40. Oxford: Routledge, 2014.

Bagchi, Barnita. "Ramabai, Rokeya, and the History of Gendered Social Capital in India." *Women, Education, and Agency 1600–2000*, edited by Jean Spence, Sarah Aiston, and Maureen M. Meikle, 66–82. London: Routledge, 2010.

———. "Speculating with Human Rights: Two South Asian Women Writers and Utopian Mobilities." *Mobilities* 15, no.1 (January 2, 2020): 69–80.

———. "Towards Ladyland: Rokeya Sakhawat Hossain and the Movement for Women's Education in Bengal, c. 1900—c. 1932." *Paedagogica Historica: International Journal of the History of Education* 45, no. 6 (December 1, 2009): 743–55.

———. "Two Lives: Voices, Resources, and Networks in the History of Female Education in Bengal and South Asia." *Women's History Review* 19, no. 1 (2010): 51–69.

Barton, Mukti. "Rokeya Sakhawat Hossain and the Bengali Muslim Women's Movement." *Dialogue & Alliance: Journal of the International Religious Foundation, Inc.* 12, no. 1 (1998): 105–16.

Bhattacharya, Atanu, and Preet Hiradhar. "The Sentimental Nightmare: The Discourse of the Scientific and the Aesthetic in Rokeya S. Hossain's 'Sultana's Dream.'" *Journal of Postcolonial Writing* 55, no. 5 (2019): 614–27.

Bhattacharya, Nilanjana. "Two Dystopian Fantasies." *Indian Literature* 50, no. 1 (231) (2006): 172–77.

Bhattacharya, Prodosh. "Two Occidental Heroines through Oriental Eyes." In *Reorienting Orientalism*, edited by Chandreyee Niyogi, 116–34. New Delhi: Sage, 2006.

Hasan, Md. Mahmudul. "Early Defenders of Women's Intellectual Rights: Wollstonecraft's and Rokeya's Strategies to Promote Female Education." *Paedagogica Historica: International Journal of the History of Education* 54, no. 6 (November 2, 2018): 766–82.

———. "Marginalization of Muslim Writers in South Asian Literature: Rokeya Hossain's English Works." *South Asia Research* 32, no. 3 (November 2021): 179–97.

———. "Muslim Bengal Writes Back: A Study of Rokeya's Encounter with and Representation of Europe." *Journal of Postcolonial Writing* 52, no. 6 (2016): 739–51.

Hossain, Yasmin. "The Begum's Dream: Rokeya Sakhawat Hossain and the Broadening of Muslim Women's Aspirations in Bengal." *South Asia Research* 12, no. 1 (1992): 1–19.

———. "The Education of the Secluded Ones: Begum Rokeya Sakhawat Hossain 1880–1932." *Canadian Woman Studies* 13, no. 13 (Fall 1992): 56.

Kosambi, Meera. *Feminist Vision or 'Treason against Men'?: Kashibai Kanitkar and the Engendering of Marathi Literature*. Ranikhet: Permanent Black, 2008.

Logan, Deborah. *The Indian Ladies' Magazine: Between Raj and Swaraj*. Bethlehem, PA: Lehigh University Press, 2017.

Manchanda, Rita. "Redefining and Feminising Security." *Economic and Political Weekly* 36, no. 22 (2001): 1956–63.

Mookerjea-Leonard, Debali. "Futuristic Technologies and Purdah in the Feminist Utopia: Rokeya S. Hossain's 'Sultana's Dream.'" *Feminist Review* 116, no. 1 (2017): 144–53.

Nussbaum, Martha. "Commentary: 'A Piece of the Pie': Women, India, and 'the West.'" *New Literary History* 40, no. 2 (2009): 431–48.

Quayum, Mohammad A. "Gender and Education: The Vision and Activism of Rokeya Sakhawat Hossain." *Journal of Human Values* 22, no. 2 (2016): 139–50.

———. "Hindu-Muslim Relations in the Work of Rabindranath Tagore and Rokeya Sakhawat Hossain." *South Asia Research* 35, no. 2 (2015): 177–94.

Quayam, Mohammad A., and Mahmudul Hasan, eds. *A Feminist Foremother: Critical Essays on Rokeya Sakhawat Hossain*. Hyderabad: Orient BlackSwan, 2017.

Rajan, Rajeswari Sunder. "Feminism's Futures: The Limits and Ambitions of Rokeya's Dream." *Economic and Political Weekly* 50, no. 41 (October 10, 2015): 39–45.

Ray, Bharati. *Early Feminists of Colonial India: Sarala Devi Chaudhurani and Rokeya Sakhawat Hossain*. London: Oxford University Press, 2002.

Ray, Bharati, ed. *Women of India: Colonial and Post-Colonial Periods*. Thousand Oaks, CA: Sage Publications, 2005.

Ray, Sangeeta. *En-Gendering India: Woman and Nation in Colonial and Postcolonial Narratives*. Durham, NC: Duke University Press, 2000.

Sarkar, Mahua. "Changing Together, Changing Apart: Urban Muslim and Hindu Women in Pre-Partition Bengal." *History and Memory* 27, no. 1 (2015): 5–42.

Sengupta Kumar, Parna. "Rokeya Hossain and the Politics of Ritual Fasting." In *Food, Faith and Gender in South Asia: The Cultural Politics of Women's Food Practices*, edited by Usha Sanyal and Nita Kumar. London: Bloomsbury Academic, 2020.

Spivak, Gayatri Chakravorty. "Teaching for the Times." *Journal of the Midwest Modern Language Association* 25, no. 1 (1992): 3–22.

Tharu, Susie J., and K. Lalita. "Rokeya Sakhawat Hossain." In *Women Writing in India. Vol. I: 600 B.C. to the Early 20th Century*, 340–42. New York: Feminist Press, 1993.

WORKS BY ROKEYA HOSSAIN AVAILABLE IN ENGLISH

Hossain, Rokeya Sakhawat. *The Essential Rokeya: Selected Works of Rokeya Sakhawat Hossain (1880–1932)*. Edited and translated by Mohammad A. Quayam. Boston: Brill, 2013.

———. "Woman's Downfall" [*Istrijatur Abanati*], translated and introduced by Mohammad A. Quayum. *Transnational Literature* 4, no. 1, November 2011. https://dspace.flinders.edu.au/xmlui/bitstream/handle/2328/25491/Womans_Downfall.pdf;jsessionid=F1B2A670783053E9625C2AD7AE231A4F?sequence=1.

———. "Nurse Nelly," translated and introduced by Mohammad A. Quayum. *Transnational Literature* 5, no. 1, November 2012. https://dspace.flinders.edu.au/xmlui/bitstream/handle/2328/26494/Complete%20translations.pdf?sequence=1\.

Hossain, Rokeya Sakhawat. *Sultana's Dream: A Feminist Utopia and Selections from The Secluded Ones*. Edited and translated by Roushan Jahan. Afterword by Hanna Papanek. New York: Feminist Press, 1988.

SECONDARY READING ON SCIENCE FICTION AND UTOPIA

Ashcroft, Bill. *Utopianism in Postcolonial Literatures.* New York: Routledge, 2016.

Atwood, Margaret. *In Other Worlds: SF and the Human Imagination.* New York: Doubleday, 2011.

Bloch, Ernst. *The Principle of Hope.* Translated by Neville Plaice, Stephen Plaice, and Paul Knight. Cambridge, MA: MIT Press, 1995.

———. *The Spirit of Utopia.* Translated by Anthony A. Nassar. Stanford, CA: Stanford University Press, 2000.

———. *The Utopian Function of Art and Literature: Selected Essays.* Translated by Jack Zipes and Frank Mecklenburg. Cambridge, MA: MIT Press, 1988.

Gordin, Michael D., Helen Tilley, and Gyan Prakash, eds. *Utopia/Dystopia: Conditions of Historical Possibility.* Princeton, NJ: Princeton University Press, 2010.

Hassan, Narin. "The Quest for Postcolonial Utopia: A Comparative Introduction to the Utopian Novel in the New English Literatures." *Studies of World Literature in English* 10, no. 2 (2001): 362–64.

Jameson, Fredric. *Archaeologies of the Future: The Desire Called Utopia and Other Science Fictions.* New York: Verso, 2005.

Mannheim, Karl. *Ideology and Utopia: Collected Works, vol. 1.* Oxford: Routledge, 2013. First published in 1936 in the International Library of Psychology, Philosophy and Scientific Method.

Pfaelzer, Jean. "The Changing of the Avant Garde: The Feminist Utopia (*La Transformation de l'Avant-Garde: L'Utopie Féministe*)." *Science Fiction Studies* 15, no. 3 (1988): 282–94.

Williams, Raymond. "Utopia and Science Fiction." *Science Fiction Studies* 5, no. 3 (1978): 203–14.

RELATED SPECULATIVE FICTION

Pre-Twentieth-Century Literature

Bellamy, Edward. *Looking Backward*. Mineola, NY: Dover Publications, 1996. First published in 1888 by Ticknor and Company (Boston, MA).

Butler, Samuel. *Erewhon*. New York: Penguin Classics, 1970. First published in 1872 by Trübner and Co. (London)

Cavendish, Margaret. *The Blazing World and Other Writings*. New York: Penguin Classics, 1994. First published in 1666 (Newcastle, UK).

Claeys, Gregory, and Lyman Tower Sargent. *The Utopia Reader*. New York: New York University Press, 2017.

More, Thomas. *Utopia*. Translated by Paul Turner. New York: Penguin Classics, 2003. First published in 1516.

Morris, William. *News from Nowhere*. Oxford: Oxford University Press, 2009. First published in 1890.

Scott, Sarah. *Millenium Hall*, Peterborough, Ontario: Broadview Press, 1995. First published in 1762.

Schreiner, Olive. *Dreams*. London: A&C Black, 2003. First published in 1890 by Frederick A. Stokes Company (New York).

Verne, Jules. *Journey to the Center of the Earth*. New York: Penguin Classics, 2009. First published in 1864 as *Voyage au Centre de la Terre* (France).

Vogel, Julius. *Anno Domini 2000, or Women's Destiny*. London: Hutchinson & Co., 1889.

Wells, H. G. *The Time Machine*. New York: Bantam Classics, 2003. First published in 1895 by William Heinemann (London).

Wolstonehome, Elizabeth C. *Woman Free*. Congleton, UK: Woman's Emancipation Union, 1893.

TWENTIETH- AND TWENTY-FIRST-CENTURY LITERATURE

Alderman, Naomi. *The Power*. New York: Little, Brown, 2016.

Atwood, Margaret. *The Handmaid's Tale* [1986]. New York: Anchor Books, 1998. First published by Houghton Mifflin Harcourt (Boston, MA).

Bogdanov, Alexander. *Red Star: The First Bolshevik Utopia*. Translated by Charles Rougle. Bloomington: Indiana University Press, 1984. First published in 1908 (St. Petersburg).

Butler, Octavia E. *Parable of the Sower*. New York: Grand Central Publishing, 2019. First published in 1993 by Seven Stories Press (New York).

Doyle, Arthur Conan. *The Lost World and Other Thrilling Tales*. New York: Penguin Classics, 2007. First published in 1912 by Hodder & Stoughton (London).

Hopkinson, Nalo, and Uppinder Mehan, eds. *So Long Been Dreaming: Postcolonial Science Fiction & Fantasy*. Vancouver: Arsenal Pulp Press, 2004.

Imarisha, Walidah, and Adrienne Maree Brown. *Octavia's Brood: Science Fiction Stories from Social Justice Movements*. Oakland, CA: AK Press, 2015.

Jemisin, N. K. *The Broken Earth Trilogy: The Fifth Season, The Obelisk Gate, The Stone Sky*. New York: Orbit, 2015–2017.

Kavan, Anna. *Ice*. New York: Penguin Classics, 2017. First published in 1967 by Peter Owen Ltd. (London).

LeGuin, Ursula K. *The Dispossessed: An Ambiguous Utopia*. New York: Harper Perennial Modern Classics, 2014. First published in 1974 by Harper & Row (New York).

———. *The Left Hand of Darkness*. New York: Berkeley Publishing Group, 1987. First published in 1969 by Ace Books (New York).

Okorafor, Nnedi. *Who Fears Death*. New York: DAW Books, 2011.

Perkins Gilman, Charlotte. *Herland*. London: Minerva Publishing, 2018. First published in 1915 as a serial in *The Forerunner*.

Piercy, Marge. *Woman on the Edge of Time*. New York: Ballantine Books, 2016. First published in 1976 by Alfred A. Knopf (New York).

Russ, Joanna. *The Female Man*. Boston: Beacon Press, 2000. First published in 1975 by Bantam Books (New York).

Wells, H. G. *A Modern Utopia*. New York: Penguin Classics, 2006. First published in 1905 by Chapman and Hall (London).

Williams, A. Susan, ed. *The Lifted Veil: The Book of Fantastic Literature by Women*. New York: Carroll & Graf, 1992.

Ready to find
your next great classic?

Let us help.

Visit prh.com/penguinclassics

PENGUIN
CLASSICS